Fire in His Eyes

Secrets & Seductions Series
Book One

by
MJ Nightingale

Published: MJ Nightingale 1st January, 2014: authormjnightingale@gmail.com

Editing: Brenda Wright and Keriann McKenna
Cover Design Andrea Michelle
Proofreader: Claudette Rossignol

This book is intended for a mature audience of eighteen and older.

Acknowledgements

First and foremost, this book couldn't have been written without my wonderful husband. He picked up the slack when I was consumed by writing. He is an amazing father, and my best friend. Thank you, Anthony, for encouraging me, and being there. I love you! Always Remember and Never Forget. And, even though I didn't use your suggestions for certain scenes in the book, you know what I mean, I still like to hear your ideas. They gave me comic relief.

A big, big thanks goes out to my absolutely wonderful editors, Brenda Wright and Keriann McKenna. They selflessly volunteered to help me see this project through. They helped to make *Fire In His Eyes* a reality when it was in its roughest form. I have to thank my mother for the third round of edits. She and a friend, Shannon White proofread the book before it went into this second edition. Thank you so much.

I also need to thank my sister who encouraged me to do this. She was the inspiration behind the character of Ana, and will be the heroine of my next book.

I had fantastic beta readers who gave me awesome advice, encouragement and support; they saw holes in the story when I was too close to the project to see it. They pointed them out, they gave me their ideas and feedback.

And I want to thank Andrea Michelle for designing a great new cover for the boxed set and the new cover for Fire In His Eyes that will come out in September of 2015.

Prologue

Haunted by the Past

I WOKE FROM the nightmare stifling the cry that wanted to tear itself from my throat by pressing both my hands over my mouth. I began to rock back and forth in my bed quickly trying to get the horrific images out of my head, but they wouldn't leave me. I hadn't had this nightmare, this dream, this remembrance of the past, in a very long time.

I stared in the dark at my vague reflection in the mirror. I was only able to make out the outline of my body sitting, rocking in my queen sized bed as my long brown hair cascaded over my face. I tried to control my breathing, but despite my best efforts, I was there again.

I was walking down the dark, narrow alley, a little drunk, on my way to my friend Marah's apartment when I was pulled beyond her door by an unseen large figure. I stumbled, and nearly fell, but was jerked forward by a strong hand attached to a massive man in a grey hoodie.

"What?" I mumbled and croaked out, still too confused to panic. Everything was happening so fast.

"Shut-up, you slut!" The gruff voice hissed in the darkness as he dragged me to the very dark recesses of the alley and threw me down onto the pavement behind a dumpster in the back.

"Ow," I whimpered as my elbow and shoulder hit the pavement. I

tried to get up, but the man in the grey hoodie pushed me back down. He began to unbuckle his belt and then unbuttoned and unzipped his faded blue jeans.

I was immediately terrified, but in my fear I couldn't even scream. Why couldn't I scream? My mouth opened and closed, and I tried to get my vocal chords to work, but nothing came out, and then a hand slammed across my face knocking me down again.

"You slut! Dancing like that. Teasing me, teasing us all, but no, Monica wouldn't give us the time of day. You're too good for the likes of us, but you came in to our bar tonight. Miss Goody Two-Shoes, in your tight sweater, and jeans."

I found my voice, as the blood from my split lip trickled into my mouth. "Please, no," I cried. "I didn't mean to. I'm sorry."

"Sorry! Ha!" The voice snarled. "I'll show you sorry." The man in grey, pushed back his hoodie off his head. I recognized him immediately. His name was Burt. He and his brothers were trouble in this town. Always breaking the law, they had been arrested for drugs, car theft, vandalism, and an assortment of other crimes. They were all ruffians and troublemakers. His legs straddled mine, and one hand pinned both of mine over my head. I began to cry even more. I tried to move, but couldn't. I was too drunk to fight, too far for anyone to hear, and he was too strong.

His alcohol laden breath overpowered my senses and I turned my face away from the foul odor. "You dance like a whore. You dress like a whore. So, you're a whore, and I'm going to show you what happens to whores." He slapped me again, hard. I saw stars and felt him fumbling with my pants then tugging them down.

"No, please," I whimpered. He slammed himself into me, taking my virginity, as pain seared through me. It hurt so badly. "Help!" I cried softly.

He grunted above me, pushed a few dozen times as I continued to whimper, and cry out softly.

"Hey! What's going on here?" I heard a startled voice call out.

"Help, please!" I managed to get out.

"Get off her! Burt? Monica?" It was a small town.

Burt hastily got off me, and quickly pulled up his pants. He ran, knocking Marah's brother, Richard, down on his way out of the alley.

Richard and Bonnie, his girlfriend at the time, helped me up. They took me to Marah's.

I didn't call the police. I was too ashamed. I was seventeen, drunk, and I believed it was my fault. I swore everyone to secrecy, and blamed myself for a very, very long time.

Chapter One
Back in the Saddle

"**L**ISTEN TO ME! You have to get right back in the saddle. You've kept yourself on the shelf way too long." Ana's voice coming through the phone brokered no argument. What Ana had to say was true, an understatement, to say the least. I hadn't done much SADDLE RIDING in my life and just recently found myself enjoying it.

When I didn't respond and merely sighed in response, Ana continued. "Come on, Monica, you had fun with Dan, don't let the disappointment of it not being long-term make you afraid to try again. You didn't even love him. You both knew that relationship was going nowhere. You just liked the sex." That, too, was an understatement and so like Ana to say. Blunt and honest to the core. The truth was, Dan had been fun. He was safe, funny, and a good friend with benefits. I never had to worry about him hurting me, and he taught me a lot about myself and about sex. I denied myself for over ten years until Dan came along because I was too afraid of getting hurt and reliving that nightmare. How he laughed when he met the twenty-eight year old "virgin."

"I know," I groaned into the receiver. "It's just that Dan wasn't complicated. He was fun and nice."

"Nice and easy and safe. Too safe. He was a friend, and

I'm glad I introduced you, but he's been transferred out of state, and you need to have a real relationship."

"I'm not looking for a relationship. I'm only thirty and have plenty of time for a relationship."

"Listen, Mon, you've done wonders in the past three years; you've dropped a ton of weight, finally got the counseling you needed all those years ago, learned to enjoy the pleasures of the flesh, but now you gotta live, too! Dan was safe, but I don't want to see you dry up like some old hag on a shelf."

"Ana, I'm only thirty," I repeated. "Plenty of time. Dan's been gone only a year."

"But a year without sex is a long time. You need to learn how to trust and have fun. You had that nightmare for a reason, Monica. You haven't been out on the town in over a year. You haven't had a date, a real date, since Dan left. You're getting into those Obsessive Compulsive Disorders again. I noticed your dishes the last time I was there."

"I just like things neat," I replied.

"Your patterns all faced in the same direction."

I winced, even though she couldn't see it. What she said was true. I made a lot of progress in three years, but these last few months, I noticed old patterns creeping back in. Defensive patterns that made me feel in control. Counting my steps, placement of objects, repetitive patterns. "Dan made me feel safe, Ana," I repeated her earlier words.

"But you didn't love Dan. Yeah, he oiled the tubes, but sex is better when it is with someone you love, not a partner to practice with, that is why you gotta put yourself out there. You gotta take a risk. You gotta stick more than your toes in the water, you gotta take the plunge, grab the bull by the horns!"

"You're such a horn dog!" I giggled. My sister was a nympho at eighteen, I swear. Knowing she would just keep hounding me until she got her way, I knew I would have to give in. The determined free spirit that was Ana, always got her way. She had our grandfather, and father wrapped around her little finger, and at thirty-four, had a slew of romantic entanglements on her hands. At thirty, I guess I was about to embark on relationship number two, or three, if you counted the unrequited love I had for my high school crush. "Okay, what do you suggest I do?" I relented.

"Yessssss!!!!" she hissed. "I knew you would see it my way. Well, I know this club down in Tampa . . ." Ana began.

"A club!?" I panicked, the old fear resurfacing, as I held the phone to my ear with one hand and twisted my long brown hair around my finger with the other. "You never mentioned a club before!"

"What do you want to do? Go to the grocery store and check out guys for rings, or have me drag you into Home Depot and ask every cute guy if he is single? You're such a social virgin! You want a loaf of bread you go to the bakery, if you want a man you go to a club." I couldn't help but laugh at the way my sister spoke. We were like night and day, but she was always the one and only who could pull me out of my funk. "Listen, I will be with you," she added reassuringly.

"All right, give me some details, please." You couldn't argue with Ana for long. When she had her mind made up, it was just a matter of time before you gave in.

"All right. The place is called the Blue Martini, and it is ladies' night tomorrow night so all the single guys will be on the prowl and buying us drinks to get us into bed. Wear something tight and sexy. I'm wearing those black slacks and that glittery gold tank top, the one with the sequins. Wear a skirt and show off those long legs of yours, okay?"

"But tomorrow is Thursday, and I have to work on Friday. I can't stay out late and get up in the morning for work!"

"Puh-lease, Miss Teacher Prude. You're thirty, not dead! Stop with the excuses. WE ARE going! We will be home by three; and you will get up at seven, and be to work by seven twenty. Throw in a movie for the kids to watch and you can take a nap when you get home. I'll pick you up at nine."

"I never let my students watch movies!" I replied appalled.

"Well, you will on Friday!" And she hung up.

I LOOKED IN the mirror in my bathroom, put the finishing touches on of my make-up, and was pleased with the outcome. I used a bit more mascara to draw more attention to my large brown almond shaped eyes. I chose to wear a form fitting denim skirt and my beige crocheted halter top. The golden tan I sported from many days in the sun during spring break gave me a nice glow. I didn't need much make-up, just the mascara, a bit of shadow, and lip gloss completed my look.

I heard Ana's SUV pull up in the drive way, and the front door opened as she came bouncing into the living room. "Are you ready, Mon?" she called out.

"I'm in the bathroom. I will be out in a sec," I replied.

"Okay!" Ana hollered back.

I finished with my mascara and walked out into the living room where she sat on my new suede sofa, channel surfing. I had just remodeled the house over the summer, doing the work myself, even the tiling. I was proud of the woman I was becoming; confident, independent, and no longer afraid of her shadow. I just wished I hadn't wasted so much time, and had gotten the help I needed after I was raped when I was seventeen. But I tried not to dwell on that any longer.

"You look fantastic, Mon! You need heels, though. God, your calves are amazing! Rock solid, and your arms. The weight training is doing wonders for your tone!"

"Thanks, Ana!" She always complimented me lately. Three years ago, when I finally decided I needed help, she'd been by biggest supporter. I barely left my house. But because of the therapy, I'd been able to deal with the rape, had lost the eighty pounds I'd gained and began to work out and tone my body. I no longer hid in my home, no longer avoided the male species like the plague, and had begun a work out regime. I biked twenty miles a day on the weekends, ran five during the week, and did weight training every other day. The weight had been another issue. Over the years, I put on weight to make myself invisible to men so they wouldn't find me attractive. I hid in nondescript clothes, and tried to blend into the background whenever I was out of my home, which had been for school or work only. Therapy helped me learn these things about myself. It helped me face my demons, deal with my guilt, my OCD, and why it had developed in the first place.

"You look like you're twenty! I'm so jealous!" Ana patted her belly.

"Ana, you look good, too!" And, she did. She had long auburn hair that she got from our mother, and hazel eyes. She was tall for a woman at six feet, to my five eight, and held herself well, despite being just a tad overweight. Being diabetic, she carried the few extra pounds around her middle. Nothing like the situation I'd found myself in after eating myself into obesity to thwart any male advances. Her face was like a porcelain china doll, with a pointed chin, a smattering of freckles across her cheeks, and a heart shaped face. She'd never been without a suitor or male companionship for longer than a few weeks. This was one of those times.

"Okay, go get those heels. I'm ready to par-tay!" She got up from the sofa, and followed me into my bedroom. "I love what you've done to the house. It looks great. You will have to come by my place and give me some decorating tips."

"You're the queen of clutter, woman. My tip is to buy a shed!" She laughed as she looked at the floor of my closet and picked out a pair of brown sandals with a three inch heel.

"Ooo! These," she said, handing me the pair she stooped down to get.

I leaned on my queen sized bed, and strapped on the heels.

"Let's rock'n roll." I followed Ana out of my room, down the hall, and out the door.

Here we go, I thought, a bit nervously.

WE GOT TO the Blue Martini, a little after ten o'clock, and the place was nice but not too crowded. It was very large with an open floor plan. There were several bars that served drinks spread sporadically throughout and a large dance floor in the center. It also had six pool tables near the back. I followed Ana through the bar until we found an area deemed appropriate for us to sit.

"Don't worry, by eleven this place will be hopping," Ana stated as if reading my mind. "I wanted to make sure we got a seat at the bar." She got up onto one of the tall, leather stools that framed the heart-shaped bar, and I got up onto another one of the chairs beside her. The lighting was nice, not too dark, but the music was thumping.

"What will it be, ladies?" The bartender asked. "First drink is on the house tonight!"

"Club soda for me, and a d-i-r-t-y, d-i-r-t-y martini for my sis," Ana winked at him as she stressed the dirty and made lascivious eyes at the blonde hunk of a bartender. Ana usually didn't go for blondes, but this guy was a real beefcake muscle-head, and that was her type. She loved the body builder types. He also looked to be in his mid-twenties to late twenties. Another plus for her, she liked them younger.

"Be right back, ladies," he drawled and winked back at Ana. From the corner of my eye, I saw her draw her tongue across her top lip as he turned to the wall of alcohol behind him to mix my drink.

"I'm designated driver tonight. I may have one drink later, but nurse that one. I only want you to have three tops or you will never forgive me tomorrow. If someone buys us drinks, don't worry, I'll dump them when no one is looking, so just sip that one."

She didn't have to tell me that. I wasn't much of a drinker anyway, not anymore, but once an older sister, always an older sister, and breaking her of the habit of bossing me around wasn't worth the effort. "Yes, ma'am," I responded.

Our drinks arrived and I took a sip of the delicious cock-tail. I loved martinis and indulged in one every now and then. A group of rowdy guys to our left began to cheer as someone at the pool table sunk the eight ball. Ana and I both glanced over.

"Oooo, army bucks! So buff!" she drawled and elbowed me in the ribs. I looked over at the five guys around the pool table and appreciated the view immensely. "So, which one do you want?" she inquired.

"We just got here!" I grumbled.

"Let's get their attention, and then go dance. Then they can watch us!" She laughed shrilly and sure enough they looked our way. I was embarrassed, and began to turn away when one of the guys caught my eye. He lifted his beer in our direction, and took a long sip as he watched me over his bottle of Corona. I smiled at him and turned around. My heartbeat accelerated. He was hot, incredibly hot. His ice blue eyes sparked with fire almost knowingly. How was that possible? He definitely seemed interested.

"Gotcha," Ana muttered, and swung back around to me. How were these things so easy for her, I wondered. I laughed at her, and she said, "Hey, he is still watching, let's go dance." She grabbed me by the elbow before I could respond, and yanked me off my stool. That must have looked attractive, I thought to myself. "He's a hunk if I ever saw one, and he is the one." I followed her and the music grew in tempo the closer we got to the dance floor. She positioned me so that the guy had a good view of us dancing, and every time I glanced his way, he was still watching us. I liked to dance and knew I did it pretty well. Another song came on and blue eyes kept watching us. A few guys came over and tried to dance with us, but Ana just kept steering us in another direction, not rudely, but enough to say we weren't interested in them. I glanced at ice-blue eyes every now and then, and he would tilt his bottle at us, or wink. God! He was gorgeous and my heart rate hitched another notch. He wore black jeans and a white t-shirt with a Tommy Hilfiger logo on it, and the t-shirt showed that he had a fine physique. Very fine. His head was shaven, and his face was rugged, with a strong chin and angled cheek bones. He had a tan that indicated he spent a lot of time outdoors. The way he kept looking at me, though, just kept my senses heightened; it felt like he was undressing me right there on the dance floor. I couldn't blame him though because I was doing the same thing to him.

AFTER FOUR OR five songs, Ana and I went back to the bar. The place was filling up and we didn't want to lose our seats. As soon as we sat down, Adonis began to make his way over to us. My heart rate picked up another notch. He sat on the stool next to Ana because that was the only one available at the bar, but still kept staring at me. I picked up my drink and took a big sip.

"Want another?" he asked. His voice was like velvet, smooth and clear.

I nodded.

"Here, switch with me," Ana said and got off her stool. Blue eyes slid onto her seat not breaking eye contact.

"Hello, gorgeous!" Blue eyes said and inched closer to me.

"Hi," I replied nervously taking another sip of my drink, not realizing I finished it.

He turned and called to the bartender, "Another one, please," he indicated to the bartender that the drink was for me, and the bartender nodded.

Blue eyes, then turned to me and smiled. His teeth were perfect. "My name is Victor Ciccone. And you have to be the most beautiful girl I have seen in long time."

"Thank-you," I said shyly.

"You're welcome!" He laughed. "You didn't seem this shy on the dance floor. You can move! I was imagining you moving like that under me in my bed."

"Y-you did?" God, that was a stupid thing to say. I wasn't used to this flirting business. I had no experience. I wasn't Ana.

"Yes, I did. And, it was good. I pleased you very much." He gazed down the length of my body and that look was a caress. I could see from his face he liked what he saw. It was a compliment without words. I was surprised I wasn't more nervous, but Ana was right there watching us. He was incredibly attractive. Oh my, if my heart beat any faster I was afraid it was going to burst right out of my chest. "So, what is your name? I want to know what to moan in my sleep when I dream about you tonight." *Was this for real? Did guys really talk like that to pick up a girl?* I didn't know. But, it was definitely working on me. This guy was turning me on, and he hadn't even touched me. Yet!

"My name is Monica Michaud," I said as I reached out my hand to shake his. It was like electricity. A shock went through my entire body. I felt warm all over, and I knew it wasn't from the drink. I only had one. The guy was pure animal magnetism, pure sex appeal.

He didn't let go of my hand, or break eye contact. He held it and used his thumb to caress the top of my hand. He pulled me closer, and we were mere inches apart. He tilted his head to the side and put his face into my hair behind my ear, and inhaled. "You smell delicious. I bet you taste good, too," he whispered in my ear. He softly kissed my cheek and trailed light feathery kisses from my temple to my lips. I gasped at the sensations he evoked in me. "Dance with me?" he asked and began to draw me out of my chair.

Wordlessly, I followed him. It wasn't a fast song, but it wasn't a slow song either. He drew me into his arms and we swayed rhythmically in time to the music. His body and mine melded together on the dance floor. The electricity between us sizzled. After one song ended and another began his hands began to roam across my back, my sides, and I just held on enjoying the feelings he evoked in me, He turned me slightly and our eyes met, and, that is when his lips claimed mine. They were soft and cool, probably from the beer. His tongue darted out, and slid along my lips and I opened for him wanting more. My nipples hardened at the sensations he was creating. This man knew what he was doing and I wanted more. He explored my mouth with his, he tasted of lemon and beer, and I tentatively began to respond. He moaned my name into my mouth. The hand that caressed my back now slid along my arm then grasped my face, and his other hand, the one that had been stroking me along the side along my ribcage did the same. I was lost in the pleasure, completely oblivious to my sister sitting not eight feet away. The kiss went on and on. He slowly began to ease back, and end the kiss. "You do," he said and sighed sadly.

"I do what?" I asked, a little shaken by, what seemed to me, the abrupt end of the kiss.

"Taste great," he answered and then laughed, his blue eyes glittering. "But that isn't the only part of you I want to taste."

I stared at him shocked. My eyes widened into saucers at his suggestion, but yet, I yearned for whatever this man was willing to offer.

"You have beautiful eyes. Lonely, big and brown eyes. I want to see them full of passion for me. But another time. Let me bring you back to your friend."

He began to lead me back to my sister, and I muttered just that. "She is my sister."

He turned to look at me, surprised. "You look so different. Both of you are beautiful, though in your own way."

I couldn't help but smile at his sincere compliment. We didn't look much alike. Once back at the bar, he helped me back onto my stool, and again sat beside me, his smile dazzling.

I was speechless and terrified and excited at the same time. Nervous, too. But, a part of me knew that this man would be worth it. Instinctively, I also felt he wouldn't hurt me physically, and although his words were evocative, I saw glimpses of tenderness, and restraint in him. He was as sexy as hell, and when he smiled his crooked smile he had a dimple. Whatever inhibitions I still had, I knew he would break those down, he would teach me and please me to no end. This man was wild and dangerous, untamed. But I saw kindness there, too.

He broke the silence first. "I want to see you again."

"I would like that," I said immediately and licked my lips not realizing I'd done it. I don't know where those confident words came from, but I was glad they came. He nodded his approval, and then sadly shook his head and I felt a sudden sense of loss. He could see it in my eyes.

"Don't worry, Mi Cara, I'm not done with you yet, but just for tonight, though I am. I have to work early tomorrow, and I don't want to rush what I wish to do to you. Give me your phone number," he demanded as he slid his phone towards me.

With shaking hands I picked up his cell phone and typed in my phone number, and then handed it back to him. "Just one second, Monica," he stated as he scrutinized his phone and hit a few buttons. At that moment, my phone began to ring; I looked at my clutch and began to retrieve it automatically, when his hand stilled mine. "No, don't worry, Monica. That was me calling. I wanted to be sure you gave me the right phone number and not a phony one. I can't let you get away, now that I've found you. And, now you have my phone number, as well."

"Good, no, I mean yes, good, I'm glad I have your number, too," I stammered.

Victor laughed and his eyes crinkled in the corner, and then he was shaking his head again. "Tomorrow night?" I nodded. "Good, I will call you with the details then?" He got up from his stool, as did I, and he grasped my shoulders and kissed me again. It was hot, and more demanding than the last time. It was an exploration, and it was thrilling and primitive. It was unadulterated lust and left me wanting. He pulled me close to him and slid his hands around me, lightly running them down my back to my rear making me feel the most erotic sensations. He lightly squeezed my ass with both hands and pulled me even closer so I could feel his arousal through his jeans. It felt amazing as a pool of warmth rushed to my loins. Then, again, all too abruptly for my liking, he ended the kiss leaving me yearning, and wanting more. He turned to my sister. "It was nice to meet you both."

Ana took and shook his proffered hand. "Nice to meet you, too." She smiled at him.

He turned then, and began to walk out of the bar. His backside was almost as hot as his front. I watched him as he approached his friends who were by the entrance, the friends that he'd been playing pool with earlier. There was a bunch of back slapping and "Hoo-yaying," going on, as he turned and glanced my way one more time. His crooked smile lit up the room and again did that racing thing to my heart. Then, he was gone.

"Oh, God, I creamed my pants watching that guy kiss you." Ana's comments broke the spell that Victor had put me under. I laughed at her usual tasteless description, and breathed for the first time in what seemed like an hour. "Okay, let's get you home and tucked in to bed. No point in staying and letting sloppy seconds try to pick you up. That guy was hot! He will call you and he seems nice." I smiled at her as she twirled a long tendril of her auburn hair around her long index finger, and blew a kiss to the bartender, and then added, "Plus, I got to drive all the way back here and take that bartender home at two."

"Wh-what?" I stammered and looked at my sister with confusion. "While you were dancing, and doing other things, and when it seemed you wouldn't come up for air for a very long time, I might add, I had a nice talk with the cute bartender. We got a date later." She winked at me. Ana got off her stool, blew the bartender another kiss, grabbed my clutch and led me out the door. It was only eleven thirty when we left the Blue Martini, but the night, in my opinion, had been a rip-roaring success.

Chapter Two

The First Date

I T WAS NEARLY one o'clock when Ana pulled into my drive way. I started to get out, when her hand stopped me. I glanced over my shoulder to see what she wanted. "Let me know the minute he calls," she demanded.

"He's not going to call tonight," I mumbled sleepily. The ride home sobered me emotionally, a little. That guy was so gorgeous, he probably met another girl in the parking lot, and he probably forgot me the moment he got into his vehicle. I finished getting out of the car.

She rolled down the passenger side window after I crossed in front of her car. "Oh yes, he will call . . . and if he doesn't you've got his number," she stated matter-of-factly.

"Ana, Victor could have any girl he wants. Why would he even give me a second thought?" I worried aloud.

"Because you're a babe. Good-night sexy. And, call me!" She was backing out of the driveway before I could even turn around.

I took my keys out of my clutch, laughed and waved. "Bye yourself!" I walked into my small two bedroom bungalow on a quiet cu-de-sac, headed straight to my bedroom, and began to get undressed stripping out of my shirt and skirt. Work tomorrow. Ughh! I thought.

I was removing my make-up when the sound of my phone ringing stopped me short. Hell! Could it be? I grabbed my purse, rummaged through it and looked at the caller ID. Victor! I answered.

"Hello, gorgeous! I told you I would call you tomorrow and it is tomorrow." He laughed softly at his own joke, as did I. "What are you doing?"

"I'm getting ready for bed," I answered honestly.

"Really?" He sounded surprised. "I'm glad you're not at that night club giving some other guy a shot at you."

Hearing him say those words warmed me up a little inside. Again honestly, I answered, "Well, I left shortly after you did. Truth is, I have to work tomorrow, I mean today, too. And after meeting you, I didn't see the point in staying any longer." I held my breath waiting to hear what he would say about that.

He paused long enough to make me start to doubt myself. "Thank-you," he finally whispered. Then, "I want to have fun with you, Monica. A lot of fun."

"I'd like that," I replied huskily as I slipped under the sheets of my bed in my bra and panties. Having fun with him, I instinctively knew, was going to be the best fun I would ever have in my entire life.

"Mmmm, I like how that sounded," he growled. His voice had dropped into the sexiest sound I'd ever heard. "Earlier, you said you were getting ready for bed, and I am imagining you undressing right now. Are you undressing, Monica?"

I laughed at his throaty tone but I would play along. "Actually, when the phone rang I was already pretty much undressed, so I just got into bed in my bra and panties." I heard him clear his throat. "Take off your bra, Monica. You'll be more comfortable," he commanded.

I laughed, but did what he asked, putting the phone on the scarlet coverlet next to me. I called out, "Taking my bra off now. Ugh, yep I got the clasp. Off the shoulders. Done." I heard him laugh again. "I'm back," I said as I pulled the phone back to my ear.

"Very funny, but doesn't that feel better, Monica. Don't those cool sheets on your nipples make them harden?" It wasn't the sheets that did that, it was his words and the way he said them, and I told him so.

He groaned. "I'd better stop, baby. I don't want to have our first time be on the phone." I blushed knowing he was talking about phone sex, and I was glad he couldn't see that. "So, what do you do, Monica? For work, I mean?" He asked in an obvious attempt to change the subject.

"Work? I'm teacher, high school English!" I lay down on the pillow with the phone pressed to my ear. I heard him groan through the receiver. "What?" I asked, "Bad track record in school, or something?" I teased.

"No Monica, that's not it. I'm just picturing you with a bun in your hair, a pencil behind your ear, and a ruler in your hand. God, even casual conversation with you has me imagining all kinds of naughty things. I'm hot for this teacher. I've always wanted to screw a sexy teacher." And, the conversation with Victor was back to sex just like that.

I laughed. "I'm pretty hot for you, too, Victor," I admitted. "I have never just met a guy and felt what I felt –so instantaneously." That was the biggest understatement of my life. This man had me imagining things I hadn't even thought of or heard of before.

"I get off work at three tomorrow, Monica. I'm going to come home, take a nap, shower and change. Then I'm coming for you, and we're going to fuck, and it's going to be the best sex you've ever had in your life." The way he said the words left me feeling anxious and wanting. I was speechless, yet wanting him to do exactly what he said. I felt a wetness in my pussy, and wished he were here right now. I had the sudden urge to touch myself. How could his words alone do this to me I wondered. "Where do you live?" he asked. I told him I lived in Hudson in Pasco County, an hour from Tampa and gave him my address. "I live right in Tampa so I should be there around eight o'clock. Is that all right? I will take you to dinner, take you home, and I want to be crystal clear about this, then I'm taking you to bed. Ok?"

"Ok," I answered. "I'm looking forward to it. Very much!" I can't wait, I screamed inside.

"Are you on the pill, Monica?" he asked tone suddenly serious.

"Yes," I replied a little caught off guard by the sudden change in the direction of the conversation.

"Good, baby. I don't want any accidents. And just so you know I'm clean, I just had a checkup. I want to feel every inch of you when you tremble around me. Is that okay, Monica?" he asked. His husky tone was back. When I didn't answer right away he added, "But I'll bring condoms if you want me to."

"N-no, that's okay. I trust you. I had some tests done, too," I added to reassure him. I wanted to feel him as well. His description sounded so good to me. The way he was speaking was making me hotter and hotter. But then an image of my sister popped into my head. Unprotected sex cost her so much early on in her life. "B-But," I stammered, "Just for a little while maybe we should. We don't know each other at all. You don't know me."

"I'm not worried about that Monica, not with you. Even

though, you're sexy as hell, I know an innocent when I see one. That makes you even sexier to me," he added. "But if it will make you feel better. I'll bring protection, okay?"

"Okay," I whispered lamely, and then added after a slightly awkward pause, "Victor, I'm very excited about tomorrow night. I'm so glad you called."

"Me too, baby. I'll respect your decision. Good night, Monica. I'll see you tomorrow, well tonight actually. Wear a dress for me." With that he hung up.

THE SCHOOL DAY dragged on slowly and I did end up showing a movie because even though I had maybe five hours of sleep after talking with Victor, they were filled with dreams of him with those ice blue eyes on fire for me. Our talk on the phone kept running through my mind all day too. While the students watched the film, I spent the day dreaming of him.

I called Ana on my lunch break and filled her in on my plans with Victor for that night, but I didn't give her any details about the suggestiveness of the phone conversation. They were too delicious to share. She was happy for me that he'd called and that I would get to see him so soon. "Okay, so dinner is first. That will take about two, maybe three hours with drinks, then hanky-panky by eleven," she stated gleefully getting right to the point. I could hear her clapping her hands together in the background. I laughed. That was just like my sister, such a horn dog. "Now, don't drink too much," she cautioned, but then added suggestively, "You're going to want to enjoy yourself, and the alcohol may dull the pleasure."

"Ana, please. I'm at work," I squealed behind my hand in the teacher's lounge.

"Prude," she teased but then became serious for a second. "I'm going to call your house at eleven o'clock to make sure you're okay, and that he isn't some kind of maniac or something. If he is, just say on the phone, you didn't talk to mom today, and I will rush over, grab a shovel out of the garage and bash his brains out. Okay?" That was my sister, too, very over-protective.

"Ana, I'm a big girl now," I pointed out, and after last night's phone conversation I seriously doubted I would be backing out now. If he did half of what he promised, I considered myself very lucky indeed. She really was over the top sometimes when it came to my safety when she put herself into all kinds of risky situations. But she was the older sister, and she believed that gave her license to do as she pleased.

She interrupted me firmly, "Code words are-I didn't talk to mom today. Got it?" She stated emphatically. She wouldn't be taking no for an answer. I had no choice but to give in.

"I got it!" I laughed while shaking my head. "Okay, let me go now. I have one more class today, then I'll go home and make myself sexy. I will talk to you later around eleven, I guess."

IT WAS SEVEN o'clock and I'd just finished straightening my hair. My hair was long and naturally wavy, but in the Florida heat it could get quite frizzy if I didn't blow it out or straighten it. It reached about half way down my back when it was straightened, and was one of my best features.

Deciding what to wear though was going to require some thought though. Victor wanted me to wear a dress. I didn't have a lot of sexy clothes or dresses. Dan and I hadn't gone clubbing or dancing and had only gone out to family style restaurants that didn't require some kind of dress code. I had a couple of cocktail dresses for work functions, and some gowns for when I chaperoned prom or homecoming. I was stumped. I did have one black cocktail dress. But a little black dress? Too cliché! I looked through my closet for the second time, and realized I didn't have anything sexy enough in any other color. I was a teacher, and a bit on the conservative side. I almost panicked, but then I thought I could always wear one of my shifts from work and take it up a bit and forgo the blazer. The navy blue would do. It had a nice shimmer and a low cut square neckline that revealed a bit of cleavage and the rounded tops of my size c cupped breasts. I took the dress off the hanger, dropped my towel on the floor and held up the dress against me to see if I could make this work. It was fairly new. I had only worn it a couple of times and it was form fitting enough to be considered sexy, but not slutty. It would have to do. I was thirty not twenty-one, anyway. The dress went to just above my knees. I could easily cut the bottom and hem it up five or six inches. Satisfied with my decision, I put the dress aside for now.

Next, I want to my lingerie drawer. Here I was able to choose more quickly as I had a large selection. I loved the feel of pretty things under my clothes, as it gave me a feeling of confidence knowing what I wore underneath wasn't quite so conservative. I put on a black lacy bra and matching panties. I knew they looked good against my olive skin tone and turned in the mirror to see how they would appear from all angles. Not very innocent looking. Perfect!

Now to attack that dress again. I threw on a t-shirt and went out into my back screened lanai where I kept a portable sewing machine on a small table. I laid the dress on it, quickly cut six inches from the bottom, folded it up an inch and set a new bobbin in the sewing machine with blue thread that matched the dress. Within ten minutes, I finished the job with a nice hem and a little back slit to make it moveable. Thank-you mom, for making Ana and I learn how to sew. Why we ever thought it was a pointless skill when we were younger, I'll never know.

I made my way back to my room, donned the dress, and liked what I saw. The navy material had an elasticity that hugged my body. It fit like a glove. It had a shimmer that made it dressy with just a hint of sex appeal. The dress now reached me just above mid-thigh. It was perfect. I was five foot eight, and had great legs. I'd always thought my legs were my absolute best feature. I was a runner too, and had great definition in them especially my calves. When it came to shoes, I picked out a pair of dressy black sandals with only a two inch heel. I'd noticed that Victor was only a few inches taller than I was, and I had three inch heels on the night before, so two would do for tonight. I knew guys liked the height advantage.

Back in the bathroom, I applied a bit of make-up—the usual black mascara, a bronze eye shadow with some shim-mer, and a rose gloss to my lips. On my way to my bedroom I glanced into the living room and realized it was just a few minutes to eight. Victor would be here soon. I was excited and nervous at the same time. So, I quickly put in some sapphire studs for a bit of sparkle, but no necklace. Soon, I kept thinking as I finished with the earrings. Just the thought of him made me simmer with heat and anticipation. I put my shoes on leaning against my bed, spritzed a bit of perfume into the air and walked through it, and went back into the living room. I took my ID, some money, my credit card, and keys and transferred them into a small black clutch. That is when I saw lights in the driveway. My heart beat faster and lurched into my throat. He was already getting out of his car as I walked to the front door. I had it open before he could even knock.

"You look fantastic, Monica. Sophisticated, yet sexy as hell. What a combination!" And just like that, without hesitation Victor grabbed me around the waist and pulled me to him, holding my body against his. His eyes possessed me, and I was mesmerized by them as his head dipped and he began to kiss me. My eyes closed involuntarily, as his tongue teased my lips seeking permission to enter. This man knew how to kiss. He tasted good, minty and something spicy, too. His hands were in my hair, holding me in place. One hand began to drop down my back, as it made its way slowly to my rear and began to caress and squeeze me. "Firm ass, nice. I can tell you run. So do I." His words were spoken between passionate kisses that trailed down from my lips to my chin then neck and collarbone and then back up again. He gave each and every one of those parts some sensual attention. I was breathless and had never felt this desired before. He knew seduction intimately. I could do nothing but hang on, moan my pleasure, and well just hang on. He held me with one hand in my hair, and the other cupping my rear and pressing me into his erection. Through the soft material of my dress and his black dress slacks, I felt every inch of him, every inch sending waves of pleasure through me. His kisses began to slow, he dipped back to my neck inhaling my scent, and I could hear him softly breathing as he tried to gain control of himself. He was just as affected by this passion between us as I. It made me smile inwardly, and I was glad he seemed just as affected by me as I was by him.

"Dinner first, Mi Cara. I'll taste the rest of you later," he promised in my ear, and gently bit my lobe just below the sapphires I had put in my ears earlier. He pushed me back slightly to gaze into my eyes. "You smell great, by the way. You – are – irresistible," He punctuated each word as I watched the fire in his eyes blaze. I could lose myself in those eyes. He then turned me around and gently cupped my behind and pulled me into him so that I could feel his arousal against my ass. "Real nice ass," he whispered.

I fumbled for my keys as he distracted me senseless with his hands on my rib cage just below my breasts. My heart still hammered inside my chest and I wondered if he could feel it. I don't know how I did it, but I managed to close and lock the front door. His hands lightly brushed the sides of my breasts causing my breath to hitch, and then they were back down on my ribs and hips. He gently held me at the waist, turned me around again and gave me a soft kiss on the lips. It was tender, yet still full of restrained desire. Pulling back and breaking the kiss, still with one hand possessively around my waist, he steered me towards the passenger side of his black Lexus. It wasn't a new car, but it was in good condition. He held open the door for me and helped me get seated before he smoothly closed the door and proceeded to come around to his side of the car. I watched him walk. He was graceful, but fast, and moved like a panther stalking his prey. While crossing in front of his car, his eyes were locked on to mine never breaking contact. He slid into his seat, and started the engine. Everything this man said and did turned me on like nothing had ever done before. He exuded sex in every look, every touch. What was I getting myself into, I wondered. Was I ready for this? My mind had so many questions, but I was going to listen to my body tonight.

Victor reached over to turn on the radio and music imme-diately filled the car. He dropped the volume a tad so we could talk. "I love music, you?" he asked, making polite conversation. I did, but I didn't recognize this artist, it was up tempo with a lot of bass.

"Yes, I do. I'm horrible with names though. I like whatever is on the radio, contemporary, rock, pop, whatever," I told him rambling on as his hand was now on my leg stroking it; once again he was touching me and keeping me from any coherent thought.

He leaned over and gave me a quick, gentle kiss on the cheek, and then a lop-sided boyish grin as he straightened back into his seat and began to concentrate on driving. It was my first chance to really take him in tonight. He was so incredibly handsome, like a Greek god. He had classical features; a strong nose and chin, and chiseled cheekbones. And if what I felt beneath his shirt proved to be true, he was ripped and fit as well. I knew he ran, but he must also work out. I couldn't wait to see his body later. His head was shaved closely and his facial hair was a little longer. He had what look liked a day of stubble. He looked good morning sexy. Incredible! The urge to bite him popped into my head. The sensations that his stubble evoked as it swept along my neck and throat, had been purely erotic. The combination of that roughness and his soft smooth lips had me panting when we kissed earlier; it had been strangely titillating as well. He caught me admiring his profile and so took my hand in his and drew it to his lap while he drove one-handed with the other. He was using his thumb and fingers to caress me between each of my fingers and the top of my hand. God, even this was causing my heart to palpitate. It seemed he was always touching me somewhere, the contact sending bolts of electricity running through me. It kept me on edge, and most definitely kept me from thinking clearly.

"So Victor, are you in the military," I asked, trying to clear my thoughts. He also knew what I did, and I wanted to learn more about him.

"Not anymore." He offered no more than that for a little while looking pensively out the window focused on driving. "My friends, the ones you saw me with last night still are, but I'm not in the military any more. I was for ten years and I loved it. I miss it and them. We still hang out though." He paused again, and it seemed he was choosing his words carefully. "I'm a contractor now in new construction." I was about to ask another question, when he gazed at me sideways and said, "I saw a Chili's not too far from here. Not fancy, but they make a great margarita? Is that okay with you?"

"Sure, I like Chili's" I answered. There weren't too many nice restaurants in Hudson, but Chili's had great food, and Victor was right about the margaritas. They were delicious and used top shelf Cuervo rather than some bitter knock-off tequila.

In just another minute we were pulling into the parking lot of Chili's. It was only a few miles from where I lived. Victor stilled me when I made to get out of the car, and he came around to open my door for me, giving me his hand to draw me out of the car, and with his hand on the small of my back he steered me towards the entrance. I wasn't used to guys opening doors for me, being gallant. I like it, a lot. Even though I barely knew him, and I knew his focus tonight was on seduction, those little things, those touches, and his demeanor and actions made me feel safe, protected.

We were seated right away by the hostess when we walked in, and then a waitress who was right behind her asked if we would like to order a drink.

"Two margaritas, doubles," Victor responded casually then glanced at the young waitress focusing his attention on her. I was a little bothered by the once over he was giving the adorable young blonde. My heart clenched when he took her arm and turned it to remark, "Hey, nice tattoo!" I had a bit of a hollow feeling in the pit of my stomach; it was a feeling I didn't like, but his touching her bothered me. It made me feel a little insecure, a little jealous, frankly. I tried to put those feeling aside to reflect upon later, and then glanced at the young pretty blonde again, she couldn't have been more than twenty. I might have taught her a few years ago, but didn't recognize her or the name I read on the nametag, Nicole. She was very pretty, but the tattoo she had on her arm wasn't anything remarkable, just some tribal bands with the words Hot! Hot! Hot! above them.

The girl giggled, batted her eyes and blushed to her roots at Victor's attention. Forget, twenty, she was probably more like eighteen. I'll admit, it made me a little jealous that he'd noticed it and was holding her arm to admire it. The moment felt awkward to me. "Oh, that is just a temporary tattoo. All the waitresses are wearing them to promote our new spicy, bold menu items."

"Yeah, I saw the hostess with one on her arm too, and I was curious about it. So the new menu items are hot, I do like things that are hot," and then his gaze swept across to me, landed on me. He was staring hard. Those eyes. They tormented me, and when he looked at me like that I felt like the only woman in the room. I let out a shaky exhalation of relief; he was just being polite, making conversation I told myself. The girl turned and left us then, and we made casual conversation about the various menu items, work, and friends, but conversation with Victor always seemed to be anything but casual. They were filled with innuendos and suggestions. He had a way of making everything sound erotic, and naughty. It kept me on edge and disconcerted. He told me about the things he missed from his days in the military, the camaraderie of the enlisted, the travel to faraway places, the routine, and P.T. It turned out he was a real physical fitness buff. I was too, now. We had that in common. Check. We both ran every day. Check. He liked to run races, marathons, and had even done a few triathlons, something I'd been thinking about training to do for a while now.

Our drinks arrived and we both eagerly took a sip. It was cool and refreshing. We ordered our meals, and the waitress just slipped away unnoticed as we continued on with our conversation. I told him about my teaching career, and he remarked that all those teenaged boys must be failing because how could they possibly concentrate on work when they were all mentally undressing me. I laughed. He was such a flirt. He was so terribly sexy, and made me feel electrified.

Dan had been handsome in a cowboy rugged sort of way. But never had he made me feel like this, so wanton with expectations of what I didn't know. He'd been a trusted friend who I knew wouldn't hurt me and the only person I had willingly wanted to have sex with. He had been like a teacher, a confidante, someone who understood my situation and was willing to take it slow and be patient with me. Dan knew about the rape, and had helped me to get over my fear of sex. He had been patient and had always made sure I was ready and willing. Victor had no patience, I could tell, and there would be nothing slow about what we were going to do later tonight. Victor was exciting, pure sex on wheels, no holds barred. But, he made me want to do things I had never dreamt of, had only read about in romance novels or seen on television. Dan was about the basics, teaching me about my body, and how not to be afraid. Victor scared me a little, but not in a fearful way, in an exhilarating, adrenalin-charged way, in a curiosity kills the cat kind of way.

Our dinner arrived, steaks with green beans for me, a baked potato for him. We ate, leisurely, talked, and more margaritas arrived. I didn't even notice he had ordered them, or that I had even finished the first one, but the waitress was taking the empty glasses away. He sat next to me on the green faux leather seats, and his hand kept straying to my thighs, brushing them lightly, stroking them gently. My senses were on high alert, and yet my brain was dulled by the Cuervo, a sensual heady combination.

"Are you ready?" His eyebrow arched devilishly asking my permission.

"Yes." I was ready.

He called the waitress over, paid the bill, and helped me to scoot across the seat holding my hand behind his back as he escorted me out of the now crowded restaurant. I trailed behind him through the waiting patrons near the restaurant's entrance feeling a little light-headed from the two double margaritas. We were back to his car in quick time, and he swung me around and pressed me against the passenger side of the car pushing his erection into me. He buried his head into my neck, and confessed in my ear, "I have been hard for you all night!"

His lips found mine, as one hand began to stroke my thigh inching up higher under the hem of my dress. Instinctively I raised one leg and pulled him in closer to me. My pulse quickened as his fingers inched closer to my loins. When the tips of his fingers reached the lace of my panties my legs began to shake and I felt a quivering rush deep inside of me.

Heat pooled at my core. I moaned his name and breathlessly groaned out, "Oh Victor, I can't wait to feel you inside of me. I want you, inside of me." And like magic granting my wish, two fingers moved my panties aside, and he slowly, achingly slow, began to insert them into the center of my being. Victor's other hand caressed the side of my breast, as he continued to kiss me in a crushing kiss that drove me wild. He devoured me. He consumed me. I couldn't think. I could only feel, as this sense of fullness began to fill me. His thumb circled my core, two, then three times, slowly, leisurely, and I groaned and pushed into him. I was wet, so very wet. In and out, over and over again with those wicked fingers, I felt myself begin to move in time to his rhythm. A building pleasure and excitement coursed through my veins. I clenched around his fingers as he began to withdraw them once more, he insert them again, and again. I felt like I was going to cum. I was close.

I had to feel him, too. My hands had been roaming restlessly over his well-defined back, and the muscles there. I scratched lightly at first, then dug into him alternating with caresses, my palms on his back. I slipped one hand between us and felt his dick through his pants. It was big, and hard. I felt it pulsing in my hand through the material, and he savagely broke the kiss, and tilted his head, back to say my name. "Monica, softer. Not so hard, baby." I lightened my touch. He returned to kissing me.

We heard laughter behind us, and both froze frustrated and panting for air. He rested his forehead on mine for a second breathing hard, trying to regain control, and then he pulled back and gave me that grin. The grin that was just a little lop sided, and made that delicious dimple appear in his cheek. It was sexy as hell.

"Your place, now!" His eyes, ice blue, glittered and smoldered with white flame. How the heck we were going to make it to my place without ripping each other's clothes off, I didn't know.

Chapter Three
Oh, Fuck Me!

THE DRIVE TO my home was done quickly and silently. As I fumbled with my keys and the lock in my excitement, I could hear the incessant ringing of the telephone. I reached to the wall and picked up the receiver of my cordless phone as Victor trailed behind me. I was mumbling something about my sister calling to check in, but clear thoughts were eluding me as his hands were already on my back and ass, and lifting the hem of my dress. I put the receiver to my ear, but couldn't concentrate, and barely heard my sister say, "Hi! How was dinner?" Victor had turned me around and had me up against the wall in the hallway between my kitchen and living room. He was already trailing kisses along my neck, and collarbone and stroking my thighs. I was feverish with desire and a fine film of perspiration coated my entire body.

Ana was talking, but I wasn't hearing a thing. "I DID see mom, she was great, fantastic," I panted into the phone and I dropped the receiver onto the charger with a clatter as Victor's hands tweaked my nipples through the material of my dress. Not caring if the phone was off or on the hook, I let my hands fly and roam his back and shoulders once more.

As soon as the phone was forgotten, his hands left my nipples; he reached for the hem of my dress, and yanked it over my head, stepping back to take in my body. The look he gave me was the biggest compliment he could have ever had given me—his eyes were on fire with desire for me. "You're so fucking beautiful, Monica. Let's fuck."

His words were harsh, but what a fucking turn on. I was getting wetter. Burning, yearning for what my body knew only he could provide. He reached for me, and lifted me up right under the arms. He was strong and carried me just like that and set me on the sofa behind us. He separated my legs and positioned me while still standing and stroked my thighs; instinctively I wanted to close them. My back was against the side arm, with one leg up on the sofa bent at the knee and the other hanging off the side. "Don't move," he commanded. It took all of my will power, but I didn't move and watched as he slowly undressed, first taking his belt off, then his shirt, his slacks, and lastly his boxer briefs folding them neatly and placing everything on the floor beside the sofa. He was gloriously naked standing in front of me. His erection, once sprung, was massive. He had at least a good eight inches, and the girth! Oh, my! He must have seen my eyes widen in surprise. "Don't worry, it will fit," and laughed at my dazed expression. Spread eagled before him, I was feverish with desire.

He knelt on the carpet in front of me, and urged my hips off the sofa with his hands, as he slid my panties down slowly just a few inches. "Always wear a matched set for me, Monica. I like that." After removing my panties and gliding them off my legs, he allowed me to lean back on to the sofa, but kept one hand under my rear caressing it, squeezing it. His other hand grasped my thigh almost pinching it as he slowly began to allow his head to descend, keeping his eyes locked on to mine. "I'm going to enjoy this as much as you will, Monica. I like pussy, I like to kiss it, taste it, suck it." Oh, my! I had never had this done to me before. With his shoulders spreading me wider and his hand holding one leg, he dipped down, and the moment his tongue touched my center, my head flew back. It was fricking awesome. I felt every lick, every lap of his tongue. He sucked on my core, licked and licked. My head began to toss back and forth of its own accord. I had no control. He licked me and my muscles quivered, and pulsated. I tried to squeeze my legs together because the feelings were so intense. His whole head was in there. He rubbed his nose against my sensitive flesh, and lashed me with his tongue and lapped at me until I thought I would scream. My hips began to gyrate of their own volition. The excitement in me grew until I was nearly ready to explode; his finger on his other hand explored my ass, and tentatively poked me. The pleasure was so intense, and without any thought, I screamed, "Oh, my god! Fuck Me!"

"I will later," he grinned up at me momentarily while I squirmed and writhed uncontrollably, and then he continued licking, and sucking. I never knew pleasure like this. He licked, sucked and tasted just as he had promised. I moaned my pleasure, and bucked some more. And then I exploded into a million little pieces and reared my hips toward him pushing myself onto his face, as he sucked on my crazy over sensitive nub, and I exploded again.

"Fuuckk!" That garbled scream had come from me. He finally lifted his head after my second orgasm in quick succession, and smiled at me. He watched me as my eyes went from cloudy pleasure to reality. I tried to reach for him, but I was still panting and out of breath. He got up from his knees and lay himself between my legs, and crawled up onto my body, putting his weight on one forearm as he lay beside me.

"Now, it's my turn," he murmured. The man had such control. One hand reached over the side of the sofa, and fumbled around. He showed me the condom he held, and using his teeth ripped the package open. I scooted sideways as he placed the condom over the head of his penis, and then he took my hand in his, and placed it on his dick. With his hand on mine, we rolled the condom down, and I watched his eyes close with pleasure, as I tightened my grasp around him. I continued to hold him, and he then pulled me to him and went in for a kiss. Deep into the kiss, I could feel his hands begin to roam. He played my body like an instrument. All the while he was stroking me, first my legs, then my abdomen, flat now, and then finally my breasts through the bra. Other parts of my body became alive with desire for Victor and my hands began to roam and explore his exquisite body, as well.

He broke the kiss with these words: "I want to see your breasts now, Monica." And, he pulled both cups of my bra down. "Lovely, almost perfect!" He said teasingly. I gave him a puzzled look. "I like bigger tits!" His smile was mischievous as he dipped his head and began to pay each one of them exquisite attention. While licking one, he was squeezing the other gently. He rubbed his palm on the already excited flesh and my nipples tightened and hardened even more. Small fires of longing shot through me again, licks of pleasure, and then his teeth were on the other nipple, biting gently as his tongue titillated and toyed with the tip. I began to squirm beneath him. I had to touch him, too. I scratched his back lightly by instinct alone and felt between us to find his cock. Like in the parking lot, he was granite hard and I could feel pulsating beneath the skin. His dick was hot, as the blood rushing into it pumped through his engorged penis. My fingers shifted to grasp him all the way around, the tips barely reaching, I stroked him. Once, twice. He groaned around my nipple. His teeth released my nipple, and cool air from the ceiling fan made it pebble even harder if possible. He scooted a little higher, took my hand, the one that held his dick, and then his massive cock plunged deep into me, penetrated me to my very core. As he sank into me, he groaned his pleasure quite audibly. He stilled for a moment allowing my body the time it needed to stretch to be able to accommodate his massiveness. It was exquisite pleasure, and we fit so perfectly. It was slow torture as he began to move. In, then out, almost. In again. Slowly. He built the fire within me unhurriedly and deliberately, stoking the flames of our desire. He began to move faster. He kissed me crushing his lips onto mine, and plunged his tongue into my mouth as his dick charged again and again, deep, and full, so fulfilling.

I felt the quaking within me begin to build again, and feeling it he slowed his tempo. "Not yet," he grounded out in a guttural gasp. "Wait for me!" he demanded. He plunged again, picking up the speed, rubbing against my center, grinding into me, diving into me. I was burning, slick, my wetness began to seep down my legs. He screamed my name, I screamed his a fraction of a second later as I felt his seed spill into the condom. He collapsed on top of me breathless and panting and his weight felt good to me to.

When he tried to pull away a minute later, I begged, "Not yet! It feels so good. I want you inside me like this. I can't believe how good it feels." I didn't want to lose this connection, this oneness I felt with him still inside of me. He complied for a little while. But then, slowly he withdrew and took the condom off. I felt empty. He then twisted crosswise and sat up on the side of the sofa and retrieved a couple more condoms and smiled at me mischievously.

He scooped me up onto his lap, and with one eyebrow raised inquired, "Bedroom?"

Spent for now but happily so, I indicated over my shoulder with my chin. He walked briskly to the room I indicated and he laid me down gently on my bed. He got in next to me and turned me on to my side away from him, spooning me from behind. "Now go to sleep, Mi Cara, because I'm going to fuck you again in the middle of the night, and again in the morning." And, he did!

Chapter Four

The Morning After,
The Next Night, and Sunday

VICTOR WAS UP early and had me again, as he promised. He was an amazing lover and the bedroom gymnastics we had competed in last night had me exhausted and a little sore. By seven, he asked if I could make him coffee, and if I would join him in the shower. I glanced at him and caught his mischievous expression. One eyebrow was raised very temptingly. How could he possibly still be able to do this again, I thought. But, I wasn't about to complain. I gave him a quick peck on the cheek, and hopped out of bed wrapping the sheet around my body.

"Hey, don't hide your body," he ordered. So, bossy! "I like to see what I'm going to fuck!" He laughed as I just held up my arms letting the sheet drop as I continued exiting my bedroom giving him a nice view of my backside.

I walked into the kitchen completely buck naked, and I quickly opened the pantry in my large eat in kitchen and grabbed what I needed. When I started scooping the coffee into the filter and poured the carafe of water into the chamber, I heard the shower turn on. I hastily finished making the coffee, swiped the counter with a sponge, and then made my way into the bathroom wondering what Victor had in store for me now. Before letting him know I was also in the bathroom, I admired his body through the smoky glass doors. In the early morning light slanting through the window, I could see more clearly that he did indeed, have the most meticulously amazing body. He was lean in all the right places, probably didn't have an ounce of body fat, but was incredibly well-defined. His chest and arms were magnificent. The man was strong and fit and not only did it reveal he did run, but he worked out with weights and must spend a great deal of time at the gym. He wasn't body builder huge, but he was stacked with rippling muscles just underneath his smooth tan skin. I felt those muscles last night and this morning under my fingertips as my hands roamed his whole body.

"Knock, Knock," I said as I stood just outside the shower door. He slid one door open marginally and peeked at me.

"Get another condom, Monica, from my pants pocket and get in," he grumbled as he opened the door wider. I scrambled into the living room and reached into his pants pocket and found the condoms he had been using, and hastily made my way back into the bathroom. I stepped into the steaming shower, he took the condom out of my proffered hand placing it on the window sill, and then he turned me in front of him so that I was immediately under the spray of the shower head with the luxuriant water cascading down my aching body. "I'm going to wash you. Would you like me to do that?" he purred into me ear from behind me.

"Yes, I-I would like that," I stammered. The way he spoke thrilled me and sent goose bumps popping along my arms.

"So hesitant. I like that about you. I can tell you don't have a lot of experience. It makes a guy feel good to know that what he is possessing is so untried and unexplored. How old are you, Monica?" he whispered seductively as he positioned my hands on the wall on either side of the shower head.

"I'm thirty. You?" I asked nervously. What was he going to do with my hands splayed on the wall like this? I felt helpless, exposed. I had never showered with a man before and it made me feel a little vulnerable, and exposed.

"I'm thirty-five. But you, Monica, look younger, much younger. You have great skin." I peered over my shoulder and he was lathering up my loofah sponge and he began scrubbing my back with it in large circles. It felt delicious, decadent even. The sponge went lower over my hips, back and forth on either side, then around each of my butt cheeks and then through the crack that defined my rear. The sensation of someone washing your body is indescribable. The combination of the hot water, the soap, the sensual movements, and his husky words had me panting already and he hadn't even reached any of my erogenous zones. It was Victor's voice, so sultry. It must be. How he could caress me with just his words, I didn't know. Just as I had that thought, his hand dipped between my legs and the sponge parted my lips through the soft curls there and found my core. He massaged the soapy lather over my center. I groaned under the spray, water trickling into my mouth from my parted lips. I pushed myself into his hand, as he reached around me to slide his other wet slippery hand up my rib cage capturing my breast and squeezing it gently. Resonances of pleasure continued to come out of my mouth. The water so hot, the rubbing, the slickness of it all had me wanting.

"Bend over, Monica. Put your hands on either side of the tub on the edges there." He growled and indicated pointing at where he wanted me to place my hands. He backed up enough to give me the room to do it while he fumbled with the condom he had placed earlier on the window sill. I did what he asked but missed the pleasure I felt from his grasping my breast and rubbing me with the soft sponge. "Spread your legs, baby. Wider," he urged. I did. I felt his erection press into my backside. "I need you to bend your head down a little lower." Again, I did as he asked. I couldn't refuse him anything. I was pliable, like putty in his hands. "I'm going to fuck you so hard from behind, Monica, and you're going to love it!" I believed him. He placed his hands on my hips and gripped me firmly and with no hesitation charged into my pussy, penetrating me so deeply that it hurt a little bit, but then the pleasure of his slamming into me over and over again and the hot water cascading over my sensitive skin soon made me forget that momentary discomfort. He had a good strong rhythm going right from the start and ripples of sensation almost immediately coursed through my vagina. "Touch yourself, Monica. Use one hand to pleasure yourself. I won't let you fall." He held me firmly, and continued his punishing deep thrusts. Tentatively, I removed one hand from the tub and found my clit easily. It was already swollen and engorged. I flicked it back and forth with light touches and eventually increased the pressure there swirling two fingers over myself again and again. He plunged and hammered into me over and over. My breathing became ragged. I was close, so close. His hold on my hips intensified and his fingers clenched and dug into the flesh of my hips, but even that felt good. My body was alive, like it had never been before and I enjoyed every sensation. I felt his dick getting harder. It filled me. "I'm going to come soon, Monica! Oh, god baby!" The walls of my vagina that had been rippling now clenched and began to spasm around him at those words. My pussy squeezed and released him repeatedly as he slipped in and out of me with furious intensity. I continued to rub myself furiously increasing the pressure. A cord of electricity sent shock waves from my pussy to my nipples causing them to tighten into hard pebbles. Victor screamed, "Oh, fuck." It was a garbled and strangled sound. I loved it; it made me feel powerful. I was doing this to him, making him feel this way. My legs began to give way but he held firm and slid into me two more times as I then found my own release and screamed his name.

After that and because my legs were weak, he scooped me up and grabbed a towel on his way out of the bathroom after discarding the used condom into the waste paper basket. Dripping water on the floor, he made his way back to my bedroom, where he stood me up and gently wrapped the white fluffy towel around me. I leaned against the bed. He used another towel to dry himself off rubbing efficiently and quickly. He stooped beside my bed and picked up a black duffle bag, I hadn't noticed earlier. He must have retrieved it from the car when I was making the coffee. As he began to dress, he spoke. "Monica, I had a lot of fun last night with you and again this morning. I hope we can do this again. I have to leave, soon. I have to pick someone up from the airport, so I gotta run, and I have a family thing to do today."

"Okay," I replied. Trepidation began to descend on me, but his next words warmed me.

"But, I want you to come see me tonight. Bring an overnight bag. I will text you my address. Can you come at eleven? I know it is late, but I don't know when this family thing will be done." He had just finished pulling on a tight black T-shirt over his head. He looked so good in black. He had on faded blue jeans already, not fastened yet.

"Yeah, I can come. Tampa, right?" I asked. It was Saturday and I had no plans this weekend.

"Yeah, it isn't hard to find. I have a roommate. I hope you don't mind that. Also, she is a girl." He looked up at me from tying his sneakers and must have seen a flicker of apprehension cross my face, and added, "She's just someone I used to work with on base. Just a friend, purely platonic. I just moved in with her a couple of weeks ago until I can save up for my own place. I lived on base before that for the last six months"

"Oh," I stated lamely when he paused.

"Yeah, she's been a really great friend. I've known her forever," he smiled looking down at me.

I smiled back. How could I not, when he looked at me like that. "That's nice." Again, lame, but with him leaving soon I was beginning to feel a little lost.

He looked at me puzzled, and then dropped a bomb. "I want to be honest with you, baby. I like you a lot and we could have a lot of fun together, but, Monica, don't fall in love with me. I'm not in a good place in my life. I've got some money issues, and I'm starting over. I don't want to lead you on. You're the first girl in six months that I have wanted to fuck more than once, but don't set your cap for me. It's not going to happen." His eyes searched mine.

A lump began to form in my throat, and I just nodded. I tried to hide the disappointment and met his gaze and smiled.

"I want to be honest with you, babe. I don't want to hurt you," he whispered and gave me a peck on the lips looking at me. "Can you handle that?" He searched my face.

Again, I nodded. The lump was still there. I couldn't speak. Last night had been amazing, this morning too. I wanted all this man had to offer, but apparently all he could offer me was mind blowing sex. Would that be enough? It would have to be enough. "Yes, I can handle that." I replied trying to harden my voice.

"I will make it easier on you." He was all seriousness now. "I won't do romance. No gifts, no flowers, no fancy restaurants, okay. The minute you want out, let me know." His eyes still searching mine looked for doubt.

"Okay," I said and straightened my shoulders a little to show him I could handle it, and directly met his penetrating scrutiny. God, I was so disappointed. A thousand possibilities died in that moment, but maybe his feelings for me could grow.

"So, are we still on for tonight?" he questioned and laughed softly eyebrows waggling mischievously.

"Yeah, I'm game. Why not?" I shrugged my shoulders nonchalantly trying to appear indifferent.

"It'll be fun while it lasts, baby." His eyes searched mine and I feared he may have seen my doubts, but then he shrugged too. "Bring a bathing suit, we can swim on Sunday."

"Okay, sounds like fun," I said. He straightened up and grabbed my shoulders and gave me a firm kiss on the lips. I was still in a daze over his revelations that it took me a moment to respond and open for him as he plunged his tongue into my mouth. The kiss lasted pretty long and was pretty intense, but somehow this time it didn't make my toes curl.

He pulled back and looked at me questioningly, "You okay?" His ice blue eyes pierced my brown ones.

"Yes, I'm fine," I responded hastily. "I'm looking forward to tonight." I smiled clutching the towel with one hand in the front, and used my other to tuck a long wet curl behind my ear.

"Beautiful and vulnerable. What a sexy combination?" His eyes, so intense stared into mine. He shook his head to break the magnetism between us. "Okay, I really have to go," he said glancing at my bedside clock which read nine o'clock. He gave me another quick kiss, grabbed his duffle bag off the floor and slung it over his shoulder. He lifted one of his hands and tenderly stroked my cheek with it, turned and left. I stood there until I heard the sound of the front door closing softly with a click. I was very confused, and sad.

I spent that Saturday morning cleaning my house, and puttering as I was too distracted to grade papers. I went to Target, bought a new bikini bathing suit, and tried not to think of the things Victor had said. All day, I lied to myself saying this was another Dan. Victor was another teacher, someone who could show me the ropes. It would be fun while it lasted. Deep down I knew I was in big, big trouble.

VICTOR TEXTED ME his address around five o'clock with a. 'I'll see you later'. I had been putting it off all day, but knew I had to call my sister. She would want the details. I would give her just enough to satisfy her, but keep some things to myself. I called her at about seven when I worked up the nerve and felt calm enough to deliver the abridged version of the evening's and morning's events. Ana, was happy for me, maybe he's the one she said breathily, and I laughed because it was expected of me to do so. I told her my plans and gave her Victor's address as well. Of course, she wanted an even more detailed run down of the events of the past two days, but instead of the blow-by-blow, I gave her just the briefest of rundowns of the previous evening and morning. How many times, and in what rooms. Her reply was something of the sort, "You finally came up for air?" and, "Atta girl!"

When I got off the phone, I still had a lot of time to kill, so I tried to grade some papers and went for an extra five mile run. At nine, I packed a bag with the new swim suit I had purchased earlier in the day, a couple of pairs of shorts and a couple of tank tops for the next day. I gathered the necessities for my make-up bag and some other essentials. At nine-thirty I realized I hadn't eaten, and I made a small Caesar salad for myself minus the croutons I loved, I had to watch those carbs you know, and lastly washed the dishes by hand.

At ten, precisely, I shut off the television, picked up my overnight bag, and went out into the garage. I opened the back of my white Ford Escape SUV and put the bag inside, and then got into my car while hitting the button for the garage to open. I was on my way. I had butterflies in my stomach, and uncertainties. It seemed like it had been days since I had seen Victor, but in reality it had only been thirteen hours. A very confusing thirteen hours.

I MUST HAVE driven more quickly than I thought because it was a quarter to eleven, and I was minutes away from Victor's place. I didn't want to get there too early, or appear overly eager. I had to stop for gas anyway because I was driving on fumes, a bad habit of mine since I hated pumping gas and didn't like the smell of the fumes. I was pumping the gas when I heard the tell-tale ding from my cell phone that indicated that I had a message. I finished pumping, and as I had prepaid using my ATM card, got into my car, and checked my message. It was from Victor.

Victor: *You must be close. I just got in myself. Too tired. I had a long day. See you soon.*

Hmm, that sounded cryptic. I texted him back.

Monica: *Yes, I will be there shortly, I'm just a few miles away. I* *had to stop for gas. We can just watch television or something.*

Victor: *Ok sounds good. See you in a bit.*

I was there in five minutes. I parked in the visitor parking section near building two in Victor's apartment complex, and made my way over to the lobby. I searched for and found his apartment number and heard the tell-tale buzz. The soft click of the lock releasing moments later proved I was expected. I looked up the flight of stairs and he was there standing at the top, looking gorgeous and yes, very tired. Kind of sad, too, actually. He started to make his way down stairs meeting me halfway. He took my bag from me, and held one of my hands with his as he guided me upstairs. His apartment was just to the right of the stairs in an open breezeway, and the door was open slightly. He let go of my hand, and muttered, "Fuck, the Cat!" as he lunged two steps quickly to the door and peered in.

"You have a cat?" I laughed. He didn't strike me as a cat guy.

"Yes, I do. Love that stupid thing, too." He turned to me with a relieved expression on his face. "She's on the sofa. Belonged to a friend of mine first, but he didn't come back from Iraq."

"Oh, that was nice of you to take it in. I'm sorry about your friend," I said apologetically giving him a sympathetic smile.

"Don't worry about it. I have had her for years." He paused as he placed my bag just inside what must be his bedroom. I saw the cat on the sofa, a beautiful, very fluffy, and monstrous looking long haired white Persian. He then turned back to me. "Well, accept for the six months I lived on base. Anyway, her name is Mrs. C." He looked up at me mischievously and his eyebrow did that adorable little lift thing.

"Strange name for a cat," I stated confused as I turned back around from admiring the spacious apartment. The kitchen/dining room/living room area was all open and tastefully, yet simply decorated. As, I turned back towards where he stood it hit me what the C stood for, and then I wrinkled my nose and said, "Oooo, you're so bad!"

He laughed, "Well her name was Cat with a *C* before I had her, and my roommate's name is Kat with a *K*, well Katerina really but everybody calls her Kat for short, so it was getting to be a little confusing, so I changed Cat's name to Mrs. C. I just made it a little more colorful. A sweet pussy, needs a sweet name," he joked. He reached down to scratch the cat on the head, and she purred up at him melodiously pushing her head against his hand. "See that, same reaction whenever you please a pussy." Victor had a way of making everything sound dirty, yet enticing.

I laughed my mood lifting a little. I loved his little jokes and innuendos. He strangely reminded me of my sister. The guy had sex on the brain. Awesome, right? I thought so.

"So, the bedrooms are here and here." He pointed to opposite ends of the living room. "This one is mine on the right. I have my own ensuite bathroom. We got a balcony, but it overlooks Del Mabry, so we don't use it much. But out back is an awesome Olympic sized pool and really big courtyard. We can grill over there and have parties and gatherings."

"It's very nice. I wish I had a pool. I love to swim." I envied people with pools in Florida. I was saving up to have one built.

There was an awkward silence for a moment as he was done pointing out the various features of the apartment. He broke it.

"So, a movie then. I'm sorry, but I'm really tired tonight. I had a rough day, and not too much sleep last night, if you know what I mean, but I will make it up to you tomorrow, Monica," his usually twinkling eyes, just faintly sparkled at the suggestion.

"That's fine, Victor. I'm okay with just relaxing tonight," I told him.

"My roommate went out with her girlfriends so we have the place to ourselves for a bit. She probably won't be back 'til sometime after two."

I sat down on the sofa in the corner as he headed towards the television and flicked it on. He gazed at the media cabinet to the right of the screen and selected a DVD from the many that lined the shelves. "Oh, I love this movie. You like Tom Cruise?" he called over his shoulder.

"Yeah, I do, actually," I replied. Tom Cruise was sexy as hell, and despite his occasional public displays of weirdness, I thought he was a pretty great actor, but he had nothing on Victor.

"Have you seen The Last Samurai?" he probed as he popped open the case and removed the DVD from its casing.

"No, I haven't," I indicated as I got more comfortable on the sofa popping one leg underneath me.

He came over to the sofa and sat next to me removing the pillows and putting them on to the floor, and proceeded to lie down with his legs stretched out and his head in my lap. "Comfortable?" he inquired.

"Yeah, I'm good," I whispered as I gently began to scratch his back in circular motions.

"Mmm, that feels nice. Keep doing that." He whispered as he flicked the remote to bypass the upcoming attractions. He pressed play and the movie credits began to appear. "I really am sorry, Monica. I feel bad. I had a rough day, and know you probably hoped for me to be more entertaining. But I just can't. I have a lot on my mind, and it isn'thing I can talk about with you yet, okay?"

"Sure, Victor," I said. "We all have bad days. No problem." He sounded so sad that my heart went out to him. I hoped he would feel better and maybe more comfortable around me, maybe even willing to confide in me, someday. But, he had told me this morning there would be no promises. Our days might be very limited. It looked like that 'someday' would never come. I continued to brood over that as I continued absently scratching his back.

"Mmm, so relaxing," he muttered again. "Just keep doing that, okay?"

"Okay," I muttered. He fell asleep with me scratching and running my fingers across his back within fifteen minutes. I tried to concentrate and enjoy the movie, but my mind was racing ahead of me until I was so lost I couldn't even follow the story line. So instead of watching the movie I just lay my head back and closed my eyes. After a little bit or so, I found myself getting sleepy; and I, too, began to doze off.

I didn't know what time it was when I heard a click and glanced towards the door. I saw the knob turning and knew instinctively that it must be his roommate. A woman, very tall, older, maybe in her late thirties or early forties, and little bit on the husky size with short sandy brown hair came in through the door.

"Hi," she whispered. "I'm Kat, and you must be Monica. He's sleeping?" she inquired indicating Victor.

"Yes, he is," I whispered back. "He was exhausted."

She came over to us and looked down at him. "Well, we

better get him to bed." She began to gently shake his shoulder. "Come on, boy, time for bed," she whispered.

Victor sleepily opened one eye. "Kat?" he muttered. "I had a bad day."

"I know, big boy, I know. Come on, Vic, Mon and I will get you to bed." She automatically shortened my name like my sister did, and from the way she handled Victor I could tell she was very nurturing. I instinctively knew I would like her.

"Monica?" He turned as if he were surprised to see me and began to sit up. I got up and held on to one side of him, with Kat on the other and together steered him towards his room. He unfastened his jeans, and she pulled them down until he sat on the side of his bed, and then she pulled them the rest of the way off one leg at a time.

She began to make her way towards the exit. I laughed softly, and said, "It seems like you've done this before."

"A time or two," she nodded. "And don't worry about me, Mon. I'm like the Mom around here for these lost boys," she whispered. "Goodnight, we'll get to know each other in the morning."

"Okay," I whispered. "Good night, Kat." She seemed pretty cool.

The door clicked shut, softly. Victor was already lying down on his side of the mattress, and he must have taken off his t-shirt when I was talking to Kat. "Wear my shirt and come here so I can hold you. I quickly got up and stripped out of my white t-shirt and black capris. I took off my lacy blue bra, but left the matching panties on. He sleepily muttered with one eye open, "Nice." I took his t-shirt and pulled it over my head and scrambled in next to him in the middle of the bed wiggling my rear into him so that we were spooning. It felt nice to by lying with him like that. Dan had never slept over, and neither had I at his place.

"Your shirt smells good, like you." And, it did. I clutched a handful and brought it to my nose inhaling his scent. His maleness, his scent, woodsy and spicy was intoxicating.

"So, do you," he whispered in my hair. "It's nice to have someone to hold on to at night, again." And, with that he fell back to sleep softly snoring. He had said that I had been the first woman he had wanted to be with in a long while more than once. I held onto that. I had a little glimmer of hope. Just a little.

It took me awhile to relax, although I was very comfortable lying there in Victor's arms, again a million thoughts raced through my mind. It took me awhile to fall asleep with Victor's steady breathing in my ear, but eventually I did.

He was up before me the next morning. I heard him in the kitchen talking to someone, probably Kat. The smell of coffee and eggs probably woke me. I quickly got up, and pulled on my capris from the night before, but left his t-shirt on. I hastily went to the bathroom; I finger brushed my hair, and brushed my teeth after retrieving my tooth brush from my bag on the floor.

After that, I peeked out of the bedroom door anxious to see him, and both Victor and Kat turned towards the sound of the door opening.

"Morning, sleepy head. It's after nine," Victor teased. He was at the stove stirring a steaming pan of eggs. He cooked, too.

Kat laughed. She was sitting at the table in a long nightgown, sipping a cup of coffee. "Yeah, Victor has already run ten miles, showered, and made us breakfast at this ungodly hour." Her murmur of displeasure made it sound that this was a common occurrence.

I laughed and joined her at the table. "Is there anything I can do?" I asked.

"Not a thing, Mi Cara. Eat and enjoy!" He placed a plate of scrambled eggs with a bit of cheese before me, and a cup of coffee. He was in a much better mood this morning and seemed very refreshed. He placed a light kiss on the top of my head and then returned to the kitchen island to grab some plates for him and Kat then joined us at the table. We ate, and I enjoyed the teasing motherly-son banter between the two.

I learned that Kat was divorced, and forty five. She had grown up in the military, joined the military and had two grown children in Ohio where her ex lived. Military life was all she knew. She worked at MacDill Air Force Base in shipping and receiving and loved her job, and country. She was a gung-ho patriot. Victor, when in the military had been in charge of fitness, and did PT with the troops to ensure they were in top physical form and able to meet the physical fitness qualifications of the job. "Yeah, for one month out of the year, I would let him boss me around and scream at me, at what a lazy fat ass I was, but the rest of the year, I do the bossing around," she teased.

"That's right, Sergeant!" Victor laughed, but made the statement with respect and gave her a mock salute. I didn't know about military ranks, but felt somehow that she must have out ranked him when he had been in the military.

As we finished breakfast Victor announced to Kat that he was going to take me canoeing in Pinellas Park this morning. We would join her and some of his other friends that lived in the complex all later for the pool party they were having around three. It was a surprise to me as he hadn't even mentioned these plans to me, but it would be nice to have a little alone time with him this morning, I thought.

"Okay, well, I will clean up, since you cooked, and you both go on ahead," Kat stated as she began to clear the dishes from the table.

Victor took my hand, and we went back into the bedroom. "We will shower when we come back, Monica, Is that okay?" He was now in the bathroom brushing his teeth.

"Sure," I muttered, as I quickly pulled my blue panties down, and then pulled on a pair of fresh white ones. I had brought two pairs of shorts. I selected the denim for canoeing instead of the white ones. Hurrying, because the water was now off, I turned and pulled off his t-shirt, and slipped into my bra, and to go with the denim I chose a pale pink t-shirt with the American Idol insignia on it. I was still a fan of the show despite all of the changes in judges and format.

He came out of the bathroom and saw what I wore. "Cute. You like reality TV?"

I blushed, "Yeah, my one guilty pleasure."

"You will have plenty of guilty pleasures before I'm done with you," he smirked with that crooked grin. And the fire in his ice blue eyes was back, which I was very happy to see.

"Have you ever been canoeing?" he asked as he gathered items from his dresser to put in his pockets. He also took a small framed photograph and put it frame face down, I noticed. I hadn't seen it last night as it had been dark in the room last night and we hadn't put on the lights. Earlier, I had been in too much of a hurry to get out and join Victor and Kat for breakfast that I hadn't scoped out my surroundings either. I didn'tice that there weren't a lot of personal possessions in the room, though. He also had several boxes in the corner that he had yet to unpack.

"Lots of times, actually. I'm a farm and wilderness girl. Grew up in a village in Maine, spent my summers fishing, camping and hiking. My dad loved the outdoors, and so do I," I informed him as thoughts of the photo slipped from my mind.

"Really, awesome! A farm girl. Mmmm," he teased, looking at me through the reflection in the mirror, and then giving me a bit of his own history. "I grew up just over the bridge in Clearwater. My parents are Italian. They were from New York originally, obviously." He pointed at himself. "They retired here, when I was . . . hmm, fourteen, I think. So I'm a city boy, but I love the great outdoors and Florida." He fastened his watch on, and turned back to me. "Ready to go?" I nodded. He looked pleased. I was too. We had our obvious differences, but we had a great deal in common as well.

The ride to Pinellas Park was about thirty minutes from his apartment complex. On the way there he was quiet at first, but eventually he started to quiz me on the music and the artists. Of course, I reminded him that I was horrible with names, artists, and song titles. He laughed and said what do you call your students, "Hey, You?"

"Sometimes," I said with a straight face, then I laughed also.

We parked and made our way to the rental hut. It was a rough structure made to look like a large tiki hut. He rented a canoe for the two of us and handed me a paddle and a lightweight life jacket as park policy required we wear them. For about ten minutes, we paddled in silence enjoying the fresh air and the bountiful flora and fauna around us.

"Monica, I don't want to ruin the mood, but I want to be as honest as I can with you, ok? Those things I told you the other morning I meant."

My heart hammered into my chest. This was the only man I had ever been excited about, but he kept warning me off.

"Okay," I said hesitantly and I waited for him to continue.

"My life is complicated. I have a lot going on with switching careers, seeing what direction my life is going to take. I'm still in the reserves, so one weekend a month it is all about that. Two weekends a month I have family obligations, and it's all about them. I don't have time for a full time relationship. There are things going on that I don't want to talk about with you. I'm busy right now with trying to start up this new business. I can tell already, you are a good girl, who deserves someone who will put you first, but I just can't do that right now, if ever. I can give you one weekend a month maybe, and one or two nights a week." When I didn't respond right away, he continued. "Look, you can even see other people if you like?" Then he waited.

Other people? I only met him four days ago, but instinctively knew no one could compare. It just wasn't in me to juggle two guys at once. I also didn't want to be just a casual occasional sexual encounter. Again, I wondered why he was pushing me away. I chose my words carefully.

"Victor, I like you, a lot," I emphasized. I'm willing to take what you can give me for now. I like my life; it is simple and not complicated. I'm not interested in seeing two guys at the same time, ever. It is just not who I am. Can't we just enjoy the time we have together when we're together and worry about the rest later. If it's because you want to see other girls when you aren't with me then. . ." I lowered my gaze and left the thought unfinished. It bothered me too much to think about it at the moment.

His smile was like diamonds. "No, Monica that's not it at all. Please believe me when I tell you it's not that. I don't have time for one relationship, let alone two. Please don't think that. I just don't want to be unfair to you. But, I was hoping you would say something like that. I don't like to share, but I can't commit. I just wanted to give you the opportunity so you weren't waiting around for me all the time. I can't do dates, work stuff, family gatherings. I've already explained I can do one weekend a month, and maybe one or two nights a week. Don't fall in love with me. I'm pretty busy. I don't want entanglements, arguments, or drama because you're home twiddling your thumbs for three weekends a month resenting me. I just want to draw the line in the sand. This is all I can offer. If you're sure that you can handle this, then I'm game." He pulled the boat to shore, and then carefully stood to cross the boat to sit beside me. I was feeling a little lost at the moment. He cautiously placed his hands on my face and whispered, "You're so beautiful, Monica." Then he kissed me for the first time that morning. In the warm spring breeze it helped to melt some of the ice that had formed around my heart at his words. It was soft, and tentative, not rushed or demanding like the others we had shared. When it ended, he gazed into my eyes, and asked me one more time, "Are you sure?"

"Yes, I'm, sure," I whispered putting my head onto his chest inhaling his scent.

After a minute he pulled us apart, and gazed down into my eyes. My emotions were in turmoil; and I was never any good at hiding my feelings, and so probably seeing the confusion and uncertainty there, he stated. "You don't ask a lot of questions, Monica." *Because I was afraid of the answers.* "If you did ask, I want you to know I don't have the answers right now. But, I promise, I will share my burden with you when I'm ready, ok?"

"Okay," my voice quavered. It was the tell-tale sound that I felt like crying. He kissed me again, long enough and tenderly enough to give me a little hope that this relationship or whatever it was going to be wasn't doomed from the start.

WE WERE BACK in his apartment by noon, and we found a note on the kitchen counter from Kat.

Over at Joe's, helping prepare the food. See you at three.

–K.

He showed me the note and grinned at me maliciously. He explained that Joe was hosting this barbecue, had even flown in lobster from Maine this morning. Joe, as did many military people, rented a condo in this complex to be close to the base, but far enough away to be able to party without the ever watchful military police at MacDill Air Force Base being present. He also explained that the note meant we had the apartment for the next three hours to ourselves.

"Three hours, whatever shall we do?" he hinted.

"What do you have in mind?" I asked giving him a flirty smile.

He took my hand and led me to the bedroom, and set me down at the bottom edge of the bed. "Monica, I want you to do something for me. You trust me, don't you? Will you do this for me?" He looked so boyish, so innocent in that moment, but my fears from earlier hadn't completely evaporated.

"What is it?" I asked nervously searching his eyes for answers. This day was just full of surprises. It wasn't going as I had hoped in the least.

"I want to shave you?" He coughed and then looked down at my crotch.

"What?" I squeaked sharply. Not an attractive sound at all,

but his request had really thrown me for a loop. It had been way out in left field, way out of the ball park.

He laughed and explained. "I love to eat pussy. Seriously, a lot of guys don't like it, but I do. Weird, I guess. But the hair, sometimes, well it just distracts me from what I want to do. Okay?" He had a kid in the toy store look that was getting denied his heart's desire for a moment as his lower lip jutted out into a pout.

I had always kept myself neat and trim down there. I swam a lot and didn't want flyways in my bathing suits. How embarrassing? I must have turned fifty shades of red. I felt my face flame. And he was talking about shaving it all off! I had my doubts about him and about us, but the attraction I felt for this man was real; it made me willing to do anything he wanted. I who hadn't felt attraction to any man, who had hid away in her own home for nearly ten years, only going to and from school, to and from work, was now experiencing all kinds of strange, wonderful, erotic experiences. I was too afraid of saying no, too afraid that doing so would bring this, whatever it was, to a crashing and resounding end. With those thoughts whirling in my brain, I nodded my compliance and I haltingly said, "Yes. Okay."

His smile lit up the room. "Okay, stay here. I'll be right back." He rushed into the bathroom and I heard cabinets open and close, I heard rattling and banging, and then he came out a few moments later with an armload of stuff which he dumped onto the bed. I laughed nervously at his obvious delight.

He placed a towel at the foot of the bed on the floor and then asked me to stand while he put another towel on the bottom of the bed on top of the covers. "I want you to take your pants and panties off and sit here, with your ass at the edge of the bed, Okay? Then you can lie down and just relax while I work." With my eyes like saucers and my heart racing, I followed his directions as he watched me undress and sat at the edge of his bed.

I laughed at the mischief in his eyes. "This wasn't exactly how I had hoped we would spend these three hours alone together."

He laughed too. "You just wait, Monica. Be patient. You're going to like, no love, how this is going to make you feel." I lay there as he opened up his shaving kit and took out what looked like an electric razor and changed and cleaned the attachments, "You'll have to buy one of these, Monica. I will do it the first time, but then the day before I come to see you I want you to make your pussy pretty for me. Will you do that for me?" Those eyebrows again, raising and lowering suggestively, oh, how they could turn me on. There was a bit of the devil in this man.

"Okay, Victor," I murmured and nodded slowly as he began to descend between my legs until I could only see the top of his head. I felt so exposed, and not in a good way at that moment.

"I'm going to trim it close using a number two attachment," he explained. "It's going to tickle, but don't squeeze your legs together while I'm working or may have to punish you," he laughed mischievously into my crotch. I could feel his warm breath there; it sent a shiver through me and thoughts of the two nights ago on my sofa came unbidden to my mind.

I heard the buzzing sound seconds later. Before it even touched me though, he patted and stroked my pussy. "Thank-you for doing this for me, baby. You're going to enjoy it as much as I. I promise," he assured and then I felt the vibrations come over my flesh as he trimmed my pubic hair with his number two attachment. It tickled, but not too badly, and so I was able to remain still. He made quick work of it, running the bristles of the comb over me again and again until the job was done. When he turned off the trimmer he purred, "Nice. It looks good, but it will look even better." He then instructed me to go take a quick shower, and then use some of his shaving cream and the razor blade he handed me to remove the rest of the hair. "Don't miss any," he said with eyes twinkling, "and rinse well so there are no strays. I will clean up in here and wait for you." Darn, he wasn't going to shower with me I thought. The least he could do after what had transpired this morning was to finish the job properly.

I grabbed his t-shirt, the one I had worn to sleep in, off the bedside table and marched into the bathroom to finish the task he had set before me.

I turned on the shower and laid the supplies he had given me on the edge of the tub; when the water was hot enough, I stripped out of Victors' t-shirt and got in. I did the job, and when it was done I was as bald as, well, Victor. I didn't'tice that the skin was very sensitive and the sensation of the water coursing over me felt unusually good. I washed my hair while in there as well, and rinsed my body carefully to ensure there were no strays. I stepped out of the shower, and dried myself off, combed all the tangles out of my hair, and wrapped in a towel I emerged from the bathroom planning to get dressed. However, Victor obviously had other ideas. I discovered him completely naked lying on the bed, and music playing from his bedside radio. My heartbeat jumped frantically to see him lying there waiting for me. The look in his eyes told me everything I needed to know for the moment, and I dropped the towel.

His body glistened from the overhead light and the sun shining through the window. He sat against the pillows, his hands folded behind his head. "Come here Monica," he beckoned me with his rough words as the fire jumped in his eyes. I went around to his side of the bed, my legs shaking in anticipation. He looked at me and inspected our handiwork. "Good job, baby," he complimented. He reached for me with his hands, took both of my hands in his, and rubbed them together. I was startled slightly because his hands were oily and warm, and then he spoke softly. "I want you to suck my cock. Have you ever done it before?" My mouth went dry, and I shook my head in the negative. "Good, because I will teach you how to do it the way I like it."

The oil was warm I noticed as he continued to massage it into my hands. He swung both his legs to the floor. "Take off my shirt and kneel before me, please." I did and my face was mere inches from his enlarged cock. I noticed for the first time that he too was completely hairless. It made me smile. I guess this made it fairer. "First, hold me and rub it, stroke it, but don't squeeze it too hard, and look up now and again at me, so you can see how much you are pleasing me." I followed his directions to the letter. He leaned back a little from the side of the bed carrying his weight on his arms that were positioned slightly behind him. He smiled when I looked up the first time. "Now swirl your tongue around the tip a few times and keep stroking with one hand, mmm, that feels good, support yourself on the floor with the other hand if you need to." I did. I looked up again, his eyes were half-closed and heavy-lidded but he watched me still. I could see the ice of his eyes on fire. "Now, open your mouth wider, Monica, and take me into your mouth a little deeper each time. Yes, your mouth is hot. Lower your hand to the base of my penis.

Just use your thumb and forefinger and stroke me up and down, that way you can get more of me into your pretty, fucking mouth, yes, that's it. You're a natural, baby," he groaned his pleasure. Hearing his excitement and passion had me really turned on. I was making him feel these things. I stroked faster as his groans became more consistent. "Suck me, baby, that's it," he encouraged. "Faster. Deeper. Yes, I love fucking your beautiful mouth." And then, "Now, slower," he ground out. "Make it last." One of his hands fisted in my hair, so that he could then control the pace. I sucked his cock, and twirled my tongue around it, licking it like it was an ice cream cone. I kept peering up into his beautiful eyes, glittering eyes. He tasted like salt, and his dick was massively hard underneath the velvety skin as I continued to stroke and suck. I rubbed the tip of his cock back and forth across my wet lips and saw that he liked that a lot, and he grinned his approval at my initiative. He stopped giving me directions, and I just used my instinct to guide me, but kept peering up at him to see if he approved. His moans and encouraging words weren't enough; I desperately needed to see his eyes. I sucked him again, deeper, all the way to the back of my throat, and continued to stroke him with my index finger and thumb that grasped him like a vice. I sucked his dick for twenty, maybe thirty times like that, breathing through my nose. All the while he groaned my name; he would say oh yes, or baby, or suck it. I was so turned on because he was enjoying it so much. It made me feel power-ful. All of sudden his hands were out of my hair, and around my waist; he lifted me onto the bed on top of him, but then spun me around so I was facing backwards. "Keep sucking," he pleaded. I bent down and did. He rubbed my ass, and inserted a finger there. It felt strange, but good. "Tight," he murmured. He pulled on my feet until I was lying on top of him with my feet by his head. His finger then slid into my pussy. It was wet, and sent me soaring, as he inserted first one, and then two long fingers. He finger fucked me while I sucked his cock and it made me so much wetter, I kept deep throating him, and was enjoying every minute of it. He rolled to the side taking me with him, his cock deep down my throat. I felt his warm breath on my pussy, and sensitive without the hair it felt exquisitely delicious as I groaned around his cock in my mouth. He pulled me a bit higher and then his tongue found my sweet spot, circled my engorged clitoris, and flicked it with his tongue, two, three times. I twisted and began to buck and shake, but kept sliding my hand along his shaft, sucking and twirling my tongue around the tip. His groans were muffled as he ravaged and ate my pussy. He devoured it. I exploded. It felt like everything inside me shattered. He screamed then too, as his semen flooded my mouth, and I drank it, barely tasting it, a little salty, and slimy in texture. "Oh, fucking yes, no, stop, too much." I was still sucking his half limp dick and he had to pull me off him, and spin me around. His face was wet with my juices, and he used the back of his hand to wipe it off before claiming my lips for a quick passionate kiss. It was short, we were both still panting, and he pulled me to him and just held me until our heart rates returned to a regular beat. My head was on his chest, and I could hear his heartbeat pounding in my ear until it returned to normal. After a minute he chuckled. "Holy hell, batman, you can suck my dick anytime. You're a quick learner."

I laughed at his silly joke, and replied, "You're a great teacher," and hugged him a little closer. This weekend wasn't all that I hoped it would be but at least he could please me and still wanted to be with me for now. He pulled me closer, held me and pulled the sheet up over us with his other hand. We cuddled like that and dozed until it was time to go to the party.

A FEW HOURS later, he was in the crystal clear pool swimming and I watched him from the lounger I had claimed to get a little sun. After our nap, we had cuddled and kissed for just a few minutes, had quick showers because of our earlier encounter, and then headed to Joe's apartment to help set up for the barbecue. His friends were nice, really nice and easy to talk to. The single guys teased me about breaking their hearts and asked why I hadn't set my eyes on them first at the Blue Martini, when Victor would just break my heart. They obviously knew something I didn't, but I didn't want to pry. Joe was especially nice, an older man in his fifties, months away from being retired, but still liked to party with the young guys, he said. When I asked if he was the Dad to the group, like Kat was the mom, he roared with laughter. "Hell no, little lady! I'm the big older more experienced brother!" and he winked at me knowingly, making me blush.

We stayed outside until dusk and enjoyed the camaraderie, ate lobster, joked, drank a few beers, but it seemed all too soon when everyone began to chip in and start to clean up. We were back in his apartment by eight and we both knew I would have to leave shortly so I began to gather my things. Kat was in her room, putting away laundry as we said goodbyes in his bedroom. He helped me to put my things away into my overnight bag and I noticed the picture from earlier was gone, and then we walked out into the living room.

Victor called out to Kat. "I'm walking Monica to her car. Can you buzz me back up?"

"Sure," she yelled and then popped her head out of her room. "Nice meeting you, Monica. Hope to see you again. It was nice seeing Vic smile."

"It was nice meeting you too, Kat," I said as Victor ushered me out the door.

Victor just shook his head. We made our way quietly to my car, him carrying my bag with one hand and holding my hand with the other. He put my belongings in the car, and then followed me to the driver's side door. He leaned me up against the door and kissed me. It was the sweetest kiss he had given me so far. It made me feel a little better about this weekend and then he held me, and pleaded, "Please, don't fall in love with me, Monica. I'll give you what I can, but I'm afraid it can't be enough." His words chilled me. Why was he afraid of hurting me? Why was he dooming this relationship from the start? It hurt. He sighed and I looked into his ice blue eyes. "I have something for you, Monica," he added. "It's a temporary tattoo, remember the girl from the restaurant?" I nodded and looked down to the palm of my hand to see the tribal band tattoo, with the words, Hot! Hot! Hot! above it. "Put it on, somewhere on your body, anywhere. That's where I will fuck you next. Go now. I'll call you Tuesday."

I got into the car, and couldn't even speak to say goodbye because of the lump forming in my throat. This man ran hot, then cold the next minute. He was tender one second, then was warning me off. This man had secrets, he wasn't willing to commit, yet he wanted my body and I wanted him. I was confused. He shut the door and stood there and watched me back out of the parking space, out of the lot, and onto Del Mabry Blvd. The ride home was a difficult one. What had I gotten myself into, I wondered?

Chapter Five
Trying to Keep Me at a Distance

VICTOR DIDN'T CALL on Monday. He didn't call Tuesday, either. It made me feel horrible inside. I couldn't even explain how I felt. My dream on Monday had been first pleasant then painful. I imagined he had met someone else, and that I had been nothing but a fleeting pastime. I thought about him all day, too and was so distracted at work. I wanted to call him badly and when he didn't call again that night, I was so disappointed. He had reiterated how busy he was, and I didn't want to appear needy, so I didn't call. I waited pathetically for him to make the next move. As disappointed as I was by his revelations, I still hoped and prayed he would call. Late on Tuesday with no call coming in, apparently, I flicked off the television, and I got ready for bed then sadly climbed under the covers around eleven o'clock for another restless night. But, I had my cell phone next to me, just in case. It felt like I was just dozing off when the phone began to ring. It was Victor.

"Hello," I said.

"Hey, Monica, it's me, Victor," he said loudly into his end of the phone. I could hear music in the background. He was obviously out with friends having a good time I thought, a bit resentfully. His words confirmed my thinking. "I'm out with some of the guys shooting pool, but I remembered I promised to call you." The laughter and music began to fade and his voice began to return to normal.

"Hi Victor, I th-thought you forgot." I squinted at the clock. It was just after midnight. "I was sleeping."

I think he could hear the disappointment in my voice because he sighed and then said, "You sound mad. Are you mad, Monica?" His tone dropped a couple of decibels sounding concerned.

"No, I'm not mad." I wasn't, just very disappointed. "I was sleeping so my voice may come off a little huskier," I lied.

"Well, I'm glad you didn't wait up and you haven't been waiting around for my calls. Remember what I said, I want to be friends with benefits, no complications, okay?" he said cautiously.

The lump in my throat got bigger. Why did he have to keep reminding me of this? It was as if he wanted to put a wall up between us. "That's fine, Victor," I lied again. "I was in a relationship like this once before. I'm a big girl." *My only relationship! It wasn't the kind I wanted to have again. Not with him.* I wanted possibilities and chances.

"You sound mad, Monica," he stated emphatically. *God, was he trying to pick a fight?* I was getting mad now.

"I'm not mad," I replied on a sigh, "Just tired. I had a long day, is all."

"I was going to come see you tomorrow, but I think I will come Thursday, I can spend more time with you then. Is that okay? Are you available?" He asked.

I paused before answering, not wanting to sound desperate. "Sure, I've got no plans. What time?" I asked, and although I would have liked to have seen him on both days, I kept those thoughts to myself.

"I don't know yet. I'll let you know," he muttered. "Listen, the guys are calling me back. I'll call tomorrow, okay?"

I didn't want the phone call to end so soon, but he was making all the calls. "Okay. Good night." I hung up before he could say anything else. I couldn't say another word anyway because of the lump that was forming in my throat. I hadn't known him long and I knew it was silly, but I was feeling things for him I shouldn't feel already. Yearning, longing yes, but maybe even something a little more. He was trying to warn me off, but I didn't know what he was trying to warn me about. He couldn't commit to me more than a few days a month right now, but couldn't tell me why. I was all kinds of a fool for wanting him. *Would what he was offering be enough for me?* I asked myself. I lied to myself when I told myself it would have to be. But, the deeper part of my mind wondered what he was doing all those other times when we weren't together. Chin up, girl, I told myself. You've been through a lot worse. I could control my heart, couldn't I? But, that didn't help me to control my imagination. I didn't sleep too much after that.

ON MY WAY home from work on Wednesday, I stopped in at the Publix supermarket on the corner of U.S. Highway Nineteen and New York Avenue, just a few blocks from my home. I needed some fresh produce. I shopped often, every couple of days to buy fresh produce. I liked my greens fresh, and after putting my purse in the front of the shopping cart, my phone rang. I reached in and saw Victor on the display screen. My pulse quickened, and I made my voice sound up beat.

"Hey, Victor."

"Hey, Monica. You sound much better. I was worried about you," he remarked.

"I had a better day today; my students behaved and most actually did the assignment," I offered as an explanation.

He chuckled, "Well that is good to hear. I'm sure the boys were riveted." I laughed at his teasing. "Hey, I hear noise, you still working?"

"Actually, I'm at the grocery store. I needed parsley, artichokes, asparagus, and maybe carrots." I rattled off my shopping list and heard him chuckle.

"Mhmm," he muttered exaggerating boredom. "Fascinating." I laughed again.

"Sorry to bore you, Victor," I teased back.

"You've never been boring, Monica," his tone was once again serious. "Well, I just wanted to say hello. You didn't sound like yourself last night, and I was just checking on you to make sure you were okay. I'm on my way home to shower, and then a family thing came up. So, I'm glad I didn't promise to see you tonight, you would have been disappointed. But, I will see you Thursday, about nine. I will sleep over so we have a little more time together, and just leave early for work, okay?"

He'd worried about me, well that was something. "Sounds great, Victor. I'm looking forward to it," I replied keeping up my false sense of cheer. "I've missed you," I blurted out, suddenly not caring that he knew I cared a little.

"Oh, Monica," he stalled for time as I patiently waited for his reaction. "I missed you, as well. Later, Mi Cara," and he hung up.

His words warmed me and I would make tomorrow night special, I vowed so that he would continue to miss me. I was a little disappointed that he wouldn't be coming until nine o'clock, but he had told me he'd be able to spend more time with me if he came on Thursday. Shake it off, Monica, I told myself. Take what you can and what he's willing to give. Don't push too hard and don't push him away, my head told my heart. Make what time you do have special, and I began to plan.

My SISTER STOPPED by around six o'clock on Thursday. We had dinner together. I spilled everything. I had to. She kept demanding details. She could read me better than I could read myself. She could see the dark circles under my eyes, and the puffiness. She heard the hesitation in my voice.

"Listen, Mon. I took you out so you could meet someone and have a little fun, and see that sex is good with many men. Enjoy it. Take what he has to offer for now, and keep your eyes on the horizon for the next hunk. But I have a bad feeling about this guy. Don't fall in love with this guy."

"That's what he said!" I grumbled. Then, we both laughed at the joke, and the funny line often used in the comedy *The Office* we both enjoyed.

Her laugh trailed off, and then she sighed. "Seriously, Mon. This guy sounds like he has some deep issues. It seems to me, the guy is hiding something, and I don't like it. Something smells fishy to me," she stated tapping her long French manicured fingernails on the table top."

"I do really like him, and the sex is great. Better than great. Mind blowing. I have been having a lot of fun," I complained. She was worrying her bottom lip. I already really liked Victor. I wanted her support here, I wanted her to see the silver lining, see hope. She wasn't giving me any of those things.

"Well," she drawled out, "Fun is good." She smiled wickedly wicked. "But don't lose your heart to him if he won't come clean with you. Do you think you can handle that, honey?" she reached over to pat my hand.

"I won't lose my heart, and I think I can," I vowed more to myself, avoiding her searching gaze.

"Good, we're on the same page here, then?" she enquired with one arched eyebrow looking at me from her porcelain face.

I nodded.

"Well, it sounds like he's another Dan, but with a lot more sex appeal AND he seems knowledgeable. He will teach you things. That is for sure." She waggled both eyebrows suggestively. "Enjoy it. Go with the flow. Ride the wave, if you know what I mean, and if you don't, I meant ride his cock." She was trying to lighten the mood again, and I sorely appreciated it.

"Way to state the obvious, Ana!" I laughed. "I'll do that, though. The sex is really amazing," I reiterated.

"It sure as hell sounds like it. Damn, I wish I had taken him home with me," she teased and took a sip of her sweet tea. I chuckled and murmured hands off he's mine. She laughed, but then got serious again and repeated her warnings one more time. "Mon, this guy has got serious commitment issues. He's hiding something from you, and if you pressure him for answers he's going to bolt. I advise you to enjoy it, but keep looking, chicka! Don't set your cap for the first guy that rocks your world." Did I mention my sister was a psychologist? She was always full of advice, whether it was asked for or not.

"Yes, Ana." I grumbled. I knew she was right. Victor was hiding something, but I didn't want to know what it was because it might make the distance between us grow even more. I got up to clear the table. It was nearly eight and I had to get ready for Victor. Butterflies appeared suddenly in my stomach. I wanted tonight to be perfect.

Ana helped me with the dishes while we chatted a bit more, and then she kissed me on the cheek and left. She always made me feel better, and I felt a bit more confidence surge through me because of what I planned to do tonight. Victor had seduced me wholly, but tonight I was going to seduce him. Because of Ana's words, and my plan, I shook myself off and squashed down my self-imposed funk. With a much improved attitude, I began to get ready for Victor.

AFTER A QUICK shower and shave, I straightened my naturally curly long brown hair and applied just a bit of mascara and lip gloss, and lastly spritzed on some vanilla bean body spray. Wrapped in only a fluffy towel, I made my way to my bedroom to make my final decisions on what to wear, and selected a matching set of red satin bra and panties with a bit of black lace. It was sexy as hell. My sister Ana had bought most of these bits for me introducing me to the sense of power these garments instilled, to make me feel better about myself a few years ago. The week of my birthday last year, she showed up every day with a new something for me. I wore them all the time now under my clothes, and she was right, they did always make me feel better. To complete my ensemble, I put on a short satin black robe, and left it open. Perfect. Seductress. I read books. I could and would be in charge tonight. Think about sex and pleasing Victor, I reminded myself, and nothing else. Feel your inner goddess, as my sister would say. Ha!

The doorbell, rang. He was here. I quickly left the bedroom and pressed play on the CD player. Three Doors Down *Here Without You* softly played out of the two speakers from on top of my entertainment center. I opened the door, and Victor stood there gaping at me. Score. Point mine. He looked sexy and startled. He wore grey cargos and a blue button dress shirt accentuating his eyes. The shirt was open wide at the collar revealing his amazing chest. His ice blue eyes ravaged by body from top to bottom, and back again. He loved what he saw. And I was glorified by his reaction; my self-esteem needed it very much. I took his hand, and turned around leading him straight to my bedroom, the music following us as the lead singer's words spoke the things I could never say to Victor about my growing feelings for him. How he was constantly on my mind.

I led him to the foot of my bed and pushed him down onto it; he landed with a thump but still in a sitting position. He laid down after kicking off his shoes, and watched with those mesmerizing ice cold eyes on fire, glittering for me. I stepped back when he reached out to me and then turned away from him towards the mirror on my dresser. I looked over my shoulder at him, as Brad Arnold's words continued to croon and express how each moment you got to spend with the person you cared for was special.

I slowly stripped and danced for him dropping my robe inch by inch ever so slowly down my back revealing the red satin and lace bra. I swayed in time to the music and then lowered the robe to reveal the tattoo he had given me in black ink, with the words, Hot! Hot! Hot! above the tribal band just above my fiery red panties with the black lace. His eyes shot to my face, they were on fire, burning for me. As much he tried to push me away, he wanted me. This I knew. I had surprised him by putting the tattoo there. I had really stunned him. He made to move and get up, but I held up one finger and waved it back and forth, the universal sign for wait, and then I let the robe fall and flutter all the way to the floor. I continued to dance for him, swaying my hips erotically, showing him with my hands where I wanted him to touch me. The words to the song caressed my soul hope, as I caressed my body for him.

I CONTINUED MY dance in time to the music wanting him to wait, and ache to touch my body, and as the track ended and the next song began to play, I leisurely crawled up on to the bed, and straddled him. "No touching yet," I warned.

"You've planned this," he groaned his frustration but kept his hands to his side like a good boy.

"Mmh," I murmured seductively and bit my lower lip fully knowing he was watching my every move.

I sat on his thighs and began to undo his belt without breaking eye contact. I unbuttoned and unzipped his pants and gave him a little rub through his boxers. He was already fully aroused. I saw him lick his lips, and he, who was always so in control, was breathing out of his mouth. I knew he was incredibly turned on. But he resisted and continued to let me take the lead. I began to work the buttons of his shirt and pulled it from the waist band of his pants, and leaned in to lick his flat chest from his belly button up to his chest between his pectoral muscles. I felt his muscles jump beneath my palms as I stroked his chest and abductors. "Mmm, you taste so good," I breathed. I maintained eye contact the whole time. I licked one of his nipples, flicking my tongue across it, and then blew on it making them harden, then I made my way to his other nipple and did the same. I scooted up on him to continue the journey to his neck while arching my back and pressing my crotch onto his erection. He groaned at the contact. I kissed his collarbone, then neck, and then made my way to his finely chiseled chin, licking, kissing and nibbling him ever so lightly with my teeth. His hands reached for my arms but I pushed them down again, and I could feel him shaking as he fought for control.

"Oh, God, Monica. I want to touch you so bad. I have to touch you." His words sounded panicky, strange, yet filled with desire. He was getting desperate to touch me, and this was what I had wanted.

"Go ahead, baby. You can touch me, now." I gave him the permission he craved and his hands immediately went around me, to my back, and then my bottom.

My kissing and seduction continued along his face and neck and when my mouth reached his, I plunged my tongue into it, and withdrew, then bit his lower lip, sucking on it briefly and taking it into my mouth. He lost it, then.

"Monica, stop for a second," he ground out sounding like he was in pain. "I think I'm going to cum. Please stop."

Wow, I thought, and was pretty pleased with myself, but did as he asked and waited for him, not moving until he had the time to regain control. He pushed me a bit, and I sat up, and he positioned my leg off of him. He then slid off the bed as I knelt there and he removed the rest of his clothes, and stripped for me.

"I'll be right back," he murmured and went to my bathroom. He came back moments later and set the jar of Vaseline from my bathroom cabinet on my night stand then got onto the bed and knelt in front of me. Taking my head in his hands, he kissed me with a wildness and abandon that left me gasping for air. Gripping my face, his kiss deepened and explored my mouth. He was in control again I could see, but I let him take the lead as I had accomplished what I wanted to do. One hand came off my face, and he used it to reach behind me to unclasp my bra still not breaking the kiss. He drew the strap off one side and then the other, switching hands from my face to the other strap. When my bra fell, his head dipped to capture my nipple in his mouth, and he flicked his tongue across it several times and the blood in my veins rushed to my groin, and then he sucked my nipple deep into his mouth. I urged him on, with a throaty response. Desire for him pooled at my core.

He switched to the other breast giving it the same magnificent attention. My nipples were hard little stones, and it was nearly painful, yet it was exquisite torture too. He pushed me back onto the bed, yanked my panties off with one hand, stroked the outside of my pussy with his palm, and cupped me there. I watched his eyes as he worked. They were like blue fire. Amazing! I felt one finger go in my pussy, then out, then two fingers, in then out. He put those fingers in his mouth and sucked on them, and then returned to his fingers there, stroking. I was on fire, twisting and turning to meet his touch. His thumb found my nub and pressed, and circled repeatedly as I began to buck on the bed, and reach for his cock to stroke him, too. He stopped my hand after a few passes, and turned me around so that I was lying on my stomach with my ass in the air. "Touch yourself, Monica. Slowly, not too fast," he instructed. I did. His palms found my ass, and he bent to kiss each rounded mound. "You have a beautiful behind, Monica. And I'm going to love fucking your ass." He caressed my rear when I tightened nervously at his words. I had wanted to surprise him with the tattoo on my lower back, but thought he would take it to mean doggy-style. From the look on his face, I didn't have the heart to disappoint him. I guess I was going to try something new again.

"I know you haven't done this before, baby. But I'm so happy you're willing to try it. Relax, and keep touching yourself slowly, circles, Mi Cara." I felt the mattress dip as he leaned over to reach for the Vaseline, and heard the soft pop as he opened the jar. One hand kept caressing my ass, and one finger began to probe my ass. It felt strange. He inserted one finger, just the tip. It wasn't too bad, just different. He inserted it deeper, then withdrew, then did it again. "You're so tight. You've never done this before so it will hurt. Thank-you for this, not a lot of girls are willing to try it. You're so special." He kept sliding his finger in and out of my ass. "It's going to be uncomfortable for a while, I'm not going to lie, but I will prepare you, and please you." He repeated the motion four or five more times with one finger, then two, and I felt him spreading those fingers stretching me. It was uncomfortable, but not unpleasant. He then spread my legs, and knelt between them. "Monica, touch yourself faster, and harder so that when I penetrate you the pain will be less intense," he spoke the words as he continued to slide his fingers in and out of my ass faster. It started to feel really good. "Don't tighten up, stay relaxed." I watched him over my shoulder as he watched me pleasure myself between my legs. His eyes blazed as he took a condom from the bedside table and put it on his engorged penis. Not breaking eye contact with him, I watched as he moved closer. Then I felt his dick at my ass. He pushed into me slowly, just the tip, and I stretched around him. He only went in a little bit, then pulled back out to put more Vaseline onto his shaft over the condom. I turned my head to watch as he stroked himself, a couple of times, while looking me in the eyes. I touched myself, circling my clit, in the way I liked best, and began to squirm. He bent over leaning on one hand and slid his other hand under my waist to urge me into a kneeling position. Then he plunged into me, to the hilt, it hurt like holy hell, but I didn't feel anything tear. I cried out. He withdrew, and plunged again. It still hurt, but not as much. He withdrew and plunged again sliding in and out staring into my eyes all the while. He then began to yell. "Monica, make yourself cum for me, baby, hold nothing back. You're so fucking tight, baby. I'm close, baby." I was already close, too, despite the pain, but I could tell from his voice he was closer. I rubbed furiously at my clit, and began to really get into it as he rode my ass. I clenched the muscles in my vagina, and he screamed, "Monica!" I screamed out, "Oh Victor," and collapsed on the bed. He collapsed beside me, and drew me close to him and we gazed into each other's eyes. I didn't see the fire there anymore, but what I saw surprised me because I thought it looked like tears because his eyes were glistening. He closed his eyes then and turned away, but used his hand to press my head down onto his chest so I couldn't look him in the eyes, and he held me like that until we fell asleep whispering about how spectacular and special I was. It made me feel for the first time that he might care for me just a little bit. But, when I woke up at six, the alarm clock blaring in my ear, he was gone, no note, no nothing. He had simply left in the night, and I cried for the first time in a very, very long time. Then I got mad.

By seven I was running, well almost finished running. I ran five miles every day before work, religiously, and rode twenty miles on Saturdays on my bike. I did weight training three times a week after school. I was determined to keep the body I had regained after my long bout of depression. When I ran, I carried my phone with me, in case I got hit by a car, or something. I felt it vibrate at my waist. I was in the cool down part of the run, so I picked it up, and glanced at the caller ID. Victor.

I stopped running, but continued to walk. I answered the

phone. My run hadn't cooled my temper. I didn't even say hello. "Nice disappearing act. I didn't know you were a magician as well as such a great lover." The words flew out of my mouth before I could stop them.

"Sorry, yeah, that is why I called. I know it was rude. I'm sorry. I can tell you're mad, but you're making some weird sounds, too."

"I just finished a run." Was he trying to change the subject, I thought.

"Oh, yeah, me too. That's why I left. Well, I couldn't sleep last night after and when you did, I just decided to call it a night and come home and run. It helps me think, clears my head. I'm on my way to work, but didn't want you to wait until this evening before I explained. I'll call you tonight, just please don't be mad. I know you have to get ready for work, so I'll call you tonight, okay?" he rambled.

I was having a hard time buying this explanation, but I didn't think it would be appropriate to question him about it now. And, I did need to get ready for work. I didn't like what he had done, and I would let him know that when he called tonight. "Ok, Victor, I don't need an explanation, and I don't want to force one out of you. I know where I stand. You've explained you're situation. I'm fine the way it is, for now," I added.

"But you deserve more. You were incredible last night. What you allowed me to do . . ." he paused and I heard a catch in his breathing. "I'll call you later. I promise," I could almost see him wincing as he said those words. He had told me he couldn't make me any promises, and I thought he had meant it.

THE CALL FROM Victor came at six o'clock when I was sitting

down to eat alone.

"Hi, Victor," I answered, pushing my plate away.

"Hello, Monica. How was your day? Another good one, I hope?" he asked tentatively.

"It was good, Victor." I answered. "Kids behaved. Nothing extraordinary happened at work today." Then, "I do want to be honest, though, I was upset by the way you left last night. A note would have been nice if you didn't want to wake me."

"Monica, it's that I couldn't sleep and was restless. I didn't want to rummage around looking for paper. I'm sorry. I won't do it again." Hmm, another promise I thought.

I had told him how I felt, and I didn't want it to become an issue. Our relationship was tentative at best. "Okay, I forgive you, but I just wanted you to know how I felt."

"Thanks for being honest. I don't want you to lie to me," he stated. There was a pause and it was slightly awkward. "Listen, Monica, what I told you earlier, I meant. I'm not in a place in my life where I can commit to a relationship. Last night, after we had sex a part of me realized just how special you are, and I'm not a guy that goes around hurting girls. I couldn't sleep because I just kept thinking I was going to hurt you somehow, and I don't want to hurt you. That is why I left so abruptly. I just needed to clear my head and think."

Hearing that explanation made me feel a whole lot better. If he was worried that he would hurt me then he did care about my feelings, and that could grow. So, he had left out to think about me, us, and then had called. I was foolish to be falling in love with this man, deep down I knew it, but my god I just couldn't help myself.

"Victor, I can tell you're not a mean guy. And, I don't think I'm being used by you, if that is what you're worrying about. You've been honest with me about where you are right now, I respect that a lot, and even if I don't know the particulars and the ins and outs of your situation, I'm okay with that, for now," I added.

"It is the *for now* part, that worries me, Monica," he stated truthfully.

"We can cross that bridge when we get to it. Can't we? Can we not worry about that right now, Victor? Please. I'm enjoying what we have. I promise I won't put any demands on you." It was a promise I would keep, I told myself.

"Are you sure?" he asked sounding a little hopeful, well more so than when the call started.

"Yes, I'm sure." I wasn't. But, I was beginning to really care about him, but telling him that wouldn't be a good idea; I knew instinctively it wouldn't do me any good.

"Okay, I can come over again next week, or you can come to my place. This weekend is family, next is the reserves, and the week after family again, but the weekend after that maybe we can go away together and do something. Wednesday and Thursday are the best nights for me by the way."

"I will come to you," I stated. "Just let me know when the day gets closer which is better for you. I can sleep over and drive home the next morning." I was thrilled about having him for a whole weekend, but didn't mention it. I didn't want to sound too eager.

"Okay sounds good. It's a date." He laughed nervously. "I will call you a couple of times during the week, too, and you can call me whenever you want. I may not be able to answer right away, but I will always return your call as soon as I can." Something tightened in my chest a little, but it was a good feeling.

Chapter Six
Secrets and Toys

H E CALLED ME every night! On the weekend, too. It was always a little after ten, but never later than eleven. So, he must not be staying out too late. We never talked about what he did that day, and he never mentioned the people he spent his time with. We mostly talked about shows we watched. He loved the show *Friends*, watched the reruns all of the time, loved that my name was Monica because she was his favorite character. I laughed at that, and told him I used to be fat, too. He didn't believe me at first. There were no other shows he followed religiously. He was shocked when I described to him why I had been fat, and I explained to him what had happened to me. He made the right remarks about it, outrage, and anger at the violence of rape. He was angry that it had happened to me, when a woman said no, a real man had to respect that. It warmed me to hear him say so. I even told him about Dan, and how little experience I had. He told me he thought he would like Dan. He seemed like a great friend and asked if we kept in touch since he had moved to California. I told him we just exchanged dirty jokes and kept in touch on the internet through email once or twice a month; he had left over a year ago. He had been a friend of my sister's and she had introduced us. Dan had been a safe and comfortable friend, I explained, and we had only dated casually with the understanding that either one of us could move on if we met someone we loved.

Victor shared simple things about his life. He liked news programs and took an avid interest in politics, and he absolutely loved the History Channel. He liked movies, but not theatre prices so he waited for them to come out on DVD. He told me about some of his army buddies, and the people living in his building. He never talked about his family though or the people he worked with in construction. It bothered me that he wouldn't share the more personal stuff. When he did talk about his new job, I felt he didn't like it that much. When I asked him why he did it when it seemed obvious to me he didn't enjoy the work of a contractor, he was honest and told me the money was better than what he had earned in the military. I told him money wasn't everything, and he simply remarked that it helped. It sounded kind of cryptic when he said it too, but I didn't want to make an issue out of it. I loved my job, and couldn't imagine going to work every day if I didn't love it.

It was nice. Each evening he would call me and we would talk for an hour or so, and then we would say good night. The next three weeks, were great. It was hard just seeing him once a week, but the talks were nice and kept me from missing him too much. I looked forward to those calls. I called him a couple of times, too, usually earlier, he hardly answered when I did, but usually returned the call within a half an hour or so. Those calls weren't as satisfying as the ones in the evening, but nice still. He was usually busy, working late, or at a family obligation of some sort when I called, but he made time to listen to me tell him a story about something that happened at work, or something I saw on the news and wanted to hear his thoughts on the matter.

Thursdays were great. It was now the day of the week I looked forward to most. I went the first week to his and Kat's apartment, we went for coffee, his place to freshen up and talk, and later we hung out with friends of his in a local beer joint. It was called The Honky Tonk, and had a homey atmosphere. As soon as you walked in there were two pool tables, and behind that and all across the back corner was the bar and bartender. There were ten or so high stools and ten to twelve tables between the bar and the pool tables. At the far end of the bar there was a small wooden dance floor, a DJ, and a Karaoke machine. I got a little tipsy on Coronas that night, and Kat made me sing Karaoke with her to the song *Proud to be An American* by Lee Greenwood. I can't sing at all, not a bit, so I must have been a little more than tipsy to agree to it, but it was fun. Victor laughed and smiled and encouraged me mouthing the lyrics when I didn't know the words. We played a game of pool against another couple, and actually won. It was fun. We left a bit after midnight, and had a little bite to eat before we went back to his place. That night, we made love the old fashioned way. It was sweet and I still saw stars. Victor was tender, and took his time with me that night. It was the best sex I had had with him so far, and that was saying a lot. It was special because he kept whispering endearments, telling me I was special, and beautiful, and that he loved my eyes.

It had been a teacher work day the next day, so I called in sick the night before. I wasn't really needed with no kids there so I was able to sleep in. When I woke up Victor was gone, but there was a note on my pillow. It read;

Last night was fun. I enjoyed your company. You can't sing! But, the sex was great, as usual. I'll call you tonight. Drive home safely.

—V.

I kept the note.

The calls continued every night the following week, and he came to me on the next Thursday, and also the Wednesday after that. I had promised to chaperone the prom months earlier and didn't want to break my promise, so he switched his plans to Thursday so he could see me on Wednesday. Both of the nights were memorable.

On the Thursday, I wore nothing but a leather jacket, a pair of black silk panties, and a pair of high heeled thigh high boots. His eyes popped out of his head when I answered the door. When he left in the morning I slipped the panties into his pocket when I kissed him goodbye. He texted me at two in the afternoon to thank me for my little gift, and said he was smelling them right now, and that they smelled great. He promised to sleep with them all week until I gave him another pair.

When he came on the Wednesday before prom he teased me about his plans for our upcoming weekend together. Only four days away. I was excited to be able to have a whole weekend just the two of us. He wouldn't tell me where we were going, but had told me what to pack; Bathing suits, shorts, t-shirts, and lingerie. Nothing fancy he said. A whole weekend. I couldn't wait.

I had talked to my sister earlier on Friday morning and we were going to meet for coffee during my lunch break at Starbuck's. We had talked on the phone a couple of times, but hadn't seen each other in the last few weeks, even though we lived close; she worked 2nd shift at her job from two in the afternoon to ten at night. Her days off, were Thursday and Friday, and she slept while I worked, and worked when I was home. She was a youth counselor for the Department of Juvenile Justice, and did both individual and group therapy sessions in the afternoon and early evening, then had a few hours at the end of her shifts to complete paper work and such.

She wanted to see me before I left for the weekend, I was sure to warn me off of Victor. These last three weeks had been so wonderful and I told her all about it. She heard the hope in my voice. During our several conversations on the phone whenever I talked about Victor, I would hear her audible sighs through the telephone. She didn't want to see me hurt. I did get her to admit that things seemed to be looking up. It made me feel better, like I wasn't just imagining it all.

I drove down US 19 to Little Road to the new complex of shops that housed the Starbucks. Ana was already there sitting outside at the little bistro area, sipping a mocha latte, and waved when she saw my car. I parked right in front and went over to kiss her on the cheek, the usual French greeting in my family.

"Be right back," I said. "Let me get something to drink." I went into the small shop, and ordered a medium breakfast blend decaf, with Splenda, and fat free milk. I didn't like the frozen drinks, and still liked my coffee drinks hot.

I carried my drink outside and sat down next to her.

"So, a whole weekend, huh?" She beamed and the smile across my face was difficult to contain, and then added, "And, you don't know where you're going yet?"

"Nope. He wants to surprise me!" I said excitedly.

"Well text me, when you get there. Someone needs to know where you're going to be." She took a sip of her drink. "Just saying," she added and I could hear in her voice the hesitation again.

"Don't worry about me," I sighed. She would always worry, that was what big sister's did, but I wanted her to be happy and excited for me as well.

"It's not that, well it's that, but it's bartender boy, too," she said sadly.

"Bartender boy? What do you mean?" I asked surprised at the sudden turn in conversation.

"Oh, he wants me to go to some family barbecue thing at the beach and is pressuring me. You know I don't do other people's families, and I don't do barbecues. I'm not the sun goddess you are." She indicated my skin was olive in complexion. I had our father's complexion and coloring while she had our mother's. "Look at my alabaster skin and red hair, I'm a moon goddess." She took another sip and then brought the cup down so carelessly the top popped off sending frozen mocha shooting up out of the top of the container. We both laughed. My sister was so dramatic, and terribly, terribly clumsy. She always had the craziest accidents usually involving food.

"So, bring an umbrella, lotion up and wear a big hat," I offered. She had been spending a lot of time with this guy, had mentioned it a few times, but had never mentioned it was getting serious.

"I don't know," she mused. "He's really sweet. Who would have thought a bartender would be sweet. You would have thought he would be rough and tough, well he is tough and rough at times," she waggled her eyebrows at me, "But otherwise, he is just different from the guys I normally see."

Her expression was perplexed.

My sister dated losers, and bad boys. Sweet was never a word I would have used to describe any one of them. Ever since her young marriage at nineteen to an older guy, and subsequent divorce three years later after she had caught him cheating on her, my sister had gone through three to four guys a year. She usually picked guys a few years' younger, ones she could control.

"Well, that sounds like a good thing to me." I reached over to pat her hand sympathetically although I wished her problems were mine. I would have taken it as a very good omen if Victor wanted me to meet his mom, or any other members of his family, for that matter. "Ana, maybe it's time you took a bit of your own advice, and take a chance on something different."

"Ah, physician heal thyself." She laughed and shook her head still looking melancholy. "Hey, we're here to talk about you, not me. Sooo, you're going to text me where you are, and at least once every day to let me know you are good. You're going to be careful with your heart, and you're going to fuck his brains out." Ana was back.

I laughed, and made a three check mark motions in the air, "Done, done, and done!"

I PICKED VICTOR up in my SUV at his apartment at six; he had asked if we could take my car since we would have more space in the back. I was okay with that. He also said if I picked him up it would be faster as where we were going was in his direction. The city he wanted to take me was South of him, we weren't going North. It would save us a lot of time if I met him. Excited about going, I hastily agreed. He was in the parking lot when I got there, waiting for me, and he looked fresh and clean, and scrumptious. He had on khaki Bermuda shorts, and a white Perry Ellis button down shirt. He was standing next to a small travel suitcase, a cooler, a beach bag with towels and a blanket, and a small silver trunk.

I got out of the car, and went to the back of the SUV, eyeballing his luggage, especially the trunk, as he looked at my small case, and beach bag. He laughed. "Cooler is for the beach, as are the towels and blanket, and the trunk is a surprise, no peeking," he stated firmly as he placed his items and rearranged things so that everything would fit around the trunk and still give him optimal viewing. He held his hand out for my keys, and when I dropped them into his hand, he pulled me in for a kiss. It was sweet, and tender, he held me close around the waist with the hand he held the keys with, and stroked my hair and cheek with the other. When the kiss ended, he hugged me close and whispered into my ear, "I'm going to let you into my world this weekend. Trust me, okay."

I pulled back, confused, and looked at him I'm sure, with a puzzled expression on my face. This was what I had wanted. He just looked back at me. His blue eyes strangely were pleading with me, but he didn't say anything. I nodded, and then stepped up to hug him again, giving him my answer that way. He held me there for a full minute. I felt safe. I did trust him, didn't I?

"WE'RE ABOUT HALF way there," Victor announced two hours into the drive. "Do you need a bathroom break or anything?" he asked making swirling motions with his thumb on my knee. I loved how he always had to touch me.

"Actually, yes. I could use a short break to stretch my legs." He pulled over into a Seven Eleven convenience store. "We might as well gas up, Victor, while we're here. I will pay for the gas inside, forty okay."

"I'll pay this weekend, Monica," he stated firmly.

"Victor, I don't mind, really," I said. I knew money was an issue for him. It was one of the reasons he had left the military and the job he loved. I didn't know where his money issues stemmed from, because he was so close-mouthed about his past. He wore nice clothes, and had a nice car, but other than that he was always very frugal with his money. I didn't want this weekend to be a burden on him. I made a good salary as a teacher, especially since I was single, and had no debts from college due to the scholarships I had received. "You can spoil me when we get to where ever we're going. I pay for the gas and one meal, okay?"

He laughed. "Deal," he said and the twinkle was back in his eye. He looked somewhat thankful as well.

I went into the store and pre-paid forty dollars for the gas and then went to use the rest room; I also bought two bottles of water and a couple of protein energy bars. It was a long drive and I hadn't eaten dinner in my rush to pack after work and get ready. Victor must have finished pumping the gas already because he was parked up front now waiting for me. I got back into the SUV and handed him a bottle of water and offered him one of the protein bars. "Thanks," he said taking the water but turning down the bar, and then he leaned over stealing a quick kiss.

We began the ride continuing south. "So, now that we're half way there, think you could tell me where we're going?" I pleaded turning in my seat to better view him. The man was gorgeous. "The suspense is killing me."

His expression turned foreboding. "Yeah, umm, Ft Lauderdale."

"Cool, I have never been there," I replied a little confused.

"Why so grim?"

"But," he interrupted my thoughts. "It's what we're going to do when we're there that has me worried." He watched me from the corner of his eyes assessing my reaction.

"Why? What are we going to do?" I was suddenly nervous.

"Okay, I have been trying to think about how to tell you some things about me. I have been keeping you at a distance for many reasons, but I want you to trust me." Butterflies formed in my stomach. "First off, I want you to know you're the most beautiful woman I have ever dated. I've told you many times how attracted I am to you, and I am. I find you so god dammed stunning and sexy, I think and dream about you every night, well, in my dreams you have bigger tits," he laughed nervously. I was thrilled at his words. He was so earnest saying them. He looked at me again to gauge my reaction so far. His comments made me feel better. "But, I have always been a man with a great sexual appetite, I like visuals. I love to look at beautiful women, all kinds. It turns me on so much. I had a porn addiction for a while, I guess, but got it under control." He looked at me again watching and waiting.

"Okay," I responded. "So far so good. You haven't scared me away yet," I stated. I think I understood what he was talking about.

"You're not upset? Jealous?" he asked, confused.

"No. I know you find me attractive. I can appreciate a good looking man. It doesn't mean I would want to jump their bones. I could admire their bodies. I read romance novels and get excited reading them. If something is hot, it's hot."

"Yeah! You do get it! Cool!" He didn't look so worried

anymore. He continued. "So once in a while I like to go to clubs, to watch the different girls. You know a fun night out with the guys, sometimes alone if I'm not seeing anyone. I've always wanted to bring someone, a girl with me," he looked at me again.

"You want to go to a strip club with me?" I asked and I mulled it over.

"Yes, I do," he told me honestly.

"Can I ask you one question first?" Something he has said earlier had stuck in my mind.

"Okay."

Not sure if I should ask, but unable to stop myself the question came out. "Have you ever brought another girl to one of these clubs?"

He looked at me again. "One girl, but she didn't much care for it, and I'm not ready to talk about her just yet with you, okay?" I nodded. *Just yet? Good sign.* After a moment he continued, "So, as I was saying, I like the visual stimulation of porn. I like to see girls in lingerie, and naked, touching themselves. I love to see YOU in lingerie and naked, touching yourself for me, but I wanted to be honest with you about who I am." He paused and watched me for my reaction. I felt like this was some kind of test. "So, do you want to try this, go to one of these places with me?"

"Yeah, sure!" I really didn't see any problem with what he was talking about. I really believed this was something we could enjoy together.

"Really?" he was excited.

"Really, let's do it," I replied.

He looked happy. "Have you ever heard of the Dollhouse?"

I squealed. "You mean from the Motley Crue song *Girls*

Girls Girls?"

"Yes!" And, then, "Hey, I didn't think you remembered bands and names?" He was laughing at my reaction, and his hand stroked my leg.

"Motley Crue, Victor. Puh-lease! I love your close shaved head, very sexy. But, my god, in my pre-adolescent years I was always about the hair bands. Those guys were hot!" I broke out into song singing the first stanza that discussed the club called the Dollhouse.

"Okay, stop singing please," he winced in mock pain and then asked still laughing, "and should I be jealous?"

"Not, if you're willing to wear lycra pants, no shirt, and a wig," I teased.

"Well, how about just naked, and maybe the wig. But I refuse to wear lycra," he laughed. "I know that song too, but my favorite words come from the next part of the song. He sang a few bars, about being a really good boy, but wanting girls to dance for him. All the while, he glanced at me sideways raising and lowering his eyebrows suggestively.

"I've danced for you," I murmured huskily.

"I remember, baby. It is a night I will never forget. The best." His smiled at me then, and it spoke volumes. It was more than words could say, and told me he had feelings for me. I smiled back, and he leaned in for a soft kiss.

I reclined back in my seat and I sighed, and then casually said, "And, I've always wanted to try toys. But now that I know you like the dancing, I can do that for you more often." I laughed.

"What?" He sounded shocked, looked at me quizzically and then his hands hit the steering wheel and this time his smile lit up the car. "Well, then I've got a surprise for you in the trunk."

"Really?" The butterflies were back. But I was curious. "You have toys, in that trunk?"

Victor nodded mischievously. "Would you be willing to try some things with me? Some toys?" he questioned. His expression, his eyes, the fire there, told me what my answer would be.

Looking him dead in the eye I responded, "I would like to try everything with you."

His hand went from my knee to grasp my hand, and he brought it to his lips and kissed the back of my hand. It was so gallant, so Victorian, and so inappropriate after a discussion of toys. But, it was exactly what I wanted. It was romantic. He relaxed into his seat, and the rest of the drive to Ft. Lauderdale flew by.

WE GOT TO our hotel a little after ten and freshened up a bit before heading out to the Dollhouse. Victor surprised me with a sky gold shimmery cocktail dress. It was a simple design, and revealed a lot of leg and hugged all my contours. When I put it on for him and twirled his eyes burst into flame. He wore a tight black t-shirt and a pair of tan cargo shorts. "It's not a fancy place," he informed me, "but the girls do dress up a bit."

The club was actually in Sunny Isles Beach, just twenty minutes from Ft. Lauderdale and we arrived just a bit after eleven. It was also a bit more than just a strip club as I soon found out. When we got there, the bouncer at the door smiled at me appreciatively, took the cover charge from Victor and let us in. Once inside, it looked like a typical bar with the low lighting in various neon's, except there were groups of tables arranged around ten or so small stages, with girls dancing on each of them. The waitresses wore midriff tank tops with the

Dollhouse insignia revealing their flat bellies, short black leather miniskirts, and heels. Some wore fish net stockings but not all. Victor gave me a quick tour of the place, showing me and letting me peer into the side rooms when it was allowed. There were a couple of friction rooms on one side of the main area. He explained this is where guys could go and get a lap dance, and pay to have women touch you through the clothing, and you could pay extra to touch the girls through their clothing. Most places didn't allow it, but this place did if the price was right. On the other side of the club were champagne rooms, and VIP rooms. In a champagne room, a couple could have privacy, and watch girls through specially treated glass. You could bring your own girl in to a champagne room, or you could hire one of the dancers. The VIP rooms were for special groups, swingers, or people who wanted privacy because they were into some kind of fetish in that they needed the extra confidentiality. Victor wasn't into that, he told me, and I was glad for that. I didn't think I would feel comfortable sharing him with another girl. He asked me if I would go into one of the champagne rooms with him later. I agreed to go, and was excited that we wouldn't have to wait until the hotel later to touch.

We went back into the main part of the club and he ordered us a couple of drinks, a martini for me and a scotch and water for him after we took a table on the left near the big stage in the back. Near the center stage, there were a bunch of rowdy guys who were screaming and hooting and hollering. Victor wanted me to see what was going on and directed my attention to where the action was taking place. It was pretty hilarious, actually. It seemed to be a bachelor party going on from the snippets of conversation I could catch over the cheering of the young guy's friends. The groom-to-be was sitting tied in a chair in what appeared to be a large shower stall. One of the walls was covered in large blue tiles and the room was surrounded on three sides by large sheets of clear glass. The groom was three sheets to the wind, and all his buddies sat at three tables around those glass walls. They were pointing and laughing and calling out to him, things like, "Just wait," or, "You're in for it now, buddy!" He was laughing and pointing back at his friends but I couldn't make out what he said through the thick glass. He also kept trying to get up out of his seat, but couldn't because he was tied. He seemed to keep forgetting that. From beside the center stage, there was a red velvet curtain, and four girls in very skimpy bikinis came out. They sashayed their way around the bachelor party swinging their hips for all their worth and then entered the front of the shower stall room. The last girl was beautiful, with the biggest tits I had ever seen. As she entered the shower last, she exotically undid the tie at the back, and then turned around to the groom's friends and let the top fall. The guys went wild, and I couldn't help myself, but, I laughed and joined in with their cheering. Victor watched them but kept turning to watch me. He scooted his chair next to mine and draped his arm around me, and slipped his finger into the front of the sleeveless gold dress he bought me and stroked the top of my breast his index finger.

I relaxed into him, and quickly began to feel aroused, just by being with him and the excitement his stroking aroused in me as he lightly touched the top swell of my breast, dipping down to flick at my nipple on occasion. We continued to watch the girls in the shower room. They had large sponges and were putting soap on them. Then they turned on the shower, and it must have been cold water, because the groom-to-be jumped out of his seat only to flop back down when he reached the limits the ropes would allow, and the guys all laughed, but one of the girls quickly shut the water off, adjusted the knobs, and acted like it was all some big mistake. The water was turned back on and the girl's sponges became very soapy. The girls all took turns in front of the groom, lathering parts of his body, and parts of their own. When not entertaining the groom, the girls entertained the crowd by washing themselves, sudsing up their sponges, lathering their breasts and rubbing their breasts, and pretty soon all the girls were topless. Some girls rubbed their pussies through their bathing suits with the sponge and groaned their pleasure. Victor's caressing of my breast soon came to be squeezing, and the flicking turned to pinching my nipple through my bra. I returned the favor by rubbing his very aroused cock through his pants under the table. I heard his groan of pleasure as soon as I touched him. I squeezed him, and gave a little moan to let him know I was enjoying myself. The shower lasted about ten minutes, and we enjoyed the show and finished our first drink. We ordered another, and then watched three or four of the table dancers that were within our viewing distance. They were all quite beautiful and even though they were girls, I found it very erotic. There were all kinds of girls, too, African American, Latina, Asian, Native American, and girls from other nationalities as well. Some were lean, others more voluptuous, all shapes and sizes. Victor kept touching me subtly, on the breasts, on the ass, along my thighs, but I soon found myself squirming in my seat. We shared a couple of passionate kisses, too. We were both pretty worked up.

"I think it is time to go into one of the Champagne rooms. Monica, come." He got up and gave me his hand, and I followed him as he crossed back over to the right of the club. Victor approached a very buff looking black man wearing a tight black Dollhouse t-shirt and tight grey jeans. He was standing by several archways and Victor conversed with him briefly, but I couldn't hear what was said above the thumping of the music in the main bar. Money exchanged hands, and then he indicated which room we were to go in. The walls in the room were gold, with low lights directed against the walls and recessed lighting in the ceiling, but it was muted. A black leather sofa was against the back wall, and a coffee table in front of it. On either side of the sofa were two black leather chairs, one with arms and one without. All three faced a wall of dark glass. Victor led me to the sofa and indicated I should sit down. A woman entered and set a bucket of champagne on the coffee table in front of us, and two flutes of champagne. I settled onto the couch more comfortably tucking one of my legs beneath me. She filled one glass, and Victor asked her to fill his only half way as he was driving. I looked to the glass as a light was turned on behind it, and saw a small door open, and two girls entered the viewing room. They began to dance with each other and both wore satin negligees with garters that were very revealing. One girl was Latina, and the other was a tall leggy blond. The Latina wore a deep purple and the blond wore emerald green. They began to dance with each other when Victor sat beside me. "What do you think?" he asked not watching them, but watching me.

"They are very beautiful," I stated honestly.

"Yes, but not as beautiful as you," he whispered in my ear and began to kiss and bite and lick my neck. He stopped briefly when I was just beginning to get aroused again, and reached out to take a hold of the champagne glasses. He handed me mine, and then clinked my glass with his. "To the most beautiful girl in the place tonight, who has happily surprised me to no end." He drank and so did I. He took my glass and set it on the table in front of us and settled more deeply into the sofa. We watched the girls dance and begin to disrobe. They took their time, and helped one another disrobe. They began to touch each other sensually and kiss passionately feeling each other's asses, and caressing each other's breasts. Both of them were completely naked now. The Latina then broke the kiss and led the blond to a chaise lounge that directly faced us. The Latina sat down and straddled the chaise giving us a full view of her pussy and spread her legs wide, and I found myself involuntarily spreading my legs. Victor noticed because his hand went to my thighs and he began to caress them as the blond kneeled beside the Latina and touched her and stroked her with two fingers looking back over her shoulder at us as if she could see us. She parted the Latina and touched all her folds and caressed her. The blonde then took those same two fingers and inserted them into her own mouth, and showed us through the glass that she liked how the other woman tasted. Victor pushed me onto the side of the sofa, and pulled one leg onto his lap, and pulled my black lace panties to the side. "You're pussy is beautiful, Monica, and I love how it tastes. He inserted two fingers into me, and withdrew them and tasted them like the blond behind the glass. Victor's eyes were on fire. I pushed up and into his fingers as he inserted them into me again and again and then he turned to watch the girls again. The blond was finger fucking the Latina, using her hand like a gun, and her thumb to stroke the Latina's clitoris, while the Latina gyrated on the chaise and squirmed showing us her pussy and how wet and juicy she was. The Latina was also reaching up to stroke the blonde's breasts, and I reached up to fondle my own breasts through the thin fabric of the dress. I tweaked my own nipples. Victor must have been watching me as I did this, and muttered, "Yes, Monica, I like to see you touch yourself, baby." He kept finger fucking me using his thumb to stroke my clit, and I felt him move a bit as he shifted, and undid his own pants. I looked down to see he had his fully aroused penis out, and gripped himself tightly with his other hand. I groaned at the sight of his arousal, and because his attention to my clit was getting me very, very excited. Like the Latina, I, too began to squirm.

I turned back to the girls to see what they were doing. The Latina was having an orgasm, and I could just make out her screams of pleasure through the glass. They switched places but the blond sat at the edge of the chaise as the smaller Latina began to eat the other girl out. I wasn't a lesbian, but damn, it was such a turn on to see. The blonde's legs moved restlessly on either side of the Latina's head, when Victor groaned, and withdrew his fingers from me. "Monica, I need to be inside you now." He began to fumble in his pocket to get a condom. I stopped his hand and shook my head. His look and smile of wonder told me all I needed to know. I was giving him my trust, all of it. He pulled me up onto him, and I straddled him with my knees on either side of him. Pulling my own panties to the side, I sank right onto him feeling every ridge. His sigh of pleasure told me he felt it, too, this closeness, this intensity. Because I was so wet all ready, and I began to ride. I arched my back so that my clit rubbed against his lower abdomen, and I rode hard and fast. He alternated between watching me and watching the girls over my shoulder, while I rode him, and slid against him. I was panting hard, and was so turned on, knowing that someone could peek in and see us, my pussy just slid up and down along him. It was so slippery as I rubbed my clit into him that his huge cock would come right out of me, but I would impale myself again and again feeling his hardness like I never had before. I continued to soar. I started screaming, and I must have been coming like mad. I felt juices squirting out of me, dripping down my legs. He came, too, and was bucking off the couch into me screaming my name, and yelling that I was perfect. It went on, and on, I think I had two orgasms in a row. I collapsed. I felt sweat dripping down my back from between my shoulder blades, and I hugged Victor, hard, until my breathing came back to normal, while he hugged me back. We held each other like that for five minutes panting, his cock still inside me. Neither one of us wanted this feeling to end. The lights dimmed briefly in the room and restored to normal, and then the lights went out in the room behind us. I looked up, and Victor, said, "That means we have five more minutes. I nodded, and put my head back on his shoulder for a moment while he stroked my hair, and called me Mi Cara, his heart.

We got up, and cleaned ourselves off and straightened out our clothing. It was nearly two, and Victor said we should head back to the hotel. Once back at the hotel, we took a quick perfunctory shower, together, with no sex, although we did soap each other up, but we were both exhausted. We crawled into bed, and I turned to him and reached to give him a kiss. He controlled the kiss and didn't allow it to progress into anything, and pulled back. I could tell he had something on his mind. "Yes?" I questioned eye brow raised to lighten the mood.

"I want you to tell me what you thought about tonight, honestly?" he asked. "Do you think what we did was . . .," he was searching for the right word, "bad?"

I didn't hesitate for a second. "How can something that felt so amazing between two consenting adults be bad? I loved it, and I'm glad you shared that with me."

He smiled at me then and settled his head back on the pillow. "You didn't make me use a condom. Thank you, Monica. That meant a lot to me." He watched my expression. I knew there were tears in my eyes. I just smiled. He looked back at the ceiling. "I don't go often, a couple of times a year. Like I said earlier, I come mostly by myself, and usually just touch myself, or have a lap dance in a friction room if I'm not dating anyone. I like the variety, and the visuals, Monica. I love sex, all kinds of sex. I have an active imagination. I think about it all the time, I think about it with you, mostly." He stopped short and then looked at me, and then continued. "I don't cheat, Monica. I don't think of it as cheating. Do you?"

"If you brought another girl, or hired a girl and did what we did in the champagne room, I would consider it cheating, Victor. But watching and pleasuring yourself, no, I don't think that is cheating not at all." I reached my hand out to him, and he took it and placed it on his heart.

"Really?" he asked as he pulled me closer with the arm that was under me.

"Really, Victor. To masturbate is normal, it's a healthy normal activity, despite what some may say, and to see beautiful willing people, porn even, to help you find your release, well I don't think there is anything wrong with that at all." He watched all the while as I explained my feelings on the matter looking incredulous that I should feel this way, then laid my head onto his chest and kissed me on the top of my head. "Sleep, precious. Tomorrow we will have a fun leisurely relaxing day, and then tomorrow night I have a few more surprises for you that I hope you will like, too." *Toys, the silver trunk, I thought and smiled as I fell asleep in his arms. I'll try anything once, twice if I liked it*, I thought as I drifted off to sleep in Victor's arms.

WE WOKE UP late the next morning, and slept until nearly nine thirty. I asked if he wanted to run with me, he laughed and said sure. He was surprised I asked. I was a bit OCD about working out. I didn't miss a day, unless I was in the hospital. Actually, I was a lot OCD about a lot of things due to the rape and trauma, and guilt I had gone through. But, these were all things I had dealt with and now had control of. I didn't share those thoughts with Victor. It was obvious he was dealing with his own demons and I didn't want to confuse the matter with my own. I was pretty positive we had overcome one hurdle last night, and hoped tonight we could climb over another. I didn't know a lot about sex toys, but I read *Fifty Shades of Grey*, and wasn't a prude or anything. It was also obvious he had issues with guilt, and I knew how hard those were to overcome. You had to do it in your own time, but you also had to have supportive people around you, to guide you and make you see that you aren't the problem. You aren't to blame. Counseling and my sister had helped me through it. I was hoping I could help him if he wanted it. By showing him I wasn't appalled at his lifestyle, well, it had been a huge step. I had the suspicion that someone had found out about his likes and criticized him for it, and it had scarred him deeply.

We did five miles, and he teased me like crazy, called me slow and ran circles around me, but it was fun. We had quick showers, put on our bathing suits under our clothes, and then we went to a Denny's and had a big breakfast. When we left, we were full but both excited to spend the day at the beach.

We went to Lauderdale-by-the-Sea, one of the smaller beaches in Ft. Lauderdale, Victor told me. It was small, and not too crowded for early May, as spring break season was over, so it was mostly locals there with just a few tourists around. I liked it, we didn't have far to walk from the parking lot to the beach which was a cute hamlet maybe a half mile long with little shops and an adorable Ice Cream Shop, the actual name, that had a long line out front. We found a nice spot near the water and put out our blanket and had fun taking turns putting sun tan lotion on each other, but not too much fun, it was a family beach, after all. Victor took out two sweet teas out of the cooler and handed one to me, which I opened and took a long refreshing sip. It was hot out, nearly eighty-five degrees, I guessed, but a small breeze kept us cool. We decided to soak up the sun for a bit, ten minutes on each side and then get in the water. We lay side by side on our stomachs first, giving each other small pecks, and holding hands, and then lay on our backs for a while.

When it was time to go into the water, Victor put on his Devil Rays baseball cap, so he wouldn't burn his scalp. He looked so handsome, tan and glistening. He was so carefree and relaxed. I liked it when he was like this. I wished that I could see him like this all the time. He had an amazing body, lean and toned, muscles rippling in the Florida sun. We walked hand in hand into the water. The water was gorgeous, clear, and warm but not overly so. We went waist deep, then Victor squatted in the water pulling me to him as my legs instinctively wrapped around him. He supported me with one hand around my waist, and another under my rear cupping and caressing me under the water. He kissed me and I kissed him back, nothing erotic, just slow lazy kissing, truly enjoying each other. It was like time stood still that day for us in the Florida sun. I loved the normalcy of that day, the feeling of not being rushed because it usually seemed like we had only stolen moments together. I would cherish this day, forever.

We watched people snorkeling in the distance. The beach

apparently had three tiers of natural coral reef within walking distance of the shoreline. Neither of us had brought snorkeling gear, so we watched and held each other, but it was okay, we enjoyed each other and enjoyed watching, and hearing the younger kids come up for air oohing and aahing about the things they saw, this fish, that part of the reef, etc. After an hour so, we went back to our blanket on the beach and dried off, It was nearing late afternoon, and we decided to stroll the length of the beach and then go have some ice cream. Victor picked up a sea shell near the end of the walk, and presented it to me. It was smooth, and shiny, blacks with purple and blue swirls, an abalone shell that reminded me of his eyes. "A keepsake, Madame," he offered.

I took it from him, and closed my fingers over the shell feeling its warmth. "I'll cherish it forever," I teased at his gallant offer. But inside I wasn't teasing, and I would cherish it forever. I would put it in the top drawer of my dresser and keep it with the note he had given me. It would remind me of today as long as I lived.

At the ice cream shop, I got a chocolate ice cream cone, and he got a strawberry double scoop. He planted the tip of his cone on my nose and licked it off, when I tried to do the same, he ran away from me. I laughed chasing him for a while, and then gave up and promised not to. We found a vacant bench, sat down to enjoy the ice cream, and held hands as we watched the surf, and people. "Hey," he interrupted my thoughts, "I forgot to tell you how amazing you look in that pink bikini, you almost look as tasty in it as my ice cream," he teased and popped the last bite into his mouth.

"Ooo, you," I laughed. "I should have smashed your face with my cone."

"Race you to the blanket," he called. He took off, and I

ran after him. He beat me, of course, but I wasn't too far behind him. We collapsed on the blanket and turned onto our side and talked about everything and anything frivolous from our childhood.

We took one more quick dip in the ocean, dried off and began to pack up as the sun was just about to set; we were both surprised to find it was nearly eight o'clock. The day had flown by.

The ride to the hotel was done quietly and quickly. We had agreed to have quick showers, mine would be a little longer, I told him, as I needed to do some grooming. Then we would go out and have a nice dinner and then back to the hotel for the fun he had promised me.

BY, NINE THIRTY we were just being seated at the Pelican Landing, a casual dining restaurant at the end of Pier 66. We sat outside, and had a great view of the Intracoastal Waterway, and boats coming in and out, yachts too. Victor hoped someday to have his own boat as he loved to sail.

The lighting in the restaurant was subdued, yet bright enough we could easily see one another. We both ordered the seafood special with the vegetable of the day, and Victor also had them bring out oysters because they were purported to have aphrodisiacal qualities. Although I had never tried them before, I found that I quite enjoyed them as the little slippery suckers slid down my throat. They were good with just a squirt of lemon juice. We had one cocktail after dinner, enjoyed each other's company and the spectacular view. By eleven thirty, the check was paid and we were in the car, headed back to the hotel where a whole new dimension on our sex lives was about to be unleashed.

Victor seemed nervous when we got back to the hotel,

and it made me a little nervous, too. He was probably worried about my reaction, I told myself, and not by what might be in the trunk? I excused myself to go freshen up and give him some time as well. I rummaged through my bag, and retrieved the one piece white, almost see through satin chemise with matching lace panties I had selected for the night and made my way to the bathroom. He stopped me as I passed him, and pulled me in for a quick kiss, and said, "Don't be afraid. I won't hurt you. I just want to please you." His eyes searched mine.

"I believe you," I whispered the words as I pulled away. In the bathroom, I brushed my hair out until it shone and shimmered like gossamer, and brushed my teeth. I stripped and I used one of the hotel washcloths to freshen up my arms, face, and legs. Then I applied my lotion smoothing and massaging it all in, before I put on the little nightie. It was a simple piece, virginal almost. I had bought it last week, knowing Victor would like it because of its innocence and because he liked me in white as it contrasted well with my skin tone.

When I came out of the bathroom, he had on a nice pair of form fitting black boxer briefs. He looked like an Adonis to me, with his chiseled chest, and the glow from today's tanning revealing every ripple in his chest and arms. "You're so ravishing in white, Monica." He crossed the room to me, and swept me into his arms swinging my legs over one arm and supporting my back with the other.

"Thank you," I whispered, and then his lips claimed mine greedily. It was intense, and needy, and demanding of a response. I was breathless when it ended and he put me back on my feet in front of the small silver trunk he had placed on the small table in the room.

I looked up at him. There was hesitation in his eyes. "Show me," I said.

He slowly unlocked and opened the box, but didn't look down. He watched me instead. Intensely.

I looked down. He had an assortment of dildos and vibrators; some were really long. I touched one. It must have been eighteen inches. "This most certainly doesn't go in all the way," I stated.

"No," he laughed. "It doesn't."

I looked through the dildos, and picked up one vibrator that was his size and had an attachment that I supposed could reach and stimulate the clitoris. I examined it and then handed it to him. "This one," he laughed and at my nod he set it on the bed behind us. He lifted the box higher so another level appeared. In that level was an assortment of clips and clamps. Some had beads on them, feathers, and jewels.

I said, "Your turn. You pick." He chose two clamps with jewels adorning them and chain that connected the two together. Those he placed onto the bed as well. Next, he lifted the lid higher to reveal a third row. Here were lotions, Vaseline, a couple of strings with marbles on them, some odd shaped dildos that I later learned were plugs, a whip, and a few other things I had no clue of. "I don't know what most of these are or what they are used for," I stammered a little nervously.

He pointed to the string of marbles and picked them up. Three golden marbles on a golden cord. "These are Ben Wa balls. They can be used during sex, or before sex, you can even wear them all day to strengthen your vaginal muscles. You can also insert them in your ass, and when you come, I can pull them out of you and it will strengthen your orgasm." He looked at me, the question unasked.

"OK, I would like to try it," I stated nervously. That was going to be a lot of stuff in me, all at the same time, but I was willing to try it for him. He put the beads on the bed, and took the jar of Vaseline out too, before closing the lid.

He kissed me again slowly, and seductively, and then asked me to take my panties off as he sat in the chair beside the bed. I took them off slowly and stood before him. He picked up the Ben Wa balls and warmed them in his hands and then put them in his mouth. He opened the jar of Vaseline and inserted his pinkie into it, and then indicated I should turn around. He patted my ass and stroked my ass and gave one cheek a small slap. He took the Ben Wa balls from his mouth. "Monica, bend over and touch your toes. I'm going to insert my pinkie into your lovely ass, and then the Ben Wa balls." I bent over. He inserted his pinkie and it slipped right in because of the Vaseline, he stroked me like that a couple of times, and then I felt him push one, then two of the Ben Wa balls into my rectum. They were warm, and hard, a bit uncomfortable, but not much, one ball dangled between my legs. I could see it hanging there in that position. I could also see Victor smiling at me through my legs. "Hi, there," he teased.

"Hi yourself, handsome," I teased in return.

His smile and joking made me not so nervous, and I smiled back. "Monica, walk around a bit, and tell me how that feels."

I straightened and walked back and forth across the room passing right in front of him a couple of times. They felt strange, but the longer they were there, maybe from the sway of my hips, or the fact that they kept moving around, it felt quite pleasant if a little foreign. "They are okay," I nodded. "Probably would feel better in my vagina, though."

He laughed and agreed. "If you were just wearing them, for that, you're right they would. You would feel anticipation all the time while wearing them, and horny as hell, and frustrated if you couldn't get the job finished. Delaying gratification can be quite enjoyable, too, Monica, especially when it is finally relieved. But that isn't what we're going to use them for tonight." He laughed as I continued to walk purposefully gyrating my rear, swaying a great deal more than normal to experiment with them. When I got near him again, he stopped me for a kiss, and squeezed my ass cheeks. "Try to clench and release the balls, Monica." I did, and that felt better, the balls in my ass were helping to make my vagina walls clench even harder.

"Yeah, that's nice." I nodded and smiled at Victor.

"I love your smile, Monica." His smile was sweet when he pulled me to his chest. He kisses me on the nose, and then he really kissed me. His hands caressed my back, and made their way down to my ass cheeks gripping them, and then began to come back up, but with his hands, he very sneakily pulled the hem of my negligee up and over my head. "I really like this one, Monica. Where it again for me," he whispered as kisses rained over my neck and throat.

"Ok," I stammered as his kisses had already worked their magic on my body.

When the kiss ended, he had further directions for me. "Go ahead and lie down on the bed, face up, head on the pillow so you can watch what I'm doing." He followed right behind me and brought the clips with him. He crawled on top of me and lavished my nipples with his tongue. When they were both rock hard, he stopped, knelt between my legs and put on the clamps. "I can tighten these, make them tighter," he explained. "Using these," he indicated the tiny little nobs under the decorative adornment.

"Yeah, go ahead, make them a little tighter." I was panting a little.

He just nodded and laughed. "I'll tighten them slowly; let me know before it gets to be too much."

I nodded, and watched as he turned the little screws. When the pain started to be uncomfortable, I asked him to stop. He did. "I can loosen it a bit," he offered. When I said that it was still okay, he told me he was going to tug on the chain that connected the two clamps a little and wanted me to tell him how it felt. I nodded. He tugged the chain and both pleasure and pain coursed through me like bolts of electricity from my nipples to my pussy. I squirmed and felt the Ben Wa balls. It was like torture, but exquisitely so. "Good?" he asked and I nodded again unable to form words. He went off his knees, sat between my legs and placed his thighs over mine, and spread my legs further. He then picked up the vibrator and turned it on. I was already wet, when he inserted just the tip and withdrew it, and then did the action again, going deeper each time until finally the attachment reached my clitoris and I went crazy. His legs held mine down, and I couldn't squirm and buck as much as I would have liked to, it was so fucking hot, my mind was a jumble and my pussy was on fire. He released his massively swollen penis, and stroked himself while he watched me.

"I'm going to cum," I screamed.

"Go ahead," he panted and tugged on the chain of the nipple clamps with one hand as he stroked himself. The combination of the pleasure and the pain was exquisite. I came, and squirmed, and came some more. It didn't stop. I thrashed and practically kicked him off of me. He left the vibrator on my clit, and let go of the chain, and slowly pulled the Ben Wa balls out, one, then two. I kept cumming and screaming. My eyes rolled to the back of my head. It was just so intense. I felt like I was going mad and began to cry and squirm. He continued to stroke himself until he too, came, and spewed semen all over my pussy, and legs and abdomen. He quickly removed the vibrator, and asked if I was okay. I was unable to stop crying.

"Yes," I cried, "It was just so much sensation. Overwhelming," I panted and my crying began to lessen. He lay beside me and stroked my arms, and pulled me close until I regained some control.

"You didn't like it?" he asked. He looked worried.

"No, no, that's not it," I stated. "I just don't think I could do that every night, or I might go crazy." I knew I wasn't explaining it right, I just didn't have the words right now, couldn't form the thoughts.

"But once in a while?" he asked hopefully. His hands still continues to caress me, soothe me.

"Most definitely!" I leaned up and kissed him on the lips, then collapsed back onto the bed.

He held me for a few minutes like that, and then got up, to use the restroom. He came out with a washcloth and cleaned me up, and gave me one of his shirts to wear. I slipped it on and inhaled it. I loved it when he let me wear his shirts. I loved to breathe in his scent all night. It comforted me. He cleaned up the toys we had used and then came to bed spooning me in the position he liked best. "Thank you, Monica. You don't know how much it meant to me for you to do this, baby," his words said in a whisper tickled the hair along my nape, and he pressed a kiss there.

I wanted to tell him, I loved him in that moment, but instead I just said, "You're welcome." And, I fell asleep in his arms.

SUNDAY WAS ANOTHER late morning. We ran together again along another one of Ft. Lauderdale's beaches, had a quick breakfast at a diner, showered back in the hotel and left for home. The ride was quiet, but pleasantly so. Victor made us chef salads at his apartment for dinner and then walked me to my car. We kissed, and held each other for a long while outside my car before he spoke.

"Thank you for a beautiful weekend, Monica. You are really so special." The look in his eyes was one of wonder and disbelief, but then turned to regret. "I wish things were different in my life. I feel closer to you than ever, but I still can't make you promises, promises you deserve." He pressed my head to his chest, and held me so that I couldn't see his eyes, eyes that could tell me more than those painful words, but he wouldn't let go.

Those words crushed me after the weekend we just had. But instead of saying anything, I muttered into his neck, "Thursday, then?"

He whispered, "Thursday," and let me go. He turned and walked to his apartment without ever looking back.

Chapter Seven
No Promises, No More Lies

B UT, THURSDAY NEVER happened. I got the call at four o'clock, something had come up with family. That's all he could say. *Would say?* I didn't ask. He might be able to come Sunday though, but that didn't happen either.

The following Thursday, Victor did come see me. We watched an old rerun of *Friends*, me on one side of the sofa, him on the other. He was quiet and subdued. "I'm really miss that show," he sighed. "Come on I need comfort food," he gave me his hand and I took it. We went to Village Inn and had pie and talked about the episode. I could tell other things were on his mind bothering him. I asked about his work. He admitted to me again that he hated it. The people he hired didn't show up when they were supposed to, didn't follow directions, had no respect for other guys doing different jobs. It wasn't like the military where everything was orderly, and structured. He missed the rank and file. The respect. In the military if you didn't do what you were supposed to there were consequences. If he fired someone, it delayed the whole job, and it was a nightmare rescheduling. I sympathized. I knew how behavior problems could screw up a whole lesson plan.

I asked him as I moved my chocolate silk pie around on

the plate, "Why don't you go back to the military? If it made you happy, you should see if you can back in."

"I'd love to. I really would. The money wasn't great, but at least I felt like I was doing something worthwhile, something that mattered. It's not like building condos and townhouses for rich people who only spend a week or two in them at the most every year." He rubbed his temples.

"Did you change jobs just for the money?" I asked not sure if I should probe deeper, but wanting to help him with this decision.

"Pretty much, yeah." He replied. He pushed his apple pie away just as untouched as my own.

"Do you really need the money?" I asked. Again, I was trying to get him to way his pros and cons.

"Not really," he replied. "I changed jobs because there were expectations that I earn more." He left it at that and I didn't ask for more information. I knew from experience that when people wanted your advice they would ask for it. But, I could have asked whose expectations. I didn't want to press to hard. I wondered why he put so much pressure on himself. Many military families got by on their salaries. It wasn't a great living, but it was enough to live comfortably, gave great insurance, and a decent pension.

Victor signaled for the check, and paid for the pie and coffee. He helped me out of the booth, held my hand on the way to the car, and got the door for me.

We pulled into my driveway and he shut off the car, but he made no move to get out. I waited for the words I somehow knew were coming the moment he had arrived tonight and I saw his somber mood. "I'm sorry, Monica. I just don't feel like myself today, all week actually. Got a lot on my mind with work. I hate this shit. It's not you, okay?" he tried to reassure me when he saw my head drop. "I promise next week will be better."

"You don't want to come in, at all? For a little while?" I asked looking up at him, but he wouldn't meet my gaze.

"I don't think it would be a good idea. I'm just not feeling it tonight. I'll call you tomorrow?" he asked.

"Okay," I said flatly. I got out of the car, he didn't. He waited for me to unlock the front door, and before I could turn around to wave, he was backing out of my driveway.

I went to my room, and cried myself to sleep. It had been nearly two weeks since our trip, and this had been the first time I had seen him. It wasn't just about the sex for me. I missed his companionship, too. It was a long night, long night.

HE CALLED ME in the morning to apologize again. He laughed and said, "That episode of *Friends* got to me." I thought his laugh sounded a little bit phony although the episode had been an emotional one involving Ross and Rachel. When I didn't respond right away, he added, "Okay, have a good day. I'll call you tonight," and hung up.

He called every night that weekend between ten and eleven as usual. He asked about my day, told me about his but that was it. There was no more sharing, laughing, teasing. After ten minutes or so, we would hang up. The calls weren't the same. They didn't satisfy me or comfort me between our weekly rendezvous.

By Wednesday, I was really getting worried. I felt like he was putting this distance between us on purpose. He was in a dark place with his job, and he was taking it out on me. When he called, I offered to come up the next day instead of him driving.

"No, I don't think so," he stammered.

"Why not?" I asked.

"Mmm," he uttered. "I think Kat is having some friends over or something."

"Okay, then. I'll guess I will see you tomorrow. Bye, Victor." I clicked off my cell and hoped I hadn't sounded sarcastic.

ON THURSDAY, HE was an hour late. I had been crying, and although I had run to the bathroom and washed my face when I saw his car pull up, the tell-tale signs were there. I was no good at hiding my feelings. He looked in my eyes, and saw my pain. I saw it reflected back at me in his eyes when I looked at him. He reached out to hold my face, eyes intense he whispered, "I'm sorry. I never wanted to hurt you. I didn't think it would last." He kissed me, each swollen eye first, and then on my lips. It was so tender, my heart broke. Not breaking the kiss, he steered me backwards and softly closed the door behind him. He picked me up, swinging me into his arms carrying me straight to my bedroom. There were no words that night. He made love to me slowly, straight sex, but it was beautiful. I fell asleep in his arms, and when I woke he was still there looking at me in the dawn's early light.

"You didn't leave." The awe in my voice was apparent. I was touched he had stayed so long.

"Yeah, I didn't want to leave you. I wanted to be sure you were okay. You're okay, right?" he looked me in the eyes. His eyes were baggy, dark circles underneath them.

"I'm okay, but what about you? Did you sleep, at all?" I asked concern for him apparent in my voice.

"Not much," he turned to me lying on his side. I did the same. "Monica, we have to talk, but there are things I just can't seem to tell you. I don't think I can find the right words to make you understand." I could see the internal struggle he was battling with. "When I do, I will tell you. I wish I could tell you now, it would be such a relief to get it off my chest, not having to live with these other secrets." His eyes searched my face for answers I couldn't give him because I didn't know the questions.

"There are other secrets?" I asked.

"Yes." He closed his eyes and nodded briefly.

"Why can't you tell me, Victor? I wish you would. Maybe, your mind is making more out of it than it really is, like with the toys and other things." I was grasping at straws here. I knew whatever this next secret was it was going to be a whopper, but I hated feeling like this, and seeing him like this.

"I can't tell you because I can't have you, and I don't want to give you up." It looked like he was battling some serious demons. I wished I could help him.

"I don't want you to give me up, either!" I sat up in bed, suddenly terrified, and took his hands. "Don't give me up, please. Don't give up on us," I begged.

"I should. You'd be better off!" He turned to lie on his back looking up at the ceiling pulling away from me.

"I wouldn't," I stated firmly. "Victor, I wouldn't be better off without you. Don't say that," I was pleading now.

"Yes, you would." His voice was full of resignation.

"So, where do we go from here?" I asked grasping the bed sheets in my hand. Fear, like a knot in my stomach, made me nauseous.

"I don't know. I've got things to think about. I guess we're still in the same situation. I can't, won't, make promises to you I can't keep. I don't want to lie to you, but I guess I'm lying to you because there a lot of things I'm not telling you. Lies by omission." His laugh was cold and he still was staring at the ceiling not looking at me.

When I first woke up to see him here, I had been touched, but now just a few minutes later I was terrified and because of that I was getting angry. I didn't like the direction this conversation was going in. I didn't like it at all. "Well," I stated sarcastically, "At least you're being honest about the fact that you're lying to me." I was extremely frustrated that this conversation was going around in circles and I didn't understand any of it.

"Ouch, Monica!" His sharp eyes turned to me.

"Sorry, I didn't mean that," I tried to back track. "I don't want to fight."

His eyes softened. "I don't want to either, Monica." There was pause as he sat up. "Listen, I'm already going to be late. Let me shower quickly. We can talk tonight, I promise. We'll hash some of this out." He sat up and gave me a quick peck on the cheek and headed for the shower.

"Okay . . . tonight," I said, scrambling out of bed behind him. I'd fix him some coffee for the road. I was willing to let it go indefinitely if it meant not losing him. I knew whatever those explanations were going to be, they might ruin us. Victor thought so, he had warned me from the very start. I was foolish, so foolish, despite all his warnings to the contrary, I had gone and fallen in love with him anyway.

Chapter Eight
Dancing Around the Issues

H E CALLED AT ten on Friday night. He was in a much better mood. He had made a big decision he informed me. From his tone, and it sounded real to me, he was feeling better. He had decided he would continue with the contracting business for the rest of the year, and if it didn't improve, he was rejoining the military. He had even called his senior ranking officer, and had been told they would give him 12 months from when he resigned, to allow him to re-up without getting demoted and taking a pay cut. So, he had four months before he had to give them his decision. I could hear the excitement in his voice. A door hadn't closed on him, and knowing that really cheered him up. I would do everything I could to help him make the decision to return. He loved the military. Even if it meant him being sent overseas away from me, it was worth it if he was doing something he loved. I loved teaching, but it was a job you could do anywhere.

"That's great news. You are being pro-active. I know when I have a plan, and a deadline it makes me feel like I've got something accomplished," I said enthusiastically.

"Exactly, I do feel a big weight off my shoulders. I wouldn't have even called today, if you hadn't brought it up last night. I'm seriously going to consider this, and I've got four months to make my decision." The relief in his voice made me glad I had pressed a bit last night.

"Money, can't buy you love," I laughed. "Love what you do."

He laughed, too. "Ain't that the truth?" His tone became a little flatter, but in the next instant, he was chipper again. "Come to me next Thursday. I want to take you dancing. I want to see you and make it up to you for my crappy mood last night." He laughed.

"Really?" I laughed. "That sounds great." I laughed. The call ended a bit later, after he asked me to recap my day, and I felt good about the call. I was also a bit relieved that he hadn't brought up anything from our talk that morning. I was sure I wasn't ready to hear it.

On Thursday, I arrived at Victor's apartment a little after eight. He was outside to greet me. He swept me into his arms, and kissed me with all his might. "You look gorgeous in that red dress," he said as we parted.

"You look great, too, Vic." He had on dark blue jeans, tight, and a grey t-shirt.

"Let's go upstairs and have a drink. A bunch of us are all coming out, some of the people you met from the barbecue, and Kat, too. We're going to The Honky Tonk, you remember, we went to that place once before?"

"I remember," I said but was momentarily worried. "You don't think I'm overdressed?" I was wondering about my clothes.

"Always," he teased, "But the dress looks awesome with your tan legs. I love that you never flaunt all your assets. Just one at a time. It makes guys wonder what the rest looks like." My dress was a simple halter dress, sleeveless, conservative, but short.

"You are such a tease. But really, is the dress ok?" I didn't want to be out of place if his friends were all in jeans.

"Don't worry about it. Michael's girl, Tina, she has a dress on, too." He started walking me to the door, grabbing my overnight bag from the backseat.

I was relieved when we got to the apartment to see that Tina did indeed have a dress on. It was a green tight little thing that showed off her legs, cleavage, and half her back. Kat was wearing jeans, and so was Maria, but hers was paired with a tank top with a silvery concoction of flat discs really dressing up the outfit. Cute, I thought, I really liked it.

By nine thirty, we climbed into two cars and made our way to The Honky Tonk. We were in Kat's car. "Going to sing with me tonight, Monica?" she asked playfully.

"Hell, no!" Victor laughed, "Not if I have any say so." Everyone in the car laughed.

I punched him lightly in the arm for teasing me. "I don't sing that badly."

"Yes, you do," Kat and him said together. They both laughed harder. I pouted and sunk down in the middle of the backseat between Victor and Michael. Tina was in the front with Kat.

"No pouting," Victor teased. "I will sing to you, instead. How about that?" He laughed again gazing into my eyes. He looked so happy and carefree right now. I loved seeing him like this. I loved him.

I noticed a look from Kat to Michael in the rearview mirror. It was a surprised, pleased expression. It made me feel good to see it. I felt like his friends genuinely liked me.

"I'd love that," I stated and put my head on his shoulder for the rest of the ride to The Honky Tonk. Kat kept giving me looks from the rear view mirror. She smiled, and I smiled back.

We got to the bar, and Victor immediately took me to the dance floor. This was the first time we had ever danced a fast song together. And, he could really dance. The way his shoulders moved when he danced was really a turn on. Some of the guys were calling him to play a game of pool. "Do you mind?" he asked.

"Not at all," I said. "I'll go sit with the girls."

"I'll get you a drink first; be right back." He kissed my cheek and then went to the bar as I made my way over to the table, where Kat, Tina, and Maria were sitting. Victor came with my drink, kissed me on the top of the head, and then went to join the guys. I loved that he was so affectionate.

I chatted with the girls. Both Kat and Tina were in the military, Maria wasn't. Tina and Kat, I found out, worked in the same office, shipping and receiving. They talked shop for a while, and then Maria heard a song she liked and grabbed Tina to go dance with her. That left me and Kat. We sipped our drinks and watched the guys play pool. Victor made a great shot. He was in front of me, and wiggled his butt while making it because he knew I was watching. Kat and I both laughed. I turned to her, when she said, "You're the first girl he has brought around us in the last eight months that hasn't been a one night stand, you know?"

"I didn't know that?" I said surprised. I liked her even more now for telling me that, too.

"Yeah, you are. He likes you a lot. In fact, none of us have seen him this happy in a long time. When you're around he is like his old self again," she paused, "better than his old self, actually."

"Thanks," I said. "I'm glad. I know he puts a lot of pressure on himself. I like to see him like this. So relaxed." I was careful with my words. I didn't want her to think I was prying.

"I can't say much, Monica," she paused and searched my eyes. "I know things he hasn't told you, and I have been friends with him for nearly ten years. I don't want to break his confidence, but I like you. You're a nice girl, and I think you should know by now, he is pretty fucked up in the head sometimes."

"I know that he has a lot on his mind," I told her. "But he doesn't really confide his problems to me, and that's okay for now. We enjoy each other's company a lot," I blushed.

"You're good for him. He told me you said he should go back to the military." Kat fiddled with her bottle of beer nervously.

"Yes, I did. He loves it, and misses it. He hates what he does now," I said watching her.

"We've told him to come back for months, but he listened to you, so that is good. At least he is seriously considering it now. He never should have left to begin with. Thanks for that." She took a long swallow.

"Sure," I said lamely. I didn't know what else to say.

She looked at me quizzically, "And you're in love with him?"

I nodded and took a drink of my beer.

"Don't tell him that. He already suspects it. But don't say the words. Not yet." She patted my hand. "He really does have family obligations, Monica. He is all about his family. It's an Italian thing. He takes his responsibilities very seriously. He isn't lying about that. He won't tell you about his family because it's pretty fucked up right now. And, don't ask him about it because he will know I've talked with you, but you're good for him, really good."

Again, I nodded, and told her I wouldn't say anything.

"When he does tell you in his own time, listen to him, Monica, please, and hear him out. He hasn't said anything to me, but I can tell he wishes he could spend more time with you. He talks about you all the time." Her last comments ended on a sigh. "I really hope he gives you a chance," and with that she left to go to the ladies room. I hoped he would, too. From, Kat's lips to God's ears, I prayed. Whatever it was that was going on in his family, Kat felt I should listen to him and hear it all. I vowed right then to myself that I would. Whatever it was.

KAT RETURNED JUST as the game of pool was finishing up, and the guys joined us at the table. They joked about how Michael had cheated. To deflect, Michael reminded everyone that Victor was supposed to sing to me. He laughed and shook his head. A slow song came on, and he took my hand. "I'll sing to her, but not the rest of you fools. I'll never hear the end of it." I followed him onto the floor. The song was *She Will Be Loved* by Maroon 5. I loved this band, and this song.

Victor took me in his arms, and we swayed, and danced in time to the music. And he sang the song to me whispering the words in my ear, words I wished were meant for me. As the lead singer spoke of a man being drawn to one woman over and over again, I wished it were me and Victor he was talking about. My heart hurt that the words were written by Adam Levine and James Valentine for someone else. When the next lyrics talked about a girl with the broken smile, it hit home and I felt my emotions overwhelming me. I hugged Victor closer to me. He hugged me back. He couldn't sing anymore after that. I could hear it in his voice. The words of this beautiful song had impacted him as much as me. We finished the dance, and he kissed my ear, my cheek. There were tears in my eyes. He wiped them away. He led me back to the table, and his friends back slapped him. "I was so horrible," he stated, "that it made her cry." They all laughed harder and then I was laughing too. Kat just smiled, knowingly.

It was midnight, and the guys wanted to go to a different bar, but I had to work the next day and get up at five thirty to be at work for eight with the hour drive, going for a short run, and getting ready for work. I was glad school was over for the summer in just two short weeks, a week and half really. June couldn't be here soon enough for me. Victor gave our apologies, and Kat dropped us off at the apartment before going back to join the others. I didn't know how they did these late nights and worked the next day.

Once in the apartment, we went straight to Victor's room. His trunk was on the bed. He watched my reaction when I saw it. I laughed.

"You really don't think I'm a pervert?" he shook his head in wonder and opened the lid.

"If you're one, then so am I," I laughed. He hugged me, and took out a vibrator and closed the lid.

"Just a vibrator?" I questioned teasingly.

"Yes, just a vibrator, for tonight. And a little role playing, okay?" He pinched me on the ass.

"Ouch, that hurts," I said rubbing my butt, "But okay."

"You're a naughty girl, Monica. I'm going to have to punish you," he teased. I ran from him around the bed, and he caught me quickly. We fell on the bed because he made us fall, and then he was sitting up with me over his legs. "I have to spank you," he said lifting my dress.

"What?" I began to squirm on his lap. "Why?"

"Because no woman should have as beautiful an ass as you do. It's not fair to all of mankind," he laughed huskily as he pulled my panties down. He didn't hit me, at least not right away. He patted his hand on each cheek, and caressed them. I was getting really turned on. Then, wham!

"Ouch! Fuck! Vic!" I yelped. "That hurt."

He was caressing the cheek he had just slapped. "Nice girls shouldn't use bad words, Monica." Wham, he slapped the other cheek and immediately began to caress it.

I yelped again, but didn't curse this time. I was getting into it; the pleasure pain combo was heady. I was getting wet.

"Do you like it, Monica?" he asked. From his voice, and the erection pressing into my rib cage, I knew he did.

"Yes," I whispered.

Wham!

"Ouch!" He was caressing me again.

"I didn't hear you," he said louder.

"Yes," I was panting and squirming.

Wham! "Yes, what?" He demanded.

"Yes, I liked it. I like it when you spank me, Victor. I love it." My pussy was quivering. I was surprised too, because I was almost ready to come.

"Good girl. Now you can be rewarded." He pushed me off him. I stood in front of him between him and his dresser. "Take off your clothes. I want to fuck you in that beautiful ass again tonight, and shove this vibrator up your pussy so far you're going to fucking see stars. Do you want me to do that, Monica?" I was already stripping.

He placed my hands on the dresser and made me spread my legs wide. I could see myself in the mirror and I could see him behind me. My brown eyes were alight with desire. His blue eyes were in flames. He began with the vibrator, inserting it into me, and withdrawing it a couple of times until I was groaning, swaying back and forth and pushing down on it. I looked at myself in his mirror again. I was so wanton, my hair a wreck falling across my face, skin flushed, ass sore, but climbing every second towards that peak. He left the vibrator in me, and positioned the clitoral stimulator over my clit. He encouraged me to scoot lower so that I was really jerking and feeling the pressure building. He quickly lubed himself, held on to my hips, and pushed once then twice. I wasn't completely ready for him in my ass. It hurt. It felt awesome. He pumped into me like he was a using a jack hammer. I felt his cock all the way, every glorious inch of it up my ass, I felt it hit and jostle the vibrator. "Move, Monica," he screamed. I really began to move, pushing my ass into his cock, and we soared together. Holy hell, when the explosion came, I did see stars. Tons of fucking stars.

Chapter Nine

Absence Makes the Heart Grow Fonder

S UMMER WAS FINALLY here. And, it was both a good thing and a bad thing. It meant two months of sunshine, beaches, and more time for fun. But, it also meant a lot of time to miss spending that time with Victor. It also meant my yearly trip to visit my father in Maine. I went every year for a week, my sister and I, and it was falling on the one weekend a month Victor had off to be with me.

"Don't worry about it, baby. I'll try to switch things up. I'll see if I can get away a bit on Saturday when you come back, and pick you up at the airport."

"I'd love that," I stated. "Try, please. But, if you can't, I'll understand."

WE HAD ONE more Thursday night together before, I was leaving and I wanted to make it a night to remember. Special. I bought some new lingerie. It was a bustier in gold with black trim, and matching satin panties. The cups of the bustier were padded a bit to make my breasts look bigger. Victor would like that.

I put candles all over my bedroom, and bought new satin

sheets, in black. He would look glorious laying against them his ice blue eyes on fire for me. God, how I loved those eyes.

I had a bottle of champagne chilling in a bucket by my bed, and two crystal flutes. Sade was playing in the background to set the mood. It was perfect.

When I answered the door, his mouth hit the floor. My breasts were on full display.

"God, I love it when you answer the door like that," he stated. He dropped his overnight bag on the floor and swept me into his arms kicking the door closed behind him with a bang. He carried me to my room. "Wow, I love what you've done to the place," he breathed, noticing the candles and the sheets. And, then he was kissing me. He dropped me onto the bed, and began to strip slowly. As each item came off I gloried in his magnificent body. He folded each item and carefully placed it on the chair in the corner of my room. His chest was absolutely breath taking. His abs perfectly formed from a lot of time at the gym. His waist was narrow, his stomach washboard flat, narrowing into his lean hips, and muscular legs. When he took off his briefs, his cock sprung out ready and gloriously hard. He watched me watching, and rubbed his shaft. "Do you like my cock?" he asked.

I loved it when he talked dirty. "Yes, I love your cock. I love to look at your cock. Touch your cock, suck your cock, but I love it best when your cock is inside of me. Come here, Victor, so I can do all of those things." His eyes widened at my words. I had never spoken like that before.

He came towards me on the bed, eyes burning. He lay down next to me on the satin sheets, and I rolled onto my side, and began to touch him. His chest was first, and I kissed his ribs, each one, and then I scooted lower, leaning up on one elbow and took his cock in my hand. He sighed happily, folded his arms and placed them under his head relaxing and allowing me to have my way with him. I stroked his dick, feeling even more blood rush into it, and bent to give it a little nip with my teeth. I twirled my tongue around the tip, the ridges there that brought him so much pleasure and then put my lips over just the top, sucking hard and then softly. I began to use my lips and tongue to tease him peering up at him, and showing him how much I enjoyed sucking his dick. I murmured my enjoyment, and he groaned in pleasure. I took him deeper into my mouth, and he groaned again, his hands whipping out from underneath him to stroke my hair. God, how I loved this man. I wanted to do all I could to please him. I licked and bathed his cock with my tongue. He was delicious, slightly salty, yet clean. I stroked and sucked for a few minutes, feeling him getting harder all the while pulsing in my mouth. "God, baby. I need to be inside you."

He made to flip me over, but I pushed him back down, and crawled on top of him. I slipped right onto him, impaling myself like some wanton creature. We both groaned together as I lowered myself onto him the second time more slowly. I began to increase the rhythm arching into him. He put one hand on my hip, and his other hand reached between us putting his palm on his belly and his thumb on my clit. As I moved and grinded, he stroked and rubbed. We took our time, going slowly making it last. We climbed and soared together and when we climaxed we did it together. I collapsed onto him, my legs tucked up on either side, with him still inside of me. He stroked my back as I listened to his heart rate begin to slow. I loved this feeling of closeness with him still inside of me after we had made love. It kept the connection alive, as if we were truly one. He let me stay that way for a full ten minutes before subtly pushing me to the side, and I curled into his arm, leg over his legs, my arm bent at the elbow, fingers swirling over his chest.

"I really care about you, Monica," he said and pressed a kiss into the top of my head. I loved him, but I still couldn't tell him that.

"I hope you know how much I feel for you, too, Victor," I whispered into his chest.

His answer was, "Yes, I think I do. I do."

We made love again that night, and he woke me early and we made love again. He left at six promising to call me every day at our usual time, and I began to get ready for my flight later that afternoon. I would have to hang on to the memory of this night for the next nine days. And, it was a good memory to have.

MAINE WAS BEAUTIFUL in the summer. Big trees, oak, and maple, scented the air. The conifers, green all year round, interspersed with the other hues of green. My father usually rented a cabin when we came for a few days, at least, as he had a very small apartment in town and it was pretty cramped. He also liked to take us camping and fishing like we did when we were little. My dad was an awesome father. He may not have been a great husband, but when it came to being a dad, I wouldn't have traded him for the world. He and my mother had divorced twice, believe it or not. He was a cheater and a womanizer; my mother told us when we were old enough to understand. He was just not satisfied with one woman, and he had broken my mom's heart twice. She had kept us in the dark, because she was a great mom, who knew how much we loved our father and how much we needed him in our life. The final divorce had happened when I was in my early twenties, and I was able to handle it. I was just glad both of my parents were happy now.

The first weekend in Maine dad took us shopping at the various outlets, and tried to buy us stuff like we were still children. Dad took Ana and me to visit with all our aunts, my dad's six sisters, and some of our cousins. We also cleaned and scrubbed his small two bedroom apartment. He seriously needed a cleaning woman, and every year Ana and I would do a thorough spring cleaning in the summer for him.

By Monday, we were on our way to a little fishing village on the Canadian American border. The place was called St. Stephens. It was adorable and reminded me somewhat of my weekend with Victor in Ft. Lauderdale. The cabin was cute, and it had three rooms, so Ana and I didn't have to share, like we did at my dad's apartment. The woman was still a bed hog. We had shared a bed growing up, too. The best part about the cabin was that it was right on the water facing the St. John's River, and we could fish sitting in hand-made Adirondacks right in the back yard. We did that the first night we got there catching up with the old man. I told him a bit about Victor. Just that I had met someone, and liked him, but didn't know if it was going to be for the long term. Ana told him she had a couple of guys in the fire going, but I didn't think it was true. She had been spending most of her free time with Teddy, aka bartender boy. Dad laughed and said she was too much like him, and his only hope for grandbabies was me. Out of the corner of my eye, I saw Ana wince. She was hurt by that, but tried not to let it show. She couldn't have kids, but our father didn't know that. Her ex-husband had cheated on her, and given her a disease that had made her infertile. She had gotten treatment for it, but it had taken a severe toll on her. She had never told my father about it, she didn't talk about it at all. It was a shame because she loved kids, and dedicated her life to them in her work.

Dad told us about his new girlfriend, her name was Leandra. He liked her, but she was pushy and wanted to move in with him. He liked his space, and didn't want all her lady things cluttering up the place. After being divorced for nearly ten years, he liked his space. He was fifty eight and didn't see himself getting married again as my mom had done.

My mom had reconnected on the internet with an old flame four years ago and was blissfully happy with Tom, who took her out all the time, and loved to travel. My mom was actually sixty; she had retired early and both she and Tom spent more time away than at home reliving their youth.

The next day, my dad took us on a tour of the local Ganong chocolate factory in the morning and on a whale watching excursion in the afternoon. It was magnificent to see those mighty creatures. We were on a small commercial fishing boat, maybe a sixty footer, when a grey humpback came splashing out of the water. The thing was massive, twice the size of our craft, and rocked the boat. When we got back to the cabin, dad grilled us some peppercorn steaks and made baked potatoes.

By Wednesday, we were on our way back to our dad's place. Thursday, Ana and I spent the day visiting our friends from high school and college borrowing our father's car. We spent the morning with Tammy, my dearest friend from college. In the afternoon we went to see Ana's best friend, Louisa, and her daughter, Veronica.

Friday, we went for a hike in the woods with our dad, played cards in the afternoon, and then had dinner at a restaurant where we met my dad's new girlfriend. Ana and I were both anxious to get home, so we packed our bags for the return flight early the next morning. All in all, it was a nice visit, and we enjoyed ourselves, but the highlight of each and every day for me was the phone call I got from Victor each night. On the night before my return, he had told me, "I really, really miss you. I didn't think I would miss you this much." His words were sweet. He did sound like he was missing me. That had to be a good sign, right? I was wrong.

EVEN THOUGH IT was a five A.M. flight, I was happy about that. It just meant I would be seeing Victor soon. He had told me the night before that he would be able to pick me up at the Tampa International Airport at 11:00AM.

When we got off the plane, we exited the terminal and took the shuttles to the main lobby. I saw Victor right away. He stood leaning against a pole looking so good in faded, ripped jeans, and grey shirt, I could have gobbled him right up. I was that excited to see him. It was funny, too, because he was also standing right next to hunky bartender boy and they didn't know that the other one was picking up one of the sisters. Teddy was waving at my sister like crazy jumping up to see over the other passengers who had disembarked from the tram before us. I looked at my sister and giggled. She rolled her eyes at me and stated, "You've got your ride; I've got mine." She shrugged her shoulders and opened her arms as the hunky bartender ran in to them, picked her up and swung her around. Shaking my head, I continued to walk to Victor, and got up on my tip toes to kiss him, but he turned his face and I caught him on the cheek just barely. He was looking around nervously. "Come on, babe. I don't have a lot of time." He turned and I, a little put off, followed him to the elevators.

In the elevator without listening ears, a little miffed, and little envious at the way my sister had been met by Teddy, I remarked sarcastically, "Nice greeting."

"Sorry, I'm a . . ." he paused, "just a little distracted. I told Juli—I would be back as soon as I could, and that I was helping a friend move." He looked at me then and I saw panic.

"Who is Julie?" I asked trying not to sound suspicious.

"A, a family member," he replied and looked at his watch.

"Oh, okay, but why did you tell your family you were helping someone move, when you were coming to get me?" I was confused now. He didn't answer. Then a light went on. "You haven't told your family about me," I thought out loud.

"Umm, I . . . no . . . I didn't know where this was go-ing . . . I don't tell my family about my one night stands. Would you?" He snapped. I could see he was getting agitated.

"Umm, my sister maybe, but no, not the rest," I answered truthfully. Then added because I was hurt, "But, we aren't a one night stand. You could have mentioned me later."

"You just never came up," he said lamely as the elevator door opened to let other passengers in.

When the elevator door opened onto the sixth floor he began to walk out peering at me to see if I was following. He shook his head, and he took my suitcase then. He just seemed to notice I had been dragging it along behind me this whole time. "Sorry, about that," he said indicating the suitcase and turned a little bit abashedly. I followed in the parking lot practically jogging to keep up with his longer strides.

"Victor, please slow down," I stated breathlessly.

"Oh, sorry," he apologized again. "We're here, anyway." I looked around but didn't see his car. "My car wouldn't start so I had to borrow this one from someone in my family, this Chevy here." I was standing behind a massive black Chevy Suburban.

"Oh, okay," I stammered.

"That's why I was so distracted. I was thinking about how and when I'm going to find the time to get my car fixed."

"Uh-huh," I murmured. "Anything I can do?" I asked. So, that was why he had been upset and rushed. It made some sense. I had never seen Victor like this, he looked so rattled. Stop questioning him, I told myself. He's upset about the car, and he is a busy man. This weekend he had moved things around to come get me, I told myself. I'd cut him some slack.

He put my suitcase in the back of the Suburban, and shut the door, but not before I noticed some toys. It must be a family member or friend of his who had kids, I thought. Maybe this Julie person was his sister, and he had some nieces or nephews. He didn't mention his family much, I didn't even know if he had a sister, and Kat had warned me not to ask about his family, so I kept my mouth shut.

But when we left the parking garage, I was startled again. He had mentioned going to his place for a few hours, and then taking me home later. But, he took the exit that led to the Veteran's Expressway and my home. When I looked at him he winced, his eyes pleading with me to understand. "I've got to get the truck back, sorry, really sorry." He looked like he meant it, too. I could see the disappointment in his eyes.

"It's okay, don't worry about it," I said. "We always have Thursday." I gave him a smile and hoped it looked genuine. He patted my knee and smiled back, then concentrated on his driving, both hands on the steering wheel. I turned to look out the passenger side window watching the other cars fly past on the Veteran's. I imagined those families doing things together on this remarkably beautiful Saturday in June. I stared out the window the whole way home hiding the tears of regret that glided down my cheeks.

I felt his hand caress my knee through the white capris I wore, but I couldn't look at him. I just couldn't. If I did, I knew I would lose it. I did reach for his hand and he held it there the rest of the ride home. The whole way was silent and neither one of us said a word. I knew he, too, was just as disappointed.

At my door, he placed my suitcase down, and said, "We'll talk Thursday. Really talk, okay?"

I remained silent and just nodded, not looking at him.

He took my chin in his hands and lifted my face to meet his eyes, and the tears that I had managed to control began to fall again silently down my face. "I really, really missed you, baby." He kissed me then, on the lips softly, nothing sensual, just tender.

"I missed you too, Victor," I managed to get out.

"See you Thursday, Monica," he whispered letting go of my chin. He turned, and got into the truck. He waved goodbye as he backed out of my driveway and then I went inside. Alone.

Chapter Ten
Are We Breaking Up?

"**W**HAT THE HELL?" Ana yelled, slamming her coffee cup on my kitchen table after I finished telling her about the fiasco that happened at the airport and about the ride home. I also told her about the fact that Victor hadn't called last night either. "Well, call him now. You deserve some answers!" she exclaimed with some force.

"He was probably so upset about his car, that he just forgot," I said lamely trying to defend him.

It was Sunday night, and Ana stopped here before going to her place. She just got back from Clearwater and spending the day with Teddy and his family.

I told her about the conversation I had with Kat. She sat ruminating for a bit, wiping at the coffee that had sloshed over the side of her cup. "Well, that puts a different spin on things," she stated in a calmer tone.

"What do you mean?" I asked with confusion while wiping my running nose. Two days of crying did that to a girl.

"She is his friend, but girls don't like to lie to other girls. For a while, I was beginning to think he was married," she stated matter-of-factly.

"Married!" I squeaked. "But, he lives with Kat! I've been there." I shook my head. What a ludicrous conclusion to come to, I thought. She had only thought that because of her ex, and my dad, I told myself.

"Yeah, but you've only been there a few times. Have you seen anything personal in there? Pictures? Anything?" Her eyes widened at me.

"I saw a picture once, but he turned it down on to the dresser before I could get a look at it. Come to think of it, I didn't see it all the other times I was there. He must have moved it," I whispered, fear now beginning to clench at my heart. I felt all the color drain out of my face. I felt suddenly cold, too.

She must have seen my panic, because she then switched gears. "Okay, let's not jump to conclusions, yet. He lives with Kat, no pictures. What about his clothes? His clothes are there hanging in the closet, too?"

"Yes, he has a lot of clothes there. There is his stuff all over the bathroom. There were some boxes in the corner in his room, too," I said, giving her all the information I knew, pausing between each thought as they came to me.

"Well, those are good signs," she nodded and reached for my hand to give it a pat. "He has been in the Army a lot, used to living out of duffle bag, and boxes and stuff. So, he may not have gotten around to unpacking," she mused. "What about family? What do you know about them?" she asked.

"He has only ever mentioned 'family', but no one specific, really. His mom, she lives in Palm Harbor. His dad passed away from cancer, he told me once. He hasn't mentioned anyone else? Wow, that was all I knew! He didn't mention them often, and when he did he would always steer the conversation in another direction. I talked about my family all the time. He listened when I talked about them, and laughed at my stories, but never shared any of his own. He talked about his military friends more than anyone else.

"No, sisters, brothers?" she asked, letting go of my hand and reaching for her cup of coffee.

"He hasn't mentioned any, but the truck he drove me home in had toys in the back. Girl's toys. I saw a doll, a jump rope, a Cinderella ball. No, he has never mentioned siblings or nieces or nephews or anything, but he did say the truck belonged to family. I remember that clearly," I emphasized that point.

"Okay, that doesn't mean he doesn't have them then, so it must be."

"Kat mentioned he is very loyal and feels responsible for his family," I offered her another possible clue.

"Well, that could mean since his dad passed he feels responsible for his family and that he is the man of the family, so he has to do what his dad would have done if he were still alive. He probably spends those family weekends fixing up his mom's house, repairs and stuff, cutting the lawn, taking her shopping. If he has siblings, he's Italian, and they probably do family dinners and stuff and he helps them, too," she continued to hypothesize. Then she shook her head and added, "But, I don't know why he wouldn't have mentioned them. You've been seeing each other for nearly three months."

Okay, these things all made sense to me. "He does not talk about them much." And then, "What really bugs me though, is that I don't understand why he doesn't want to tell them about me?" I asked hoping she had an explanation for that as well.

"Now that is the sixty-four thousand dollar question. I'm stumped." She took another sip of her coffee, set it down and fiddled with the handle for a bit, and then looked at me suspiciously.

"Yes, what is it?" I could tell she had thought of something.

"Well," she started tentatively, "It has to be one of three things." Again she paused. "It's either that his family wouldn't approve of you, or he's got another girlfriend, or," a longer pause, "he's already married." This last statement was said with compassion.

"But he lives with Kat!" I repeated exasperated crossing my hands in front of me. Then, "Plus, he wouldn't see someone else, either. He told me he wouldn't do that." I was getting angry at her now.

She reached out to soothe me. "Listen to me, Monica. If it is reason number one, his mom might be old-fashioned and want him to marry some little Italian girl and give her some bambinos. If it is reason number two, he has been dating someone his family loves and approves of, but he is just not that into her, and doesn't want to disappoint them, or three," she sighed, "he's married, maybe separated, I think, but hasn't told his family because he doesn't want to disappoint them."

I wanted to cry. Because all of these explanations sounded plausible! Crap, crap, and double crap! None of those situations sounded good, or easy to overcome.

"What should I do?" I asked, overwhelmed by all the possibilities.

"Honey, you've got to ask him and demand the truth. You're already head over heels in love with him." She gave my hand a squeeze. "It will hurt more if you wait. Trust me, the longer you're with someone, the more it is going to hurt. So, yank that fucking Band-Aid off?"

I didn't know if I could do it. Could I face even one of these truths? His mom would never like me, he was cheating on me with someone else, or worse, vice versa, he was cheating on someone else with me! My stomach rolled, I felt like I was going to be sick, and rushed to the bathroom to do exactly that.

WHEN HE DIDN'T call me at ten o'clock, I called him at eleven on Sunday night. He picked up on the first ring. "Hi Monica," he said.

"Hi Victor," I paused. I had thought about what I was going to say earlier, but all of my thoughts fled the moment I heard his voice. "I miss you," I said lamely. I heard his sigh on the other end of the phone. There was an awkward silence.

"I miss you, too," he said simply.

"What are you doing?" I asked pretending he hadn't called me in two days, pretended like Saturday had never happened. It was a stupid thing to ask, but it was the first thing to come to my mind.

"Just watching television," he muttered.

"Kat there?" I asked, trying to pretend this was a normal conversation when it was anything but that. What I really wanted to ask was why he hadn't called when he said he would. Why? He probably wanted to pretend it hadn't happened either, I hoped.

"She went to bed already," he said, answering my questions, but not helping to end the awkwardness.

"Oh," I said lamely. "Yes, I just wanted to hear your voice. I'll let you go if I'm bothering you."

"You're not bothering me. I was actually thinking about calling you." I heard him sigh for the first time.

"Oh, that's nice," I offered.

"Yes, I umm, wanted to explain why I didn't call yesterday," he stammered. "I got home real late and didn't want to wake you.”

“You did?” I mumbled. Fool, I called myself because I was going to accept it. I wanted to believe it.

“Yeah, after I did what I needed to do, Kat watched, umm, I mean I went out and had a drink with the guys, and I’m afraid I got a little drunk. They guys had to carry me upstairs,” he laughed. “I was going to call you then, but the guys said not to, it was too late, and I was pretty messed up.”

He had gone out with his friends last night. I was hurt. It hurt to hear that when we hadn’t gotten to spend just an hour or so together. “That doesn’t sound like you.” I was referring to the drinking to excess. He wasn’t a heavy drinker. “I still would have liked to have heard from you, though,” I sniffled. “I miss you.”

“Are you crying?” he asked. It was the first time his voice wasn’t in a monotone since the call had started.

“No, I’m not crying,” I lied. *Pull the Band-Aid. Just do it, I thought.* I cleared my throat. My voice once again matching his, trying to keep it devoid of emotion, I asked, “Victor, are you married?”

His end of the phone was dead silent, for far too long, nothing for at least ten seconds. I heard him cough then say, “Fuck.” The word was muffled. He must have put the phone to his chest. He pulled the phone away from himself then because I had heard his next words much, much louder. “Fuck, fuck, fuck!”

I remained silent. It was a good thirty seconds before he spoke again. I gripped the receiver like it was a life line. “Monica, are you still there?” he asked with worry in his voice at the utter silence coming from my end of the line.

“Are you?” My tone was cold. I was ice. I felt like my spirit had been completely sapped. This instant was forever going to be frozen in my mind. It was the worst moment of my life.

He breathed deeply. "Yes, but . . ." he began. My world shattered.

"I don't ever want to see you again," I cried. The pain, oh my God, it hurt so much.

"Monica, wait . . ." I heard him faintly say as I disconnected the phone.

I ran to my room, threw myself onto the bed, and I cried my heart out. It felt like my soul was being ripped right of my body and my heart was being shredded into little pieces. I cried as if I had just found out someone had died, cried until I couldn't even catch my breath. I passed out cold.

I WOKE BECAUSE I heard banging at my front door. I looked at the clock. It wasn't even midnight. "Monica, let me in damn it! Monica." It was Victor. How did he get here so soon, it was an hour's drive? We just hung up not forty minutes ago. Better yet, why was he here at all?

I stumbled out of bed and ran to open the door before he woke up my neighbors. The old guy, Jesse, across the street, was really protective of me. Always reminding me to lock up and be sure to keep the garage door closed when I forgot to do so. He would be out here with a shotgun soon, if I didn't make Victor stop.

I pulled open the door, and Victor with bloodshot eyes, pushed past me into the living room. "Take it back," he said pacing back and forth, arms at his sides, fists clenched. "Take it back." He was scaring me, so I backed up against the door.

"Take what back?" I was trembling, terrified, and sad.

"You have to let me explain, Monica. It's not what you think. We're separated, have been for eight months. She threw me out. She doesn't want me," he looked at me frantically, and then shook his head in despair. "But, I can't divorce her, I can't!"

Hope surged, and then crashed. "What? You can't divorce her! Why?" I blurted out taking a step closer. He wouldn't answer. "Never mind," I suddenly added and turned my back to him. "Does it matter? You've been lying to me for months!" I screamed and cried at the same time, my shoulders shaking with my sobs.

He placed his hands on my shoulders and turned me around. "My family, we don't divorce. We're Catholic. Julianna . . . that's her name, she wants the divorce," he was begging me with his eyes to understand as his hands slid down my arms.

"Whoa, wait a minute your wife wants a divorce, and you don't," I was flabbergasted. I shrugged his hands off and began to back towards the kitchen. He followed me.

"It's . . . she was my high school girlfriend," he stammered trying to explain. "We got married right out of high school."

I was confused, so confused. "I'm playing second fiddle to your wife. Your wife, who you don't want to divorce because you're Catholic or because you love her?" He didn't answer. "But she wants a divorce?" He nodded. "I can't be the other woman, Victor. I can't be second best." The tears streamed down my face. "I just don't understand." My words came out in a strange whisper.

"Please, let me explain. Please, sit, so I can think. Stop looking at me like I'm some kind of monster, please," he begged.

I had backed up into the kitchen and I sat, more so because my legs were about to give out from under me than because he asked. He must have taken that as a good sign because he sat next to me and reached for my hand.

"Don't! Don't touch me!" I yanked my hand back away from his reaching ones, and crossed my hands over my chest.

"But, you'll listen, Monica. Please, say you'll listen." This man had hurt me, had betrayed me in the deepest way possible, but yet even knowing what he had done, I kept hearing Kat's words whispering in my ear. When he is ready, listen to him. Give him a chance. I didn't know if I wanted to listen, but I did want to understand.

I nodded wiping the tears from my eyes with the back of my hand. He put his hands in his lap, but then got up and began to pace. After a few moments he began to speak still pacing and occasionally looking up at me to see how I was taking his words.

"I went to college, and it didn't work out for me. My parents were disappointed. My dad wanted me to be an accountant like him, but numbers weren't me. I loved sports, the outdoors, and physical activity. Julianna, sh-she got a job working for her dad in his construction company right away. But, I was the man, you know. I had to support her, so I joined the military. My parents didn't like it. They didn't like it at all." He looked at me to see if I was still listening. "I did basic training, and Julianna, she . . . waited for me. I got home and two weeks later, I was sent to Iraq. I was there eight months. I came home, and she got pregnant."

"Pregnant!" I leaped out of my chair nearly toppling it over.

"Please, please, sit back down." He looked frantic and his hands reached in front of him, and he began to approach me. I slowly slid back into my chair, my heart hammering in my chest.

"Pregnant?" I whispered.

"Yeah," he smiled despite my sharp intake of breath. "I have a daughter. My one true love. Her name is Stacey. When I say I'm with family, Monica, I'm talking about her. She is who I spend every other weekend with and Tuesdays, not Julianna. Sometimes we go to my mom's on Sundays." His eyes begged me to understand. He had a daughter he had never told me about. Why? The rock in my stomach got tighter. I felt bile creep up my throat, but pushed it down when I swallowed.

"You have a daughter. A daughter you didn't tell me about?" I was numb. These lies, lies by omission were big lies.

"Yeah, and I'm sorry. But when we first got together, I didn't know where this was going. Was it going to be a one night stand, a fling, I don't expose my daughter to that kind of stuff. Plus, she still thinks I'm getting back together with her mother. I couldn't tell her about you, and so I couldn't tell you about her."

My head was swimming. It made no sense to me. I shook my head in amazement trying to wrap my mind around it.

Because I was silent so long he continued. "Anyway, the sex stuff. I love sex, and Julianna, well she didn't. She tried stuff, we tried stuff, and she eventually just came to the conclusion that I was some kind of freak, pervert. She started to push me away, wouldn't do anything but normal stuff and even then, not often. She's not like you, you enjoy it, and you . . ." he let that sentence trail off. "Julianna, she also grew up with a lot of money. She kept pressuring me to get out the military, I had a child, she would say, what if I was sent overseas and got killed, her dad could get me a job in construction she would tell me."

I interrupted, eyes pleading. "Please, don't tell me you work for your father in law," I whispered. This was too much.

"No, no, I don't, but after she kicked me out, told me it was over, that she wanted a normal life, I wanted to prove to her that I could be who she wanted me to be. I could support her like she wanted. I could get her the big fancy house, the cars, the jewelry, take her to fancy restaurants." He sat down and put his hands out and up as if in supplication begging me to understand. "When Julianna kicked me out, I went to the base and lived there for a while and then Kat took me in. I've been spending the last eight months trying to win her back. It's stupid. I know. All my friends think so, but Julianna was my love, she stuck by me when I dropped out of college, when I went to boot camp, when I was overseas, we have a daughter . . . I loved her so much. She is so beautiful. She was everything to me. I had her, my daughter, and my mom. That's it."

"You had me," I said. He looked up at me and I looked down at my clasped hands in my lap.

"Had?" he questioned. Tears were in his eyes.

Even after all he had done those tears moved me. "I don't know," I muttered. I saw him approach and he took my hand then. We just sat there. I had just one more question and I took a deep breath and asked it. "I don't want to be the reason you divorce, Victor. And, I can't be the other woman, I just can't. But, I have to know." I took another breath, deep; I filled my lungs and looked him right in his sad, beautiful ice blue eyes. "Do you still want to be with your wife, Victor?"

He dropped my hand, and leaned forward on the table rubbing his face, his eyes. Then he looked at me and said, "Before . . . before you, I was doing it for both of them, Stacey and Julianna, but lately it has been more for my daughter. I wanted her to have both her parents, a whole family. I didn't tell anyone about us because I had myself convinced if Julianna knew about you, she wouldn't let me see my daughter and push even more for a faster divorce. That is another reason why I left the military, too. If she fought me for custody, or wouldn't agree to give me partial custody, she could say I wasn't dependable, and couldn't provide my daughter with a stable home environment."

"No judge would take away your rights because you're in the military," I shook my head at that. I felt for this man, this man I loved even though he was breaking my heart, had already broken it. But, I had to know, and he hadn't answered my question. "Victor, you still didn't answer my question." He looked in my eyes. "Do you still want to be with your wife?" Silent tears streamed down my cheeks.

He looked down and away. "For my daughter . . . ," he cried.

I got up from the table. I heard his intake of breath. I turned from him.

"I can't be the other woman. I love you, Victor." I saw him wince in pain. "You know I do. But, I can't." I cried into my hands.

I heard his chair move and I felt him behind me then. He grasped my shoulders and pulled me close and even though every sense of my moral fortitude went against it, I leaned back into him to feel him one last time. He turned me around and wrapped his arms around me, "God knows, I don't want to, I didn't want to Monica, but I love you. I love you, too." He took my face in his hands and kissed my breath away. He kissed me until the tears stopped and dried on my face, He held me close, so close that I felt every long lean inch of him pressed up against me. He held me like that for what seemed an eternity and we clung to each other because we both knew we were losing something so precious. We clung to each other because we knew that our happiness was lost. We clung to each other because we knew our love was doomed.

Chapter Eleven
Pain and Phone Calls

I HATE TO admit it now, but we did make love that night. Knowing he was married, knowing he wanted to keep that marriage, knowing he had a daughter whom he loved above everything else, I didn't try to stop him when he swept me into his arms and carried me to my room. I was broken, and only this, being with him could mend the pieces. I told myself, it was just one last time. Our swan song. Our goodbye.

He lay me down on the bed, and climbed in beside me. It started out as comfort only, me crying and him trying to soothe me. Then, it was one kiss, and another. Then it was a touch. A caress. Then our clothes started to come off; the need to touch each other, feel each other just one more time consumed both of us. We needed to be one. It was slow, and sad, and painful. He sat up and scooped me onto his lap when we were both naked, and we kissed and he held me like a child. I straddled him, and slid slowly down. We clung to one another and caressed, and stroked and touched, and loved, and I rocked on top of him, and he helped me with the motion. We made love just like that, in that position, and we rode the crest together, and neither one of us cried out our release, we just kept hanging on to each other never wanting to let go.

I don't know when and how I fell asleep, but I did and when I woke he was gone. I was alone with my heart break, and he presumably with his.

He did leave a note though. It read;

I wish I had met you, all those years ago. I'll love you forever,
Victor

And that was it. I didn't hear from him for a very, very long time.

SUMMER, FLEW BY, and I licked my wounds, wounds that wouldn't heal. I threw myself into my workouts, spending hours running, and biking, just so I didn't have to think about Victor. My sister helped, tried to give me hope. Maybe he will realize one day, and surely he will come to see that you're what is best for him, she would say. Or, damn those Italian's and their pride.

I had dreams and fantasies about him every night. Sometimes I would dream that I hadn't been on the pill all these months and had gotten pregnant and had a child, to have at least a part of him always. I dreamed he would come for me telling me it had been a joke, or that he would divorce his wife for me. Other times it was that we had met up years later, and we would rekindle our love, or he would see me somewhere we both had gone, a chance meeting, and he would run to me, and tell me everything I wanted to hear. It was hard. The dreams made me happy when I had them, but sad in the light of day because I knew they would never come true. It was hard.

When, summer was over it got a little easier because I had work to occupy my mind for a great part of the day. But the nights were still torture. I forgot to eat. I lost weight. Too much. My sister was starting to worry. My birthday came and went and October arrived with cooler nights. It started to get dark earlier and that made me sad too, and lonely. But the change in the seasons also snapped me out of my depression. I spent more time outside trying to be active and keep my thoughts off of Victor. I puttered in my garden; I painted the trim on my house. I kept myself occupied. I had wasted so many years being afraid, and I didn't want to spend years being sad. So, I started going out with my friends to a movie here and there. I played cards with my mom and Tom when they were in town. I had coffee with my sister and I even went to a theme park with her and Teddy for Halloween Horror Nights at Universal Studios in Orlando sometime in mid-October.

That was a fun night. We had fun with zombies jumping out of the bush, and chasing us. We laughed like crazy when one zombie jumped out of a garbage can and Teddy screamed like a girl. It was so fucking hilarious I almost peed myself. The haunted houses were terrifying. We stayed out pretty late that night. Before leaving the park at two o'clock, we all decided to have a cup of coffee at Cinnabon's before the two-hour drive home to keep us awake and alert. We chatted like old times in the car. She and Teddy teased one another mercilessly. She complained about his driving and he complained about her choice in music. She liked him a lot, it was obvious. She more than liked him. He had a good heart. He was honest. I could tell. What you saw was what you got with him, and she too, who had been lied to, humiliated and hurt would find that very refreshing.

The song by Alicia Keys called "If I Ain't Got You" came on the radio. I liked her songs a lot. I sang the words to her song softly in the back seat of the car. Even though the lyrics of the song epitomized my feelings for Victor, I didn't cry, even though I wanted to. Alicia sang of a life not worth living without her man, and even though Victor was lost to me I didn't feel that way. I was happy with the memories we had made. I was happy that I didn't cry. It was a step, I thought. Maybe two.

WHEN, I GOT home at four thirty in the morning, ready to crash and sleep until noon I was met by the flashing light of my answering machine.

I lay down, closed my eyes, and hit play, just in case it was from my mom or dad. My eyes popped open when I heard his voice. It was Victor. I sat up in bed, suddenly wide awake my heart hammering in my chest. I hadn't heard his voice in three months.

"Hi, Monica. I just saw you. Actually, I'm at Universal, and I'm watching you right now. You lost a lot of weight, babe- . . . a lot of weight. You look happy, though. You and your sister and her boyfriend are talking and having coffee and it looks like you're having a good time. I just wanted to let you know I'm happy that you're okay. I was worried about you. I'm better too, so don't worry about me. Okay, well bye. I don't want . . . just . . . be happy, okay?"

He had seen me, watched me at Universal Studios. He didn't come to say hello. Two steps forward, I thought, one step back. And, I was crying again. Until I slept.

I called my sister as soon as I woke up. I woke her up.

"Please, come over as soon as you can," I begged. "I got a message from Victor. I want you to hear it, and tell me what you think."

"Arggh, really." I heard her grumble something to Teddy. "Okay, give me an hour, sweetie. I'll be there soon as I can."

And then, she hung up.

SHE LISTENED TO the message twice before she would say anything; it was my tenth time hearing it.

"Well," she said, "he definitely sounds sad, but happy to see you're doing better. He did love you, Mon. It probably killed him to leave you like that and wonder how you were doing, if you were coping. Maybe it's closure for him. He knows you're okay, so now he can move on, but . . ." she trailed off looking away from my eyes.

"But, what?" I was grasping at straws, trying to read between the lines, looking for clues, anything that would tell me he was happy, he had moved on, or he still wanted me and was willing to give up trying to hang on to a woman who didn't want him and probably didn't love him anymore.

"He was watching us when he called. He called when he knew you wouldn't answer," she stated. What could that have meant, I thought.

"Why? Why do you think that is important, Ana tell me?" I begged wringing my hands together.

"He has probably wanted to call you a thousand times, Mon, but was afraid to hurt you when he made contact or be rejected. Calling you when you aren't home is safe. He can't be rejected, yet he can still reach out," she stated. Sure, I thought, that made sense. He felt bad, and wanted me to know he has worried, that his feelings were real. Ana interrupted my thoughts, and continued in a rush. "I think you should call him, Mon. Find out what he means by 'he is in a better place.' You need closure, too. But, do like he did and leave a message. Call when you know he wouldn't usually answer. It's worth a shot, baby girl."

WAS IT WORTH the shot? Or was I just setting myself up for more heartbreak. I mulled over it for days. Then one lonely Thursday night, after midnight when I knew he would have his phone turned off for the night I called.

THIS IS WHAT I said;

"Hi Victor. It's me, Monica. Thanks for checking up on me. I'm . . . better. I'm glad you are too. . . . " And, then I hung up. Chicken shit! It hadn't been what I had planned to say it all. I wanted to wish him happiness, and to let him know that I hoped he would get what he wanted, his family back, and to not worry about me and that I would move on. I wanted to wish him well. I just hadn't been able to form the words.

WHEN I GOT home from work I ran to my bedroom. The machine was flashing, there was another message waiting for me. I hit play. It was him.

"Hi Monica. I'm really glad you're better, not sick, I hope. You've lost a lot of weight. That worried me. I wanted you to know that I'm back in the military, I went back early, and they took me back. I hated that job in construction, you knew that. Well, it was nice to hear your voice. Be happy, and healthy, too," he laughed a little at the end but it came out hollow sounding.

It was Friday night and I was alone, and I listened to my messages from Victor over and over again, and got rip roaring drunk all by myself on stale Pinot Grigio I had in the refrigerator. I waited until after midnight, and called him.

"Hey, it's Monica . . . hiccup . . . healthy as a horse over here no fricking worries buddy. Run eight miles every day now, more 'n you do. Haha. Glad to hear you're back where you belong, great friends in the military and you need that. Gotta go. Bye." The message sounded

better in my head.

I didn't get any messages on Saturday or Sunday from Victor probably because he expected me to be home and was afraid I would answer. I went for a hike with some friends from work on Saturday along the Withalacoochee Trail, graded some papers on Sunday to kill the time, and tried not to remember my drunken message. It really did sound better in my head.

ON MONDAY, THERE was a message from Victor. He said;

"Hey, Monica. You must have been out with the girls or your sister. Sounds like you were lit pretty good." He laughed while saying that. *"I'm glad you're getting out, really. You must be training something fierce, but you've lost too much weight. You need to eat more carbs if you're doing that kind of running. You're a pole. It will eat away at your muscle mass. Are you training for a marathon or something? You always said you wanted to do that. And, yes, the guys are glad I'm back to work and they are the best. It is nice to be around guys you respect, and respect you. How is work this year? Hope you have good students? Okay gotta go. Bye."*

At midnight I called and left him this message;

"Hi, work is good. Good kids this year. I have three honors classes and an AP class which means a lot of papers to grade at night. It's all good, though, it keeps me busy. No marathon, though. I haven't seen anything close enough to do around here. But, it is something to think about. I will eat more carbs, too. Good idea. I'm glad you like working back at the base. Stay safe, though, okay."

On Tuesday, he left this message;

"Hey, Monica. It sounds like you have great classes even if it is extra work. There is a marathon at the end of next month, every year in St. Pete. I think it's a half marathon or a 5K just for women. I'm doing PT again, so really just training the young guys, new recruits, and

keeping the old timers in peak performance. I don't think they would send me back to Iraq, though, unless it was an emergency. You never know, but don't worry about that, okay. Bye."

Tuesday night at midnight I called him. This is what I said;

"Hi Victor. The marathon sounds interesting. I will check into it. About Iraq, I can't help but worry. I worry about all the guys there. Some of my students have been sent. So, I would worry about them and you. Bye."

Wednesday the message waiting for me was;

"Monica, tomorrow is Thursday, I have some time. Can I see you?"

MY STOMACH LURCHED. I couldn't go down this road with a married man, could I? What had I been doing all week, I asked myself. Had I been flirting with a married man, or just checking on an old friend, and lover? I felt sick to my stomach. My mind had told me the latter, but my heart knew it was the former. He had a daughter who wanted a mommy and a daddy. Her mommy and daddy. If I took that from her, ruined the relationship she had with her father, she would hate us both, he would hate himself, and he would come to hate me. I couldn't do this to a child, an innocent young girl who had no clue who I was.

At midnight, I called. I left this message;

"I don't think so, Victor. Goodbye."

He didn't call for a week.

Chapter Twelve

More Truths /
Can't We Just Be Friends?

IT WAS A Wednesday, when I got the next message from Victor.

"Hi Monica. I shouldn't have just said it like that. I think you took it wrong. I wasn't trying to pick up where we left off. I wouldn't do that to you again. I care about you still you know, like a really good friend. I want you to be happy. I want . . . to see for myself you're really okay, okay? I just need to know. I want you to see I'm okay, too. Let's talk. Have a cup of coffee together. It can be in public. Outside. In the daytime. Wherever you choose. I'm free this weekend. Think about it, okay. Call me any day, before midnight. No more games."

No more games? What was that supposed to mean? He wanted me to call and really talk to him. I couldn't do it. But yet, I wanted to see him. I was desperate to see him. Could I see him and not want to wrap my arms around him, not want to rip his clothes off? Could I sit across the table from him and not want to crawl across it and sit in his lap and cry like a baby? Or would I hold on to him, and never let him go?

I thought about it for two days. Two torturous days. Two sleepless nights. I was going back and forth. Maybe, I needed to see him one more time for closure. It had been nearly four months. I could do this, couldn't I? When I got home on Friday, I would do it. I would call him. I chickened out, but after playing with my food at dinner, hardly touching it, I broke down and called him.

"Hello," Victor said tentatively.

"Hi Victor. It's me, Monica," I said. I was nervous. I hadn't even made up my mind if I would meet him, but the temptation just to hear him had been so strong.

"I know, silly. I saw your name on the caller ID. I didn't think you would call, but I'm glad you did." He chuckled.

"Yeah. Me too," I lied as my heart thundered in my chest. I was scared to death. I still wasn't sure I could see him again.

"So, things are good, right?" he asked curiously. His voice was so casual.

"Yes, things are good this year at work. You?" I asked.

"Better than good, at work. It's like I never left." There was an awkward silence. Neither of us knew what to say. "So, can you do coffee? Tomorrow? I'm free all weekend, so . . .," his voice trailed off.

"Umm, yeah, I guess I can," I stammered. My head was spinning.

"You sure?" he said. He must have heard the hesitation in my voice.

"Yeah . . . umm, I'm okay," I stalled, then added, "How about the Barnes and Noble over there on Del Mabry. I need to get some AP study guides for my students and we don't have one over here. So I can kill two birds with one stone," I offered. *Phew, made that one sound good on the fly.* I did need some new study guides for that class anyway, even though they sold them at Books a Million nearby, but Victor wouldn't know that.

"Yeah, that's close for me. No problems. I think they

open at nine," he suggested.

"Umm, let's make it for eleven, okay? I want to get my run in, and stuff." I knew it would only prolong the inevitable, but I wanted to set the terms, the time.

"All right then. I can do that. I'll see you tomorrow, Monica," he murmured. Had his voice gotten huskier? Or, was that my imagination playing tricks on me? My mind swam, cloudy with confusion and emotional turmoil.

"See you tomorrow, then," I echoed Victor's words and quickly hung up.

I sat on the edge of my chair, the phone still clenched in my hand. Crap, crap, and double crap. What the hell was I doing? How could I put myself through this? What the hell was wrong with me? I tried to tell myself it was just to be sure he was okay, too. But, I knew that wasn't it. It wasn't it at all. I must be a sadist, I thought, because I sure as hell liked inflicting pain. On myself.

I WOKE UP feeling nauseous, and I had hardly slept at all. I crawled out of bed, and went to the bathroom and puked my guts out. I was a fucking idiot. Who was I kidding? Not me. Maybe him. I rinsed my mouth, brushed my teeth, and sipped a little water, foregoing coffee on my sour stomach. I went back to my room, and put on some shorts, and a t-shirt and went for my run. My daily runs consisted of the streets within my neighborhood. I had used the car to plot my route, increasing it as my stamina increased. My new eight mile route took me out of my neighborhood, and included some nice hills for the strengthening of my calves, butt, and hamstrings. It was a great workout and always made me feel better when I was done.

When I got home it was a little after eight. Instead of a

shower, and to kill some time, I took a bath instead, soaked a bit, and shaved my legs. By nine, I was dressed and ready to go. I didn't want to look fabulous, draw attention to myself or anything, but didn't want to look like a pathetic loser. So, I selected a pair of faded jeans. A little loose, since I had lost maybe fifteen pounds, I didn't know, but something like that, since Victor and I broke up. I matched it with a loose peasant top that I thought looked kind of Soho. Well, it was a style anyway I told myself in the mirror and shrugged. I didn't straighten my hair. I left it wavy, the humidity was pretty much gone in November, but I did blow it out just and used a little mousse in case it got hotter and started to frizz.

I forced myself to have a piece of toast, and glass of apple juice. The toast would settle my stomach. Having nothing in it made the nausea worse so I ate the dry toast and sipped the juice slowly to help it go down. At nine-thirty I was twiddling my thumbs, so I got my keys, and went. I would drive slowly, have time to buy my books before he got there, and be seated with a pile of manuals between us for protection in the coffee shop. Good, I had a plan and felt a little safer.

But, despite my planning, I got there at ten-thirty and saw his car already in the parking lot; he was standing out front looking exactly the same as I imagined. He, too, wore faded jeans, and a navy t-shirt, with an Army logo on it. He smiled when he saw my car pull in the lot, began to approach, and no sooner had I stepped out of the car or even knew what was happening, he wrapped me in a bear hug. "It's so good to see you, Monica. I was afraid you wouldn't come."

"You too," I uttered into his shirt. He smelled so good, and I couldn't help but inhale.

Then while still holding me, "You're skin and bones, what the hell," he said in shock as he let me go, bent slightly at the waist, and reached out to put his hands around my waist as if to measure me. I pulled back quickly stepping into my still open car door.

He straightened, and shook his head in apology, "Sorry, I . . . uh . . . shouldn't have done that, umm, let's go inside." He indicated the front of the store. I moved out of the way of my door, shut it and began to walk. He walked beside me to the entrance and held the door open for me.

"You look good, though," I murmured rather lamely.

Once inside, the bright sunshine from outside left us a little blinded with the muted lighting and décor of the bookstore. He peered around and indicated the coffee shop in the back.

"Oh, there it is," he said as he pointed to the small tables and chairs set up in the rear of the store for customers to peruse titles before making a purchase. Butterflies flapped in my stomach. His touch earlier had made me feel faint, and the scent from his skin brought so many memories rushing back.

I needed a moment to regain my equilibrium. And to catch my breath, clear my head. "You go," I said and he gave me a puzzled look. "Order me a coffee. You know how I like it, right? I want to get those manuals so I don't forget, okay?"

"Yes, I remember how you like it," he muttered. "Go on. Get your books." He had sounded so disappointed like he knew I was evading him for a few more moments.

I took as much time as I dared. I bought twelve study guides, one for each student. These would make a great barrier on the table. No accidental hand touches, no reaching across the table. I paid for the books, brought the bag with me and headed to the coffee shop; I spotted him right away as he waved me over. When he saw my load, he quickly got up, and pulled over an extra chair, so I could put my purchases on it. So much for protection, I thought grimly. He took the bag out of my hand, oops accidental touch, and electricity to boot. The butterflies were back. I let go quickly, trying to not let on to what I felt.

"Huff, that was heavy. Thank you," I slunk into my chair trying to act nonchalant.

"I can take them to the car for you," he made to get up just as he was sitting down.

"No, no that isn't necessary," I ushered him back into his chair. He sat back down slowly. I was a bit relieved to see he looked just as nervous as I was.

He repositioned his chair moving it a bit closer so that we weren't sitting directly across from each other at the small café table. "Okay, but I will take them out for you when you're ready to leave. Is that all right?" he asked.

"Sure, that would be nice." It was easier to agree to let him take the books out for me then the thought of him watching me lug them out, walking like I was drunk or lopsided because of the weight of the books. Or worse yet, have my pants fall down around my ankles because they were incredibly loose, with him watching.

He smiled then giving me a sympathetic look. "So, I got you your coffee. Two Splendas, and low-fat milk," he paused and then added, "I, er . . . I also got you a muffin. Hope you don't mind." His look was one of concern.

"Well, I did eat, but I can pick at it. Thank you." I didn't want to insult him. He was obviously concerned about the weight loss and like my sister wanted to force me to eat more.

"Okay, and you're welcome." There was a long awkwardness between us. It had been four months since we had seen each other, well maybe a little less for him, and we just didn't know what to say to one another now that we were here. We both just looked at each other, and smiled. Victor eventually broke the silence after clearing his throat, "So I'm glad you came." Pause. "This is so awkward, isn't it," he laughed. "Let's just call the elephant in the room what it is."

I laughed. A real laugh. It broke the proverbial ice, so to speak.

AN HOUR LATER, I had eaten the entire muffin, had finished my coffee, and he was getting me another one. He talked for a while first. Telling me stories about work, the new recruits and the stupid things they did. He talked about his daughter telling me about her cheerleading camp, and the music she listened to in the car that drove him nuts. He didn't know their names, couldn't understand the lyrics. His pride and love for his daughter was evident in every word he spoke. I listened avidly wanting to know what his daughter was like. She was a part of him after all. He had never been so open with me before.

When it was my turn, I told him about work, of course. And, my AP class that I absolutely loved. I talked about my sister and Teddy. She had brought him by for a quick visit one week ago, and then brought him to meet my mom. I had nearly died laughing I told him when she left my house, Teddy in toe, mumbling, okay let's go bring you to meet my mother, the dragon lady, and get this over with. My mom was the sweetest, funniest woman you would ever want to meet. She had obviously given Teddy a lot of drivel to scare the poor guy because he turned before he left and the look on his face was frightful. Victor laughed with me and at my description.

"Your mom sounds cool, Monica. Easy going," he sighed.

"She is. You would have liked her," I stated and then realized how stupid I was to have said that. He might have taken it as a jab. I saw the look on his face and knew he had taken it wrong. "Sorry," I mumbled. "That was stupid, just something to say."

"Don't worry about it," he mumbled. "My mom is great, too. Old-fashioned, very religious, but she loves her family and puts them first. Always." Then that is when he offered to get us refills and got up before I could say anything.

When he came back to the table with two fresh coffees, he said, "That story about your sister reminds me of something I wanted to tell you!"

"What," I asked. He waggled his eyebrows at me suggestively, and it sent a shot of nerves straight through me that made me sit up straight in my chair. It reminded me of all those times he had done that with me.

"Kat . . . and . . . ," he paused dramatically, "Joe," he nodded seriously.

"Noooo . . . No way," I said picking up my coffee cup taking a sip.

His look of shock must have mirrored my own. "Yeah, I woke up one night. I heard strange noises in the kitchen. I thought someone had broken in. So I grabbed a bat out of my closet, and ran out of the room charging. Kat was on the counter, and Joe was standing in front of her with his pants around his ankles."

"Oh my God, you didn't. She didn't. He's like old." I burst into laughter covering my mouth with my hand.

"Well, only by fifteen years," he laughed with me. "But the counter, Monica, I make my food there." He looked absolutely stricken.

We both laughed long and hard over that one. The conversation fizzled after that. We just looked at each other, neither of us knowing what to say, but neither of us wanting to leave either. I saw it in his eyes, and it stung. He still loved me. I knew I still loved him. Nothing had changed. I looked down at my watch. It was time to make my exit. "Well, I should get going. I want to get these books home and review them, make up some assignments this weekend for the kids." I made to get up, and reluctantly he followed, hefting up the bag of manuals as I led the way to the entrance to open the door.

I popped the trunk and he set the books inside reaching up and closing the door. I turned and started towards my door, and he followed me. I spun around to offer him my hand to shake and wish him farewell. He ignored it and crushed me to him. I hugged him back, but not nearly as tightly. "I like your hair like that, Monica. I wanted to tell you that. Very natural."

"Thank you," I muttered into his chest breathing him in one last time.

"Can I call you sometimes? Just to talk like friends. When you're home?" he asked. Why? I wondered. What was the point? But I didn't have the heart to say it.

"Sure. Sure." I patted his back. He let go, and took a step back so I could open the door of my SUV. He stood two feet from my car not moving out of the way, watching me back out and turn, and straighten the vehicle. He waved as I turned left on Del Mabry to head home.

ON SUNDAY, MY sister stopped by for brunch, sans Teddy, and I told her about going to see Victor.

"Well, sweetie. I love you. I do. You gave it a shot, but it seems like nothing has changed for him. He would have said something if things were different. I don't think it is a good idea to keep talking to him. You need to cut the ties and move on." When I didn't answer and just sat there mute and in pain, she blew it. "Come on, Monica, you're fucking delusional, the both of you, if you think you can just be friends. You can't put fire and ice together, baby sis! One of you is going to melt! And the other one is gonna burn!"

That was true. It had been that way from the start.

Chapter Thirteen

Just Friends

I KNEW MY sister was right. But, I wanted him in my life even if it would be just on the phone, and just as friends who talked occasionally. I was all kinds of a fool. I had myself convinced it would be nice. He would heal, we would move on. The pain would be gone. It would be like it was with my friend, Tammy, from college. We didn't talk much but we knew we would always be there for each other, to listen to, and share our joys and sorrows with. Hopefully, we could learn how to cheer each other on, as well. Tammy and I lived far apart though my subconscious told me, and she was female. But Victor and I, we didn't live far, and well he wasn't a girl, either. I told myself calls would be okay though, because we would keep our distance, call for birthdays, holidays, and only rarely would we ever see each other. That would be okay, wouldn't it?

He called Sunday at about eight o'clock. We talked for ten minutes, just talking about our day.

I called Monday at ten. I wanted to see if he had caught the show on the History Channel about returning Vietnam soldiers who had been reported Missing in Action.

He called Tuesday. He had actually watched American Idol with his daughter, and thought the show was funny, with the competing judges let alone contestants.

I had deliberately not called Wednesday because I didn't want to start a pattern. These calls were supposed to be few and far between. Old habits die hard, I guess. But I was determined to try harder to resist being lured back in. I forced myself to pull out some books from work, and do some planning for my new AP class. It was late when he called on Wednesday. He sounded out of sorts. "Hi, Monica," he said. "I just wanted to hear about your day. Everyone went out tonight, but I didn't feel much like it. Nothing's on television and I got bored."

"Yes, I know. Me too. I was bored. Then I got to working on some lesson plans and time got away from me, but geesh, it's late, I better head to bed soon," It was nearly midnight, I noticed when I looked at the clock. "I . . . wanted to tell you something the other day, but I forgot. Joe's retiring," he informed me.

"Really," I muttered. "I never would have thought."

"Yeah, me too." He wants to spend more time with his grand kids. He's got two in North Carolina, and another one in Jacksonville."

"He's not moving, is he?" I asked. I knew a lot of the younger people in the complex really respected, and looked up to Joe. He was a role model for many, and a good friend.

"Na . . . him and Kat," he laughed. "But he plans on travelling more."

"Right," I laughed. "Well, if they are happy with each other, God bless them, I say."

"Yeah," he mumbled. "They are happy . . ." His words trailed off. Victor didn't say anything else, and I didn't know what to say after that. "Well, I have to get some laundry done tonight, so I'll call you . . . some other time," he ended lamely.

"Okay, bye Victor. It was nice hearing from you."

ON THURSDAY, I called at seven. Early, in case he decided to go out, and I was worried about him.

"Hi there, Monica," he answered. "I'm glad you called."

"Hi, Victor. How are . . ." my words were caught off by what I heard next.

"Who is Monica, daddy?" I heard a little girl say. I held my breath panic striking into the very heart of me.

"It's one of daddy's friends, Stacey. One of my very best friends," he told her. "Go on in and I'll catch up, okay?" A lump began to form in my throat.

"Sure, Daddy. I'll go make popcorn with Kat. Hurry up." I heard her voice trail off.

"Listen, if you're busy, I can always call back," I offered.

"No, I have a second. My wife, er, she had a work thing come up, so I got to see Stacey. Normally, I get her every Tuesday, and every other weekend. But once in a while I get her more often. We just came back from dinner, and now we were going to watch a movie," he explained.

"That's nice. Well, then you should go," I stated sincerely. "Don't keep your daughter waiting."

"Okay, but I'll call you after I drop her off at home. It might be a little late though."

"Sure, okay," I mumbled. "Bye."

I was his friend. One of his best. It hurt to hear him say that.

IT WAS TWELVE-THIRTY when he called. I was tired, watching Lettermen, but still up waiting.

"Hi, Victor," I said a little sleepily.

"Hey, I didn't wake you, did I?" he asked worriedly.

"No, I was watching television, just getting tired," I answered honestly.

"Sorry about that, but I had to drive Stacey home. Her mom lives in Dunedin now, and she wanted to talk a bit, sorry," he offered lamely. She had moved; he stayed to talk. I tried to keep thoughts of them together out of my mind, but she was his wife.

"Dunedin?" I asked.

"Yeah, she um, bought a house there, and it's a bit of a drive," he didn't sound happy about it. He was Stacey's father and I'm sure wanted to be as close to her as possible. I didn't blame him for that.

"Oh, that's okay." I said yawning.

"You're tired, go to sleep. I'll call tomorrow," he said and I could here in his voice he didn't want the call to end.

"Thanks for telling Stacey that I was one of your best friends, Victor. That meant a lot to me," I blurted out trying to keep the call going on for a while longer.

"I meant it, too," he said with sincerity. "You're the only person that really knows me and accepts me, quirks and all." I hurt for him, those scars he had ran deep.

I tried to tease him to ease his hurt. "Yeah, we're a pair of quirky birds, you and I," I laughed knowingly. "Two of a kind."

He laughed. "It's hard, Monica, this friendship thing, though," he said honestly. I could hear the regret in his voice, but he rushed to continue, "But I don't want to lose it. I missed you so much, and worry about you. I need your friendship."

I swallowed the lump forming in my throat. "I know, me too, Vic, I feel the same way." There was a silence. "I gained two pounds, though," I tried to laugh to get us away from dangerous and painful territory.

"Ooo, two pounds," he teased. "Good job, Monica."

"Hey, I'm trying." I whined. And I was, trying to eat more often and regularly.

"I'm glad." His sigh was audible before he spoke next. "Monica, I know you probably don't want to hear this, but I want to be honest with you from now on, Okay?"

"Okay," I stammered.

"My wife and I have been going to counseling. The army really encourages us to take counseling, marriage counseling before taking any final measures. It is an eight week program. It's been a month now. I just wanted you to know," he said quickly.

The lump was back. "Oh, okay. I hope it is helping."

"In a way," he stalled. "It's been, revealing. At least, I know my wife doesn't see me as a monster anymore. We have another month of counseling."

"Yeah, well. Good luck," I managed to get out convincingly.

"Yeah, thanks, but I don't think it is going to work for Julianna." He paused searching for words. "She told me tonight she still wants a divorce. She loves me, but just not like a married couple should love one another."

"Really?" I asked. I didn't know why he was telling me this. Or, if I wanted to know. I guess he wanted there to be no more secrets, if we were going to be friends.

"Yeah, I don't know why I'm telling you this." His voice echoed my thoughts. "As friends though, that is something I would tell you. I . . . just . . . don't want you to think I have ulterior motives. You're friendship means too much."

"It's okay. Victor. I think I understand," I expressed to

him sympathetically. I heard the pain and frustration there. Confusion.

"Yeah, well, I think I'm coming to accept it. Stacey even knows that we're probably going to divorce. The counselor wanted us to talk with her about it so that it didn't come as a shock to her."

"That's a good idea," I told him. It would make any transition easier whatever it may be.

"Yeah, but the kid tells us. 'Please, tell me something I don't already know. I love both of you and you both love me, so no biggie. We haven't lived together in a year.' she said." He stated with wonder.

Kids were versatile. They adapted well if they had love and support on all sides. I saw this all the time in my career. "Kids are smart today, Victor," I offered.

"She sure is," he laughed. There was another pause. "Well, I will let you go to bed. Thanks for listening."

"No problem. Good night, Victor," I whispered.

"Good night, Monica," he said softly.

ON FRIDAY, DURING my lunch break, before I knew Ana had to go to work, I called her and filled her in on what was going on. She warned me and reminded me again that we were playing a dangerous game with this friendship business, but was glad Victor wasn't leading me on and giving me false hope. I admitted to her that was what I was hoping she would say. She again cautioned me not to hope because anything could happen. She reminded me how our parents had remarried, albeit they had divorced again. I sighed, knowing this was true, having lived it myself.

Friday night rolled around, and I called Victor. He had his daughter for the weekend. I could hear her in the background with Kat. They were laughing.

"What's going on?" I asked.

"Oh, Kat and Stacey are in the kitchen cooking and baking up a storm, and I'm trying to stay out of their way," he laughed.

"You lazy SOB, you just don't want to help!" I heard Kat yell.

"Yeah, daddy!" Stacey yelled laughing.

"Are you slacking in your duties?" I accused. I could tell that Kat must be close to Stacey by the way they talked and were so easy going together. She must spend a lot of time there.

"Not you, too," he laughed. "Don't tell me you're on their side?" he whined.

"Good girl, Mon. Fight the power. Make sure he knows that the kitchen isn't just a woman's domain!" Kat called out.

"What's fight the power mean?" I heard Stacey say.

We all laughed. "You're lucky she didn't ask what SOB meant," I said, and I heard him chuckle.

"Yeah, really. That one just slipped past her," he mumbled. "That doesn't happen too often."

"So, why are the girls in this cooking and baking frenzy for which you refuse to help?" I asked continuing to mock him.

"They are . . . um cooking and prepping for a party, Joe's retirement actually. We're doing a little something for him down in the courtyard area by the pool tomorrow night. All of us from the apartment complex are going."

"Yeah, and you should be helping!" Kat complained.

"He's your boyfriend!" Victor retorted. "Plus, I refuse to go anywhere near that counter."

"Oh you devil," I heard Kat say. Then she yelled, "Tell

Monica to come. It would be nice to see her." Oh, my. Why would Kat put us in this predicament, I thought.

"Is that Monica," I heard Stacey say. "I want to meet her."

"Oh, I don't know," I hastily stated. "I'm not sure."

"She says she is busy," he started to offer as an excuse.

"Busy, my arse!" Kat snipped.

"I really want to meet her, daddy! Kat says she's cool!" I heard the girl complain. Kat told Stacey I was cool. They had talked about me. The slight panic I felt began to rise.

"Tell that skinny bit—um, Monica," Kat cut herself off, "She's expected at eight."

There was an awkward silence from both Victor and I.

"So, eight then?" he asked when I hadn't said anything.

I paused, "Eight it is, then." I felt like I hadn't been given a choice. But the temptation to see him with his daughter was just too much. It would be painful, but something I thought I should do.

AT EIGHT ON the button, I made way into the courtyard of Victor's apartment complex. I just followed the noise. It was obvious the revelry was already under way from the sound of laughter and music that filled the evening air. I walked between Victor's building and the one next to it, and made my way down the small lane of potted plants, and decorative shrubbery to the pool and lanai area. I noticed someone had strung nets of white Christmas lights over the fence, some trees, and the umbrellas. It made for a nice atmosphere in the waning light of November in Florida. I saw two tables laden with food and drinks. There were a lot of people, much more than there had been when Joe had thrown a party last summer. People stood and sat in small groups, all around the oversized swimming pool and a sign was hung across the fence that read, "Good luck Joe! Congratulations."

Victor had his back to me, and Kat saw me first. "There you are, Mon," she crossed the lanai over to me and gave me a quick hug. "Damn, girl. Victor was right. You're as skinny as pole. Not good," she looked at me suspiciously.

Victor turned in his seat when he heard Kat make that statement. "I had the flu last month," I lied to brush away any questions. "It was awhile before I was able to eat anything solid. My stomach was very unsettled." Her eyes were still suspicious. "I'm gaining it back slowly now," I tried to reassure her.

Victor got up when he heard that, concern on his face. "You didn't tell me you were sick?" He smiled but I saw a bit of doubt in his expression.

"Oh, I . . . it slipped my mind is all," I offered lamely as he crossed over to me.

"Oh, well you're better now, though, right?" he asked and offered me a halfhearted hug.

I nodded. "Yeah, I'm fine." I hugged him quickly and stepped back.

Victor took my hand and tugged it slightly. "Come on and sit down with me and Joe. Tina, Maria, and Michael are here somewhere, too." I followed him letting him drag me along, but I was looking around to see if I could spot his daughter. I had wondered if she would look like him. He noticed my glancing and knew what I was doing. He rewarded me with a breathtaking smile. "She's with Joe's two granddaughters. They came down from Jacksonville for the party."

"Oh, that's nice," I offered and smiled back.

"Yeah, Stacey and Joe's grandkids have been as thick as thieves all day. Brittany is fifteen, and Lucy is eleven, the same age as Stacey," he said as Joe spotted me and waved calling us over. "Hey, Joe has seen you. Let's say hello." Victor took my elbow and brought me through the crowd of well-wishers over to the small group around Joe.

Joe came forward to greet me.

"Hey, Monica. It's nice to see you, again. I'm glad you could make it. Thanks for coming," he said and gave me a big bear hug.

"Congratulations Joe, on retiring." I handed him an envelope with a card wishing him well on his retirement. "I hear you're planning on spending a lot of time visiting the grand-kids. That ought to be nice."

"Aw, you didn't have to do that," he said slipping the card into his back pocket.

"It's just a gift card to the new seafood place, Bone Fish Grille, the one down on Henderson Avenue. I had heard you mention you loved fish and wanted to try it," I shrugged.

"Oh, thanks. That was sweet of you, and about the kids, yes; I'm looking forward to having the time to visit them more often, but not too much time." His eyes began to twinkle and from my peripheral vision I saw Kat approaching. So that is what was putting the sparkle in his eyes just now, I thought to myself. "I've got a great reason to be spending time here as well," Joe added. Kat went right to Joe, ducked under his arm, and gave him a peck on the cheek. Joe put his arm around her back and pulled her in closer.

"Don't stick around on my account, you old codger. You'll just be underfoot," she teased.

"Not under your foot darling, but maybe under . . .," Joe was caught off guard by the swift elbow to the rib cage Kat had given him. He coughed, and then laughed, and she kissed him on the cheek while blushing.

"Oh, here come the kids," Victor interrupted. I turned in

the direction Victor was looking and saw three young girls approaching. Two were brunette, one very tall and thin, and the other shorter and a bit rounder in features. Sisters obviously, and the third girl, shorter than the rest had blond hair and Victor's blue eyes. It was startling to see this little girl with those eyes, but no one could mistake that this was Victor's daughter. She was stunning.

I leaned over to whisper, "She's beautiful, Victor. Beautiful."

He reached over and took my hand and gave it a squeeze. He was smiling at his daughter as she approached, but he was holding my hand making those circles he used to do with his thumb. It was like a shot in the gut. I hadn't expected it, but electricity shot through me, and I think him too, because he looked down at our hands and winced. He let go of my hand regretfully. "I know," he whispered back. "She is beautiful. And, it scares the hell out of me." I nodded sympathizing with him.

Victor turned in Stacey's direction and called out to the kids, "Stacey, Monica just got here!"

The little girl with the sparkling blue eyes skipped ahead of the other two girls and rushed to her dad slamming into him around the waist and gave him a hug. Then she turned and offered her hand to me. "Hi, Mon. Nice to meet you. Dad talks about you all the time. Oh, is it okay that I call you Mon? That's what Kat calls you," she rushed out.

I took her hand and clasped it with both of mine and shook her small hand. She was eleven, but looked like she was eight. "Sure," I smiled. "That's what my sister calls me, too."

"Ooo, you have a sister. You're so lucky. I wish I had a sister. It sucks growing up an only child. Nothing but adults to play with when you're home," she pouted.

Victor ruffled her hair. "One of you is plenty," he teased but was looking at me when he said it.

"It sure sounds like it sucks," I told her and it made her smile that I was agreeing with her and not taking her dad's side.

"You're pretty, Mon. I love your jeans. I would love a pair of jeans like that, but mom and dad say no way, whenever I ask for a pair of skinny jeans," she confided in me. I had just bought these this morning. I hadn't wanted to wear anything sexy, but all my casual pants had been too large. They weren't my usual style, but they were comfortable and fit well at least. Victor looked at my legs then, and I think it was the first time he noticed what I had on, because I saw a lick, just a bit, but I saw it, a flame in his eye. My heart accelerated.

"Thanks Stacey, but your dad is probably right. If you wore these, he would have a heart attack, or worse, he'd have to chase all the boys away with a stick and you would be mortified," I teased her. "Fathers can be so embarrassing at times."

"Don't I know it!" she rolled her eyes and looked back at her dad.

"Hey, I'm not that bad," he sounded wounded as he looked at his daughter. Adoration for her filled his expression.

"Yes, you are," she teased. "Well sometimes." Brittany and Lucy over by the snack and refreshment table began to beckon to her. "Okay, I gotta go get some snacks and I want to hang out with the girls. I'll be back later, Monica because I want to ask you about your fingernails. Don't let me forget." And she was off, skipping over to the buffet, and her two friends who were piling their own snacks onto paper plates.

I looked down at my freshly painted manicured finger-nails, French-tipped. I had the nail tech add a little sparkle to the pinkies, but other than that, nothing fancy. "Oh, brother," Victor laughed, "am I in trouble or what?" he joked, but clarified when he saw my confusion, "She's been begging her mom and me to let her get a real manicure and not a fake one."

"They grow up fast," I offered looking around and realizing for the first time we were standing by ourselves and that Joe and Kat were now sitting with another group of people.

"Yeah, they sure do," he grumbled. His hands rubbed his temples. "It's scary. It scares me that I won't be there every night."

My heart lurched. It sounded as though he was resigned to it being over with his wife. I squashed that feeling and put it away to ponder later. "You are," I whispered and then more firmly. "Maybe not physically, but you see her every week at least, and every other weekend for three days, and when you do, I'm sure it's quality time. The time you spend apart, the lessons you teach, and the morals are with her always. Those just don't go away," I explained.

"You're right, you're right," he muttered and shook his head. "You were great with her, by the way. You really can talk to kids," he added mildly surprised.

"I, um, am a teacher, Victor! Kids are my life." I teased. "I'm the kid whisperer."

"Well, then I may have to come to you for advice if you're such an expert," he laughed at my joke.

"Sure. Anytime." I laughed in return.

"Come on let's go circulate," he offered me his hand, and I took it. He gave my hand a little squeeze and I trailed behind him. He introduced me to a few new people and I got reacquainted with those I knew; Michael, Tina and Maria.

At one point, Victor wandered off to spend a little time

with his daughter and I found myself back talking with Kat.

After a few minutes of conversation, she came out with it. "Yeah, so . . .," she paused. "You still love him, don't you?"

I couldn't lie. I sighed. "Yes, but I'm not a husband stealer. I just couldn't do that to anyone. But, I do care for Victor, and I think we both just needed to know that the other was all right before we could move on," I explained hoping she would understand.

"I don't think you're a husband stealer, Mon. Please don't take it that way. I'm glad you're here for him. His wife, er, Julianna, she bailed on the marriage four years ago."

My eyebrow arched up at her words. "Yeah, at first it was the sex. He hasn't had sex with her in three years. He only started . . . ," she paused searching for the right words, "seeing girls a year or so ago after she kicked him out. There were a lot, mind you, but he never saw any of them more than once or twice. And at first, it was only out of anger. But since you, there has been no one, not even since you . . . well you know what I mean," she finished lamely.

I was shocked by this revelation. She was telling me Victor had been in a marriage for three years without any sex at all, a man like him, and that he had just meaningless flings before me, then it was just me. I didn't know what to say. I just stood there, jaw dropped, staring.

She continued, "But I can understand why you want to be cautious. She was a winner. She played head games, making him think he was a freak, when it was more about the money. Her folks are loaded. She never got used to Army life. Wouldn't even consider living in base housing even after Stacey came along. She would stay with her parents when he was away, or in training. Julianna made him get an apartment and never wanted to hang out with his Army buddies. We weren't her people. She never even tried to get to know us. She kept to her own circles." It was clear Kat wasn't a fan of Julianna's.

I was taking this all in. It confused me, and I couldn't seem to make sense of all the information. It did, however, make me understand why Victor had lied for so long, and it did make me understand why he was such a mess. But, what I didn't get was why he was fighting to keep a woman that didn't love him. Why he didn't understand it was more important for his daughter to see both her parents happy, than to be miserable together?

"Thanks for sharing this with me, Kat. It helps me to understand a little better why Victor has done what he did. He hasn't shared anything like this with me," I reached out to squeeze her hand.

"He would never bad mouth the mother of his child. That is just not him," she offered with a smile. "But I wanted you to know." Joe was calling her over, so we both strolled over to the other side of the lanai where Joe was talking to Michael and another guy I hadn't met yet.

"Hi, Monica. It's nice to see you again. This is my friend, Rick," Michael stated. "Rick, this is Monica," Michael added finishing the introductions.

"Hi, Michael. It's nice to see you again, too. And, it's nice to meet you, Rick," I smiled.

"It's always nice to meet a stunning woman," Rick smiled wickedly proffering his hand. He was tall, taller than Victor, leaner too, but well defined. He was quite a bit younger, with brown, close cropped military hair, and hazel eyes. Good looking, rugged. I shook his hand intending to make it quick but he wouldn't let go. "Come on and dance with me and we can get to know each other," he stated as he pulled me to an area where some couples were dancing. I had no choice in the matter, really, he was practically dragging me. But I was happy to see Michael following us and Tina not far behind.

When we started dancing it was an up tempo song, and Michael and Tina kept circling around us making it more like a group dance so that I felt more comfortable. After two songs, Victor interrupted us to tell us the kids were all going to Joe's for a sleep over, and wanted to say goodnight. I saw that he looked upset and was eyeing Michael like crazy. We stopped dancing, said good night to the girls, and Stacey hugged me. I was a little surprised at how affectionate she was. "You're so pretty. Good night, Monica. I hope I get to see you again."

"I hope to see you, too, Stacey, goodnight." I leaned down to hug her back. "And, I think you're pretty, too." I straightened and Victor wouldn't look at me. He was deliberately looking the other way.

"I'll be back in a bit," he said to Michael. "Joe's daughter is going to put in a movie for the kids. I just want to see Stacey settled." And with that, he marched off with Stacey.

"Catch you in a bit, buddy," Michael called out to his back. "We're good here."

"Right," he called over his shoulder.

I WAS A bit concerned with his sudden change in mood and a bit distracted when Rick pulled me over to a chair. "Hey, let me get you a drink, Monica, and we can get to know each other. What will it be?" he asked, referring to the drink.

"Umm, a Michelob Ultra would be nice. If they don't have it, anything light will do," I murmured absently as I was distracted in trying to puzzle out Victor's mood change.

"A beer drinking woman. My kind of girl," he stated as he

walked off. That snapped me back to reality. Uh-oh, Vic didn't think? Well, I would straighten that out right away when he returned, I thought, suddenly nervous.

Michael and Tina sat with me, asked me a few questions about work, I answered, but was edgy as heck. I would be until Victor returned and I had a chance to explain, and to let him know I hadn't been flirting or anything. But before Victor came back, Rick had returned and handed me my beer. I would deal with him first, I thought as he sat beside me in one of the pool chairs.

I turned to Rick, and gave him a polite shake of my head. "Hey, thanks Rick. I just want to be upfront with you, okay, so there are no misunderstandings. I'm thirty-one, you look like you're twenty. I'm not from here, and don't come to Tampa often. I don't do one night stands, and I'm just not interested in dating right now, ok?"

"Ouch! I'm wounded, I'm twenty-four and I dig older chicks. They can teach me a thing or two," he teased, not giving up so easily.

He was a funny guy, not a bad sort, but he was persistent. So Michael chimed in, "Give it up, man, you're not going to get anywhere with Monica," and there was a cautionary note in his voice, but Rick still wasn't hearing it. He was twenty-four, and a little buzzed.

"I don't see a ring on her finger," he joked, and kept trying to give me flirty glances.

"Please, Rick. You're a nice guy and all, but too young for me, and frankly, I'm just not that into you," I teased back using that famous line from the movie. Often humor helped to diffuse a potential situation, before it arose, so I tried that tack instead.

"Aw, surely you jest." He pouted. "I can't do anything to

change your mind, another dance maybe? I can show you my moves." When I nodded in the negative, he just shook his head, but clasped my hand and gallantly stated, "Well, my dear, at least that was the nicest put down I ever had." With my hand in his, he kissed the top.

I heard Victor's roar of anger before I saw him, and when I turned my head he was charging across the lanai towards Rick with fury in his eyes. Michael and Tina sprang out of their chairs and jumped in defense of Rick, placing themselves in front of him. I got out of my chair and tried to step in front of them, but Kat was there all of a sudden, and just yanked me out of the way.

"What the hell," I heard Rick say, as Victor pounded directly into Michael's chest trying to reach over and grab Rick. Michael went back two or three feet, but held firm barely remaining standing.

"She's mine, you fucker! Don't you lay your god dammed hands on her. I'll fucking destroy you! Don't touch her!" While he was screaming this, he was also reaching over and trying to get out of Michael's grasp.

Michael was yelling, "He didn'thing, man, and Monica told him she was unavailable. Cool it, man."

Tina had pulled Rick several feet back, and it seemed she was trying to explain things to him.

"Why'd he kiss her, then? Why goddammit?" he was struggling, still trying to swing out at Rick, but he wasn't fighting as much as earlier and Michael was able to half turn him to get Rick out of his line of vision to deflate his rage. He was panting with fury, anger and confusion and then there were tears of frustration in his eyes. Michael kept talking, whispering, and Victor's struggles began to cease, and eventually the fight went out of him. He was in Michael's arms shaking still, cursing, "It's just not fucking fair, it's just not fair," and then he saw me and ran out of the courtyard.

I pulled out of Kat's grasp, "Let me go to him," I begged.

"I think he needs to cool his heels," she said still grasping me by my upper arm.

"Kat, what if he drives in this state? Let me go," I tugged my arm again. She released me, and I ran. He was in the parking lot, pacing in front of his car back and forth when I found him. Thank goodness he hadn't gotten into the car, and something bad had happened. I wouldn't have been able to live with myself. When he saw me, he just stood there shaking his head; I just held out my arms, and kept approaching him. He shook his head one more time to clear it, and turned to me and stepped the last few feet into my arms.

"I'm sorry, Monica. I'm so sorry. Forgive me. Please. I had no right. That isn't me. I saw red, when he was kissing your hand and just assumed the worse." He panted into my shoulder letting his anger out.

"Shh, shh," I soothed. "It's okay. I understand. No apology necessary. I see how it could have been misconstrued."

"It's not fair, though," he said into my hair. "I can't have you, and yet I can't imagine you with anyone else," I could feel him breathing in my ear. I felt a jolt of sensation as his lips softly brushed my head above my ear. I heard his intake of breath. I felt his lips on my ear, a gentle bite on my lobe.

"I can't imagine being with anyone else, either," I whispered back. Those words unleashed a storm. His hands began to roam, mine did, too. The kisses made their way to my cheek, my neck, and I was kissing him, too, through his shirt on his shoulder, his chin, and then our lips found each other, and it was like coming home. It was frantic and desperate. He pushed me against the side of his car, and his hands continued their roaming exploration of my body, it was rushed, we both felt that way. One hand slid under my shirt, and cupped my breast, squeezing, possessing, and I heard him groan; he pushed his cock into my stomach so I could feel it, all of it, feel what I did to him. I jumped up and wrapped my legs around him, so I could feel that cock where I wanted it most. He pushed me harder back against the window giving me what I wanted and we didn't need words to say it. I explored his back, his arms, gripping them, and then my hands were on his head pulling him closer to me as our tongues plunged, and sought each other's out. Car lights whizzing by, eventually brought Victor out of his delirium, but just enough to have him open the back door of his car and slide inside pulling me with him. Once in the car and settled on his lap, the kisses became less about passion, but more about comforting each other. It was about showing each other how much we loved and cared about one another. It was saying all the words we just couldn't seem to voice. It was the only way we knew how to communicate. In each other's arms.

He kissed my lips, my chin, and my throat. I tilted my head back to give him access. His hand began to undo the button on my jeans the same moment mine were on his. We fumbled awkwardly but managed to get the job done. I lifted my rear, and he yanked them down, my panties next. Just in my shirt and bra, he positioned my legs to straddle him and then fiddled with his pants, and his cock sprang out unrestricted in the cramped quarters. "I'm sorry, I have to be inside you now."

"I know. I need you to," and then I slid onto him taking him in, all of him. I felt wrong doing it, like we were the criminals and Julianna was the victim, but I needed this man like I needed the very air to breathe. We had denied this pleasure so long, we had urges and they were primal; they needed to be fulfilled. We begin to move together. One of Victor's hands slid to my pussy, and he found my clit fast, and began to rub. He sought out my breasts through my shirt, and needing the contact, the feel of his lips on my already swollen flesh, I grasped the bottom of my shit and lifted it to my neck. He used his teeth to lower the cup of my bra, and he teased my nipple until it hardened even more and then suckled me there. It was rushed, awkward and fast and it ended in an explosion that faded all too soon. His face was in my hair, again. I could hear him inhale, and then his anguish and despair returned. "What are you going to do, Monica?" His words were strangled. "I can't live without you, and I can't picture you with anyone else."

"I don't know." And, I didn't. I felt all used up. Really, what was there to say? He held all the cards. I was his for the asking, for the taking, but he didn't want us, this, and me more. He couldn't make up his mind.

Chapter Fourteen
Strong Words and Ultimatums

FROM JUST OUTSIDE the car window, we heard a very angry expletive. "Fuck! What are you going to do! You're going to fucking talk it out that's what you're going to do. Discuss your God darned feelings with each other instead of me or Monica's sister, and stop pawing at each other like a couple of sexually frustrated teenager's." It was Kat's words that interrupted us. She stood outside the car.

We hastily got dressed and got of the car feeling ashamed.

"I came to check on the both of you. I was worried, and rightfully so, that Victor would be an ass and not just come clean with his feelings," Kat spoke harshly. "Vic, what the hell is the matter with you? Look at this girl. She's smart, beautiful, and she loves you more than anything else. So, instead of figuring it out, talking it out, you fuck her like some teenaged kid in the back of a car. Don't you respect her?"

"I respect her. I do. I do love her," he said, clearly shocked by Kat's outburst.

"I know you love her. You moon around all the fucking time saying life isn't fair. The only time you smile is when you talk to her on the phone, or when your daughter is over, and then it's not even real. It's wistful and you're thinking about her and putting up all kinds of barriers, making it impossible to be with one another. It is possible God damn it, you just have to make the right choice." Kat began to get closer as her rant raged. "You have this idea that you have to be like your parents. The perfect marriage. Hardly anyone has what your parents had. They loved each other. Loved EACH other. You've got this fairytale idealization of them. It's a fairytale, and you can't have a fairytale with the wrong woman."

"Why did you come out here, Kat?" his voice rose in pitch. "To analyze me? To tell me I don't know what I'm doing? I thought you were my friend." His hands clenched at his sides.

"I'm your friend, and that is why I'm NOT telling you what you want to hear." Kat was hurt now. "I came out here to check on you, make sure you didn't do something stupid, hurt yourself, or hurt her." Kat was pointing at me.

"I wouldn't hurt, Monica. Ever!" he swore.

Kat laughed sarcastically. "You already have, you big idiot. You're still hurting her AND yourself, maybe not physically but emotionally. You never listen to your heart, Vic. You're all about pride, honor, family, country! I love those things too, but don't you get it? If you don't Vic, you're no good to those other things. You can do your duty, oh, you can fight a war, but for what, Vic?" she questioned. "You do it for the people you love back home, see!" She was pointing at me, and he looked my way, and then down. Kat stepped closer to Victor and using her index finger jabbed him in the chest punctuating each word. "Do you, Victor? Do you? Do you love her enough to make the tough choices?" Tears were in her eyes, and when he didn't respond, she turned on her heel, and walked back to the courtyard.

For the second time that night, Victor looked completely defeated as he leaned up against his car, shoulders slouched in resignation. "I totally fucked this all up."

I stood not knowing what to say. Kat's words were still sinking in.

His hand went to his face, and he rubbed his eyes pinching the bridge of his nose. "Kat's way off base here. Well about some of that stuff, anyway." He looked up to see me backing away towards my car. "Hey, now. What's going through your mind? Let's do like Kat suggested and talk this out, baby." Maybe because of the look on my face, he sensed my chaotic emotions running through me. He reached for me.

I held my hand up. "Wait. I need to think." I couldn't think when he was too close. He stopped mere inches from me.

"Think about what? Us?" he said fearfully, "Even after . . ." he indicated his car behind him.

"Us? After what? That?" I indicated the car, too. His words stung me. He came those few inches that separated us and hugged me close. I couldn't concentrate with his arms around me. Maybe that had been my problem all along. He held me tight, and I hugged back. It just hurt so damned bad. He pulled back and gazed into my eyes.

He saw the tears. "I love you, Monica. You know I do."

"I know you do," I said lamely. I just didn't know what to do. I felt a panic attack coming on. I hadn't had one in years, since I had gone to counseling. The fear, and the pressure in my chest brought back the pain of the rape, the terror, the guilt. I began to perspire. I couldn't catch my breath.

"I feel like an ass asking this. But right now it is all I can think of, will you wait for me? Will you give me just four more weeks, baby? Four more weeks to figure this out?" he pleaded.

He couldn't have said this to me at a worse time. I needed

him disparately in that moment. And he wanted time. "Figure what out?" I panted and pushed him back with all my might just so I could breathe. "That you want your wife or me?" I began to pant as a tightness built inside my chest.

"I gotta finish this therapy. It's not going well. I told you that, Monica. There is hope." When I didn't say anything, I was concentrating on breathing, he continued to approach me arms outstretched pleading with me to understand, "She still wants the divorce. It probably will go that way, she's so stubborn. I know I'm an ass for asking, but it's only a month?"

"Probably, Victor? Probably!" I was shaking my head breathing in through my nose and exhaling through my mouth trying to focus on my breathing. "I know I'm an ass, you say. Then why are you asking me?" The tears streamed down my face. I was hurt. Hurt deeply. This man was willing to wait a month, keep me hanging on the off chance, that his wife changed her mind and wanted to keep him! Even though she didn't want him, didn't love him!

I took another calm steadying breath. I took another step back.

"Monica, don't back away from me. From us. Please. Friends for a month, and then the possibilities," he begged.

The possibilities? I was done with chances, and done with friendship. I blew. "Victor, friends? Really! You want to try that again. We have been playing at friendship here. This past month has been the sweetest kind of torture for both of us, and you know it. We have just been fooling ourselves just so we could hear the sound of each other's voices, be near each other again. Friends don't do this to each other. Hurt each other. Torture each other. My sister was right. We're like fire and ice. We melt, and then we get burned. You want to know

how I feel? How I truly feel? The truth is I didn't want to be
an excuse to end your marriage, so I kept quiet. The truth is I
have been hoping you would say you loved me more, and you
choose me. I have been dreaming that you would realize that
being divorced doesn't make you a bad parent. My parents are
fantastic, and they are divorced. They are better parents apart
than they ever were together because all they did was hurt
each other, and we felt that. I have been wishing that you
would admit you made a mistake in your marriage, that she
wasn't the one, and that I am. When we first got together, and
you said no promises, well I lied too, I wanted promises. And
when I knew and heard the circumstances, I felt bad, but still
I hoped you would realize it isn't a fault in your character that
made your wife fall out of love with you, but that the two of
you weren't meant to be in the first place. You made a
mistake. Yes, you made a beautiful daughter together that you
can share and love and raise, but you don't have to be
together to do that. But, you're so fixated on being perfect.
Kat's right about that. You want to be the perfect husband,
the perfect father, the perfect provider, the perfect soldier, the
perfect lover, but no one is perfect. There is no one right way.
Families come in all shapes and sizes Victor, and combina-
tions. I was hoping I could be part of yours. Praying for it.
Pleading to God on my knees for it! But you don't see that.
You just see black and white, a wife you married at twenty
two, who isn't the same girl she was in high school, your
daughter, and you. And you, what are you hoping for? You've
been hoping I would wait in the wings if things don't work
out the way you planned with your wife. You've been hoping
I don't meet anybody else if you can't have me. Well, where
does that leave me, Victor? It leaves me alone. It leaves me all
fucking alone." I paused for breath. He remained stock still, in
shock trying to absorb my words. I continued with the tears

streaming down my face, "What if she does decide to stick it out for Stacey's sake until she is eighteen, or forever? Am I second best, waiting one month, seven years, forever, having no one to love me, to make love to me? To make me feel the way only you can when I am in your arms. To be alone, loving you for the rest of my life, maybe seeing you every other Thursday night or coming home to a call on my answering machine once a month. Is that fair? You say it is only a month, and that it probably won't work out, and you imply you will probably come back to me and fool that I am, I'd take you back, but in that month, AND for the rest of my life, I'm going to wonder who you loved more, the mother of your child and your image of the perfect family, or the girl you liked to fuck. God damn you for making me say those words!" I was crying hysterically by the time I finished my rave, and I was trying to hit him to make him feel the pain that I had been experiencing, but it was no use; he just grabbed my wrists and pulled them down, and then to the side. He dragged me close enough to let go but grabbed me around the waist before I could get away and pulled me in to his chest.

"Oh, Monica. I'm sorry, baby. I'm sorry. I'm sorry. Mi Cara, I love you. I love you, please stop crying." It took me twenty minutes to stop crying and struggling, I was a mess.

"Please, Victor," I whispered, "just let me go."

He released me, but croaked oat, "I don't want to."

Not meeting his gaze, I told him, "I going to go, Victor. I should go." I began to back away. "It's okay. You do your thinking, and you can call me if you choose me. I'll pick up the phone, but in a month it will be too late." The look of shock on his face would stay with me forever. He let me walk out of his arms.

Chapter Fifteen
Realizations

THE DRIVE HOME was one of the longest of my life. Between bouts of crying, pulling over on to the side of the road, and trying to get myself under control so I could make it home safely, what normally would have taken me one hour, took three. But, make it home, I did. I had a message on my answering machine when I got home and it was from Victor. He just wanted to be sure I made it home okay he said. Let Kat know and here was her number.

I called her because if I didn't I wouldn't have put it past him to drive up and see me to check on me. When she answered, I could hear him in the background, "Is it her?"

"Yes, it's her," Kat snapped. "Now be quiet so I can talk to her a second. We were really worried about you, Monica, especially Victor. I'm glad you called. He was planning on driving up there if you didn't call in the next ten minutes."

"Well, I'm home now. It took me awhile, I had to stop a couple of times, keep falling apart, you know," I sniffled, "but I just got in," I answered truthfully the tears still falling silently.

She didn't ask me to elaborate. She probably could guess at the truth. "I'm glad you're home safe. We all are. And, I wanted to apologize to you, Monica. I hope I didn't set that whole thing off down there, but I felt Victor needed a reality check."

"No, Kat. It's all right. I had been thinking those things, and hopefully you saying it, then me saying it will get him to see the truth. I love him, Kat. Tell him I said that. With every fiber of my being. Okay? But tell him I meant the other things, too. He'll know what I mean." I clutched the phone to my ear.

"I'll tell him, sweetie. He loves you, too. He does. You take care, and I hope this idiot doesn't blow it. You're the best thing that has ever happened to him, and if he doesn't realize it, I'm going to kick his ass. Hang in there, okay?" she said. I could hear the sympathy in her voice.

"I will, and if he doesn't come for me, Kat," I choked up, "well, I want you to know that I liked you, and all of Victor's friends. You and Joe be happy. Goodbye." I held the phone to my ear to hear her final words.

"Goodbye, Monica. Talk to you soon, I hope." And, with that she hung up. I cradled my cordless phone back onto the receiver softly, and climbed into my bed with my clothes still on. I had a good long cry for all that I might lose. *Please, Victor!* I prayed. *Pick me, pick us.*

THE NEXT DAY, I woke somber, tired, and drained physically and emotionally, but I was determined not to be miserable and allow myself to waste away as I had done the last time Victor and I broke up. I went for my run, as usual, and had a decent breakfast of juice, toast, and coffee. I wasn't going to wallow in self-pity in my home, either, so I forced myself to go outside and enjoy the beautifully seasonable crisp fall day. I went outside and did some much needed weeding, pulling out all the dead plants and flowers, and annuals that had rotted to nothing in my rock garden. It felt good to be doing something like this, almost symbolic. Getting rid of the dead, the weeds, the things that destroyed, to make room for new growth in the spring when I could plant again.

I heard a car pull up in the driveway and felt a moment of fear before I shook that thought away, and wandered around to the front of my house to see my sister and Teddy get out of her SUV. When she saw me, she waved a bag of bagels and yelled for me to take a break because it looked like I needed one. I was covered in dirt from my waist to my feet.

I went inside, changed quickly, and made a fresh pot of coffee for them as she laid out the bagels and cream cheese. I was surprised it was past noon. I had been out in the yard a lot longer than I had thought—since nine that morning.

"So, what did I do to get the pleasure of your company, both of you on this beautiful Sunday?" I joked. With Teddy there, I didn't want to burst into tears or make a scene. I had only spent a few hours with him, here and there, when Ana surprised me with one of their visits.

"Nothing special, Monica. I wanted to check in with you since the last time we spoke. And, we were out getting bagels because Teddy wanted to eat something?" Ana said putting the fixings in her coffee.

"Yeah, anything!" he cracked. "Your sister keeps absolutely nothing in the house. I couldn't even find a jar of pickles. The only thing she had in the refrigerator was a bottle of vodka, some olives, and a Chinese take-out container that must have been three weeks old." Teddy reached and grabbed two bagels, and began spreading on a generous amount of cream cheese.

I laughed. "If you want to eat at Ana's place, you will have to do the cooking and the shopping," I informed him. The woman lived on take-out, coffee, and iced tea.

"Hey, if he was willing to eat anything, I would have found something for him," she waggled her eyebrows suggestively. I laughed at her usual crudeness. "But, he said, hey woman, let's get bagels, so here we are."

Teddy laughed at her joke, and then responded. "If you expect me to keep my performance levels up, woman, I have to eat," he complained and then added, "Food." He must have seen her start to open her mouth for a quick comeback when he added that. I guess he was used to her crudeness, too. That was quick thinking on his part.

Ana reached over and patted his hand. "I used to not spend much time at home, but things change. I'll shop for you, baby," she crooned. It was such a sweet gesture and a shot of envy went right through me. If only Victor and I could be this open and have such simple disagreements.

"Thanks, Babe," he said and caught her hand and kissed it.

My eyebrows shot up. Was this my sister, this domesticated creature willing to shop for her man? I shook my head in bewilderment, but I was happy for her. Teddy seemed like a really nice guy, and she was definitely at ease with him. She never brought guys around. I hoped she had finally found what she had been looking for. They were so affectionate with each other, and I had never seen her be that way with another guy before either. I took that as another good sign.

Turning to me, she asked, "So Monica, how are things going with the Victor situation?" For her to ask me, in front of Teddy, said a lot. She had obviously filled him in as he gazed at me with sympathy.

"I went last night to his friend, Joe's retirement party. And, I met Victor's daughter," I told her.

"You did!" she was surprised.

"Yes, she was beautiful, Ana. She was sweet and I think we could have been friends," I replied and released a sigh.

There was awe in her expression and then concern. "Could have?" she asked trying to read me.

I shook my head in resignation. "The night didn't end well. We had a fight." I left it at that. I didn't want to tell her about the incident with Rick and the almost fight, or the ultimatum I had given Victor. I would tell her another time. I was still too drained from the night of crying.

"A fight?" she inquired.

"Yes, Ana. And I will tell you about it. Just not right now. And, it isn't because you're here, Teddy," I said looking at him. "It's just that it would hurt too much to relive it all right now."

"I understand," Teddy said and patted my hand sympathetically, "But if you want me to go outside while you and Ana talk, I can."

That was sweet of him to offer, but the truth was I was too raw to talk about it today. "No, Teddy. That's all right. I will talk to Ana soon, just not now."

Ana piped in, "Well, when you're ready. I'm here."

"I know, Ana. You always are and always have been." I squeezed her hand reassuringly to let her know I would be okay for now.

They both stayed for a bit longer and we chatted about an upcoming trip they were planning to take to Las Vegas. It was nice, and I felt better for it. They were good together. I hadn't seen my sister this happy in a long, long time.

And although I was happy for her, it made me think about all I had lost with Victor, and all we could have if he could just see it.

IN THE NEXT two weeks, I threw myself into my workouts with a vengeance and the running, too. I had my first ever marathon, and 5K in a few days after Thanksgiving, so it was a good distraction. The nights were harder. Although I managed to cope through the days, and keep myself busy with work, grading papers, writing lessons, and eating properly, the nights were hard. After dinner and some light cleaning, I found myself sitting by the telephone waiting for a call I hoped would come, but as day after day passed, my doubts and fears grew by leaps and bounds.

I would watch reruns of *Friends*, and programs on the History Channel imagining that Victor was doing the same thing, imagining him here beside me. So many times, I almost caved and reached for the phone to tell him to forget everything I said and that I would wait the month. To tell him, I would wait for him, forever. I felt so pathetic in those moments. But then the other part of me would tell myself, that I needed to know. I needed to be sure he had chosen me, and hadn't settled for second best in his eyes.

I dreamed of him, too. Every night. He haunted my dreams. Sometimes in those dreams he came to me with open arms telling me all those words I wanted so desperately to hear, and other times those dreams were nightmares, nightmares in which he never called at all.

THE DAY BEFORE my big race, my sister came by to wish me well, she had been planning to come cheer me on, but Teddy's mom had taken ill and was in the hospital and she needed to be there for him. I would run this race alone with no one to cheer me on. My mom was out of town this weekend. After spending Thanksgiving with her and Tom yesterday, they had travelled to see his kids in Connecticut. But Ana could tell by my face that I was really upset. I hadn't confided in her yet about what had happened at Joe's retirement part, and she had been respecting my wishes to not have to relive it. But she was worried, I could see it her face. She could tell that I hadn't been sleeping and she had so wanted to support me in this race. So, I broke down and I finally told her about that last night with Victor and all my restless nights since.

"Oh, sweetie," she cried with me. "He'll call. He has to."

"I don't think he will," I cried into her shoulder. "It's been nearly two weeks and I gave him that ultimatum. I wish I could take it all back."

"If he doesn't call, darling," she said as she stroked my hair and tried to soothe me, "Call him. If you love him and he loves you, and I do think he does, he really does, you can forgive him. Love is precious, and you shouldn't deny him or yourself from experiencing it."

"But that means he loves her more," I continued sobbing.

"No it doesn't, you silly girl. It just means he is a man, a man with a lot of pride that has been fixated on this plan of his to keep the perfect family. So what if he doesn't realize it now. He will come to realize it and know that you're his one true love," her words soothed me, and gave me some hope.

"Do you really think so? I asked.

"Yes, I really do," she paused. "Give him these two more weeks, baby girl, if that makes you feel better. But then you call him. I say to hell with that ultimatum. Don't be foolish like him, and don't let pride, yours or his, keep getting in the way of a lifetime of happiness."

PRIDE. IT WAS as simple as that. I loved my sister. As I contemplated those words later on that night, a warm glimmer of hope sparked to trembling life within my heart. I was risking too much, risking it all by waiting for him to make the choice to choose me. I needed to go after what I wanted, and I wanted him. I wanted him in my life more than I had ever wanted anything, or ever would. I chose him. I would call him and tell him he could have those four weeks, two now, but I would wait. And, if at the end of those two weeks he didn't want me anymore, well, then I would worry about that later.

It was after one o'clock when those thoughts came to me. The clarity of it all seemed so simple. I chose him, and I had to let him know. I got out of my bed, my heart pounding. I began to pace thinking about what I would say. There was hope for us. It was a Friday, and I was sure he would be up, but not sure he would answer his phone or be in a place he could hear it. I couldn't wait. I had to do this now. I grabbed my phone off the charger and called Victor on his cell.

And it rang, and rang, and rang. Then it went to voicemail. I didn't want to leave a voice mail message, so I waited five minutes, and called again. Again, it rang and then went straight to voice mail. What the hell! Maybe he hadn't charged it, or it was off, or he couldn't hear it. A small doubt sprang. Maybe he saw it was me and didn't want to talk. No, he would answer if he saw it was me. I was sure, almost. Fear began to trickle through my veins. I had my decision and I wasn't going to back out now. In a panic and not thinking about the time, I tried the house phone just to be sure, maybe Kat knew something.

She answered the phone on the third ring, and I was relieved to hear her voice. I hoped I hadn't woken her, but I was a woman on a mission.

"Hi Kat, it's me, Monica, is Victor there?" I asked in a rush to find out what was going on.

"Yeah, he is here, but . . ." her voice trailed out in confusion.

"But what?" I cut her off.

"He's sl-sleeping," she informed me. "What's the matter, you sound like you're panicking over something. Are you okay?" she asked, her worry clearly apparent.

I rushed right in. "It's just that I tried his cell phone twice, and when he didn't pick up, I started to wonder why, then I got scared, but now I feel stupid because his cell battery probably just died or something, and he forgot to charge it," I rambled on.

"No, I heard it ring, just a few minutes ago and about five minutes before that which must have been you," she stated and then continued, "But before you panic again or jump to any conclusions, let me explain."

"Please do," I inserted. I had begun to make assumptions when she told me he was there but hadn't answered.

"Well first of all I'm glad you called because lover boy has been having a hell of a time these past two weeks. He's getting into fights, breaking things when he gets mad, and every other day it seems he is drinking himself into a stupor. Because of you, I might add. He loves you, Mon. He's told you that. He has even figured out that he doesn't really love his wife anymore, it's just this idealized vision he has that he can't let go of, you know." I heard her sigh, and then she continued. "So anyway, after work today he and the guys went for a drink, and they dragged him home at ten o'clock already wasted blathering on about how he was going to lose the best thing to ever happen to him. He has been passed out in his room for the past three hours sleeping it off. He probably just didn't hear the phone."

"Oh, Thank God," I muttered as my fear dissipated, but was replaced by the sad fact that I had hurt him so much.

That my ultimatum and threats, said in the heat of an argument, had hurt the man I loved so deeply that he had been just as tortured as I these past two weeks, if not more.

"So, what's up, Monica? What has you calling 'sleepy head' in a panic at one o'clock in the morning? I'd offer to wake him up for you if I thought I could," she told me.

"No, Kat. Let him sleep. But when he wakes up tell him this, okay? I want you to tell him that I love him and I will wait for him, forever if I have to. Tell him I choose him!" I cried as I began to sniffle into the phone. "I gave him an ultimatum, Kat. And I regret it so much. It was the dumbest thing I could have ever done."

"Not dumb, Monica, but not smart either. But the rest, well, that is fantastic. I'll be happy to pass along your message in the morning when he wakes up, unless you want to do it?" she asked.

I had the race tomorrow and I didn't want to make him wait. I wanted him to know the moment he woke up. I didn't want to prolong his self-inflicted torture and the agony I had caused a moment more. "Umm, actually I'm doing a marathon tomorrow in St. Pete," I informed her, "And I need to go finish the registration and stuff early, so you can tell him and as soon as he is awake. I don't want him to suffer anymore because of me. I love him so much. I'll never hurt him again. I swear Kat. I won't. Tell him that as soon as I get back in my car after the race, I'll call him," I begged of her.

"Okay, I will tell him. I'll tell him everything. Monica, this is great. You guys are perfect for each other. I will be thrilled and honored to tell him. I'm so glad you called. Everything is going to work out," Kat said excitedly. "You will be so happy together, Monica. I'm so thrilled one of you came to your senses." She was laughing, and choked up at the same time. I was too. I had finally come to my senses.

"Me, too, Kat. Tell him I love him, and give him a kiss for me," I cried. "I love that man so much my heart feels like it is going to explode." I had hope again.

"I'll tell him, Monica. Don't you worry. I'll tell him everything you said. Now go to bed, and get some rest for that big race of yours, so that you can be sleeping in that man's arms tomorrow night," she laughed.

"Yes, Sergeant," I teased. "Good night, Kat. And thank you again." Maybe, I would be sleeping in his arms. I thought I might. I had hope.

"You're welcome. Good night, Monica, I'll see you tomorrow." Then we both hung up.

I went to bed with my heart feeling lighter than it had in months.

Chapter Sixteen
A Lifetime of Passion

SATURDAY DAWNED BRIGHT and early, and although the race didn't start until noon, registration was from eight until eleven. There would be many racers needing to register. I needed to rise with the sun if I wanted to get there, register, and familiarize myself with the route. The drive to St. Petersburg was nearly two hours, but I also wanted to get in a soak in the tub for my muscles to relax before the big day ahead.

Even though I had barely five hours of sleep I felt refreshed. I thought about Victor while soaking and felt in my heart that things could work out for us. I was sure he would accept my apology, and hopefully we could see each other soon. I made some toast, had oatmeal for the carbohydrates and the extra energy I would need today, and some orange juice. I was in my SUV by seven thirty and on my way. As I drove, I listened to a weekend radio program that had me laughing and smiling. I was in great spirits. I was excited about this race and even more excited about hearing from Victor. I had really come a long way, from recluse to fitness buff, to a woman not afraid to try anything. This race, to me, was proof that I had come a long way, and I could make it to the finish line. And then the race was over, well, then there was Victor.

The radio show was done at nine and that song came on the radio. The song by Maroon 5, She Will Be Loved, a song that had played while Victor and I had danced once, and it was perfect. It was another sign to me that I would be loved by the greatest man that had ever walked into my life. I hummed along the whole way and continued to sing the melody when the song was long over.

I made the last few turns into Tropicana Field, the forum in St. Petersburg where the Devil Rays played baseball. I saw from the parking lot where registration was being held for the 5K, and then parked my car. It took a while to get to the front of the line as I hadn't been out here earlier, but I still made it to the front of the line by ten thirty. I talked with some of the other racers while waiting my turn to fill out my registration packet and pay my registration fee.

Once that was done, I had a little more than an hour before the race so I did some stretching and kept sipping from my water bottle to be sure to I stayed nice and hydrated. I chatted with some of the other racers and reviewed the map that showed the course we were to follow. I wasn't all that familiar with St. Pete, but my plan was to just follow the person in front of me until I passed them, and then do it again with the next person, and so on. I wasn't in it to win it. Not my first time out by far. But I did want to have a good time, and possibly enter another race, or this one next year and beat my own time.

There were a lot of racers, both young and old alike, all women as this was an annual race being sponsored by the National Organization for Women and it was their annual United Against Violence run. It was probably one of the reasons Victor had told me about this race and encouraged me to do it. It warmed me to know that he had probably researched the various races, and had picked it because it would mean a lot to me. That fact had just occurred to me now, and made me love him even more.

At about eleven thirty they made the announcement that there were over nine thousand racers this year, and they had beaten last year's registration by over six hundred people. That meant they raised over ninety thousand dollars in registration alone. The crowd cheered loudly, and that didn't even count the money they made on selling t-shirts, banners, water, calendars and other souvenirs people could buy to help support this great cause. It made me happy to know that this was all going to a great cause.

You could feel the excitement in the crowd as the race drew nearer. I soaked it in. I was excited, too, and not just for the race. There were all kinds of supporters there to root the woman in their family on. Knowing that Victor had picked this race made me feel like he was here rooting me on, as well. I didn't feel alone.

As I started to make my way to the starting positions, I read some of the signs and banners people held; "Go Mom!", "Women Unite NOW", "End the violence", "Grandma, leave them in the dust" which made me laugh, and "Tina and Susie, WE LOVE You". It was nice to see all the support people were giving one another. I put on the shirt I had been carrying; it was one of Victor's t-shirts. The one that he had given me in Ft. Lauderdale to wear the first night we were there. I grabbed a hand full of the shirt and brought it to my nose and I inhaled. I could still smell him in it, even though I had worn it a few times. I put my race belt on over it that showed the number I had been assigned for the race, and tied a small knot in the shirt to tighten it around my hips.

At eleven forty-five they called all the racers into the starting area to take their positions. They also asked the crowd to leave the area and to go behind the cordoned off ropes. I had started making my way there ahead of many others so I found myself in a good position for starting. We would be ending here, as well. I soaked it all in as people hugged all around me, and wished their loved ones luck. Even with just a few minutes until the start of the race, Victor was on my mind. He would have been proud of me for doing this. My thoughts were on him so much that I even imagined I saw him in the crowd just as the starting pistol cracked.

It startled me at first, and the people around me pushed past, but I recollected myself and began to run. I wanted a good time, but I had to break out of this pack which was no easy task with a group this large. It probably took me a full half mile to three quarters of mile before I could really begin to move, and then I hit it with all I had. I followed the person in front of me just as I had planned, until I passed them; then I chose another person far up ahead to follow until I passed them, too. I kept repeating that pattern until I could see the finish line up ahead.

I really pushed myself that last quarter mile. I could barely make out the LED display showing your place and time. It was still in double digits and I was thrilled. The top one hundred would be fantastic. I flew past eight people in those last two hundred yards, and came in 46th place. My time was twenty minutes and nine seconds. That was fantastic. I had run more than seven miles an hour.

It took me a while to slow once I crossed that finish line and by the time I was at a slow jog that is when I saw him. Victor! I halted completely and just stared. He was holding a sign that said, "I choose you!" and he held a single red rose in his other hand. I started walking again, and then I was running. I flew into his arms.

As my body hit his, he wrapped his arms around me, and I wrapped my legs around him both of us clutching each other as if our lives depended on it.

"Monica, Mi Cara, my heart, I love you like no one else. I have for a very long time and I want you to know that," he said in my ear.

"You, don't have to say any . . ." I began to say. I was crying.

"No, I do. You deserve to hear it and so much more." His eyes lowered to my lips and he kissed me. It was perfect. As more racers were coming in and their family to congratulate them, Victor carried me off side. He set me down and put both hands on my face holding me so that I could see into those ice blue eyes, and he gazed into mine. I could see the love there. He spoke. "Monica, the morning after we made love that very first time, I knew you weren't like anyone else I had ever met before. I knew you were dangerous."

"Me, dangerous . . ." I laughed. I wasn't expecting him to say that.

"Shh, please let me get this out," he interrupted. "I have a lot I have to say, and I want to do it right."

I looked at him and nodded.

He continued. "Yes, dangerous, Monica. I was in a bad place then, but those things I said to you, the way I spoke to you, treated you, it was meant to scare you away. I had a plan to get my wife back, and put my family back together, but I knew even then that with you in my life, I would soon not want it. I knew you would be perfect. It scared the hell out of me. The fact that I could know that about someone I had just met. That I could feel like this about someone I had just met. For weeks, I kept you at arm's length, not letting you in, not letting you see the real me. But, you didn't run away. When we went to Ft. Lauderdale, I knew you loved me then. What you did for me, what we did, and you stayed and you were perfect. That weekend was the best weekend of my life. And, it wasn't about the sex, though that was amazing. It was about you, and how I felt when I was with you, at the beach, at the restaurant, you chasing me on the beach. I knew I loved you that day on that bench eating that ice cream. That is the exact moment that I knew I was so very much in love with you." There were tears is his eyes.

He took a breath and kissed me softly on the lips showing me just how much he loved me, and continued when he pulled away. "I didn't think about Julianna at all that weekend. I was lost in you." His expression was pained. "But when we got back from Ft. Lauderdale, reality set in. I had my daughter, and then my efforts were all for her. I became so fixated on what I thought she needed. Then you went away, and how I missed you. It was all so confusing. I didn't tell you this, but each night I yearned for you." He winced and turned his face away for a moment and then back, "I kept playing it cool, kept you at arm's length. I was a fool." He kissed the tip of my nose, each of my eyes as I stared at him in wonder and awe.

He wasn't done. He had a lot more to say, and I wanted him to let it all out. I wanted to give him the chance to finally unburden his soul so we could begin again. "When we broke up that first time, it was painful, it hurt so damn much. When I thought of you, it was like I couldn't breathe. I threw myself into over drive at the gym trying to forget. I went out with the guys once, and they tried to get me to flirt with other girls. I punched Michael in the face and stormed out." He shook his head at that showing how disappointed he was himself and how he had treated a friend. "He forgave me, of course, he was only trying to help me get over you, but I didn't want to get over you, ever." He paused to kiss me again on the lips, on the cheek, to caress my cheek with his own, ensuring I was still there, still listening, wanting to show me how much he loved me while he explained.

He smiled with that crooked grin that revealed one dimple and continued. "When I saw you at Universal Studios, it was a sign to me. You were so beautiful, and I saw how frail you looked. It scared me to death. I had to reach out, but I knew I had hurt you. I wanted to give you hope, both of us. I still had this idea that we could be together until Julianna came around. That you would accept more time with me for maybe forever. It was unfair, but we were both in so much pain. But it was really because I couldn't resist you, and didn't know how I could give you up. I even thought that if Julianna did take me back, there might be some way we could still see each other now and then. But I wasn't thinking clearly at all. I was a mess." I stroked his back when he paused to wipe the tears from his face. I reached up on my tip toes to press a quick kiss to his lips. He accepted it, returned it, and then pulled back to look into my eyes again.

He took another deep breath and went on. "We began to communicate on the answering machine, and then talk, and it was like I could breathe again." He smiled and then his look grew grim. "Then there was Joe's retirement party. I saw you with my daughter and wished that we had a child together. But, I didn't want to give you false hope just yet. I had counseling for one more month. I was determined to see it through, so that if my daughter ever blamed me for the divorce, I could honestly say I gave it all my effort to try to regain her mother's love, for her, for Stacey. Not for Julianna, but for her. That was my finish line. It was my last goal."

His face contorted into one of pain, and anger. "But when that guy touched you, I saw red. I saw what I could lose, and the thought of any man ever having you, touching you the way I've touched you, I couldn't stand it. Monica, I wanted to murder him, I mean that. If Michael hadn't stopped me, I don't know where we would be right now. In my heart you were mine, and only mine. I would kill any man that took what was mine. Monica, you've been mine since the day we met."

His face was still angry. Fierce. I reached up to kiss him again, letting him know I was his. I told him, "I'm yours, Victor. There is only you."

He nodded and then gruffly repeated, "Mine!" He shook it off, then, the anger. I saw the tension leave his body. "Mine. Baby, I love you so much." His lips crushed mine in a soul searching kiss that bonded us together for minutes and eternity. Huskily, he rasped against my face, and told me the words I needed to hear more than anything, "I don't need two more weeks. I need you. I choose you!" We kissed again, and it was like rapture. The passion soared between us, and we were on fire. I could feel the burn start in my veins, and I knew he felt it to, he was panting, and his arousal so evident matched my own.

Because the groups coming in to meet the racers was getting even more crowded, we were getting closed in on again, but he still had more to tell me. When the kiss ended because we had been jostled, he laughed and went on. "After Kat told me about your call this morning, it was like a light bulb had gone off. It was you. You, through your selflessness, had shown me the way. You, who had already given me your heart, your love, your passion, were willing to sacrifice your pride for mine. You were willing to sacrifice your happiness, on the chance for my daughter's happiness, it spoke volumes. No one has loved me the way you do. Not ever, no one, and you deserved no less. I called Julianna this morning and I told her I didn't need more counseling, she could have the divorce. I told her I met someone who I loved, who I had been pushing away for Stacey' sake." He shook his head. "She said she knew. I don't know how, I didn't ask, but she had known that my pride had kept me from agreeing to the divorce." I smiled at him. I saw his relief.

"So next, I drove to my mother's house and told her everything. I was worried she would be upset, angry. Her faith is so important to her, to me. But, she was happy for me. She knows how miserable I was. She knew Julianna and I had our issues, but never once spoke badly of her because she felt it wasn't her place. I told her about you, about us. She wants to meet you. She cried and said when you talk of this Monica, you have love in your eyes again. She said go get her, and bring her to me. I must meet her, the woman that puts life and love in your eyes. She gave me this to give to you. It was hers and my father's, he said as he reached into his pocket and pulled out a box, a small box.

I began to shake. Victor let me go, and got on one knee, right there in the parking lot, just beyond the finish line. He opened the box to show me a ring, a simple beautiful solitary ring. The crowd began to cheer around us, but we were oblivious to it all, and only had eyes for each other.

"I was a fool for so long. Please forgive me. Love me just half as much as I love you and I will be a happy man. Monica, the one I choose is you. Mi Cara, will you marry me?" he breathed.

I had been crying from the moment he had gotten on one

knee. "Yes, Victor. Oh yes. I will marry you." He pulled me to him and hugged me around the waist, his head lying flat against my belly, and then I was kneeling in front of him and we kissed, sealing our fate, and tying our future to one another forever.

Epilogue

What the Future Holds

Three months later . . .

I T WAS A cool February afternoon, and Victor and I stood
hand in hand on Clearwater Beach watching as Stacey ran
towards us with our dog, Snoopy, running around her. Stacey
had named her, and the mutt loved her like no other.

After Victor had proposed, we waited until Christmas, a
full month, to tell Stacey about us, the engagement, and our
plans to move in together. Victor had included me in their
weekend outings so we could bond, keeping Tuesdays just
with her. We had gotten closer, all of us. When we told her,
she showed genuine happiness for her father and genuine
happiness to have me in her family.

Since Christmas, we had found an apartment together in
Palm Harbor, so we would both be close to work and to our
families. I had put my small little bungalow up for sale, and it
had sold quickly giving us a nice little nest egg for when we
decided to marry and buy a home together. Living together
and seeing each other every day drew us closer. Every day, he
told me he loved me and showed me in so many ways. He
sent flowers to me at work, for no reason, left chocolate on
my pillow at night, put notes in my lunch bag, and sent me
texts at work telling me he was thinking of me. When I asked

him about it, he kissed me on the nose, and told me he should have been doing those things all along, and wanted me to know every day how precious I was to him. I loved him, and my love for him grew every day. I showed him at night how much I loved him, and told him with words and actions how much he meant to me.

Stacey had turned twelve just a few weeks ago, and Snoopy had been my gift to her. Stacey had never had a pet before, she had confided in me once, and when I asked Victor to allow me to do this for her, he readily agreed. Our apartment allowed one small animal, so we had selected a mixed breed basset hound from the animal shelter. When Stacey saw him, she ran into my arms and thanked me for giving her the best gift ever. She even kissed me on the cheek, and immediately claimed his name was Snoopy before she even knew it was, in fact, a boy.

After the news had been shared with Julianna, she even allowed Snoopy to come over to her house on the weekends. So Snoopy spent the week with us, and every weekend with Stacey, one with us, and one with Stacey and her mom. I had even met Julianna, and she had been pleasant, wanting to meet me and know the woman who would be helping to raise her daughter. She accepted me, it seemed and even seemed happy to see Victor happy with me.

Victor pulled me down to the sand, onto the blanket we had placed there, and we continued to watch Stacey throw sticks for Snoopy to fetch. Snoopy bounded after the sticks and raced them back to Stacey barking at her to do it again. Eventually, the tired duo made their way back to us, and Stacey plopped down on the blanket at our feet, Snoopy's head immediately in her lap.

"Tired kiddo?" Victor asked as his daughter sighed and

leaned back onto her forearms.

"Yes, a bit," she stated, "But before we go, I wanted to ask you guys something." She looked serious.

Victor looked at me a little fearfully, and I shrugged my shoulders indicating I didn't know what was on his daughter's mind.

"What is it, sweetheart?" he asked giving her his full attention.

"I was wondering when you guys were going to get married," she blurted out. "Mom, said the divorce was final this past week and that you might be planning on getting married." She looked at me and then at her father. Victor looked to me. We had decided to not rush into a marriage, even though we both wanted to have that bond, that symbol of marriage that would tie us together for eternity, but we wanted Stacey to be ready for it. When Victor didn't speak up at first, I decided to be candid with her.

"We haven't really set a date yet, Stacey. We love each other and we want to get married, but we wanted to give you time to get to know me better," I stated honestly.

"I know good people when I see it, Monica," she gave me a dazzling smile, just like her fathers. "And you are good people. I don't think you should wait. You make my dad so happy, and I love you for that."

A lump formed in my throat. "Thank-you," I choked out over the restriction in my throat and reached out to her. She grasped my hand and squeezed it. Victor laughed quietly beside me squeezing my other hand.

"So, when do you think we should get married?" he asked her earnestly.

She turned her head to the side, apparently mulling it over for a few seconds. "This summer. Summer weddings are beautiful and romantic. We should do it on the beach." She stated matter-of-factly looking around her taking in the view.

"On the beach, huh?" He looked at me quizzically.

I laughed. Was this conversation for real, I wondered? They both were looking at me expectantly. "A beach wedding. I like the sound of that," I stated tentatively.

"Great!" Stacey laughed clapping her hands. "Let's do it in June on dad's birthday."

My mind spun rapidly counting. "June!" I croaked. "That is four months away."

"Yeah, four months is plenty of time." She brushed the note of concern in my voice away and jumped up. "I will be a bridesmaid, though, not a flower girl! Do you like purple, Monica?"

"Yes, I like purple, and lavender," I stammered. Victor just looked from me to his daughter with love in his eyes for the both of us. He reached and took ahold of my other hand, holding them both and gaining my full attention.

"I'd love to marry you in June, Monica. It would be the best birthday present ever," he stated sincerely blue eyes beginning to flame.

"Then it is settled," Stacey added gleefully and turned to whip the stick out into the breeze as Snoopy gave chase, and she after him.

I was in shock. Four months. "Monica?" Victor interrupted my thoughts as I looked at Stacey's retreating figure and returned my gaze to him. "Will you marry me in June?" he asked.

I looked into the eyes of the man I loved more than anything else in the whole world. Everything I needed I saw in those eyes. I saw the fire begin to smolder, and I knew now that only I could put it there. His heart had been ice, but now he burned for me. I had no doubts. Not anymore. No reservations.

"Yes. I will marry you in June," I whispered and crawled onto his lap. As his head dipped to mine to seal our pact with a kiss, his blue eyes burst into flames, and I melted into him. I was where I belonged.

The End

Keep reading to find out about my other books

A Note From the Author

MJ here. If you liked my debut book, please consider checking out the other two books in the Secrets & Seduction Series; *Afraid to Love*, and *Afraid to Hope*. They are available with most retailers in ebook format.

Afraid to Love is Monica's very feisty sister's story, Ana. *Afraid to Hope* chronicles their friend Louisa's journey to find her happily ever after. You will get to see more of Victor and Monica in them. I promise it gets better.

I also published, along with seven other authors, a guide to accompany the Secrets & Seduction Series entitled *The Ultimate Romance-Erotica Book Club Guide*. This book will give you some insight into my books, as well as the other authors, and why we wrote what we did. It is a behind the scenes look at the characters, who they are based on, and what I was trying to do with these interconnected standalones. I hope you will check it out.

In 2015, I released my Bounty Hunter Series – The Marino Brothers. They are super-hot books with suspense, action and plenty of erotic scenes. Each brother has his own romance in this four book best-selling series.

Next on the horizon is my five Book series entitled Mystic Nights. Tawny Sassacus and her four children have their hands full running the newest casino in Lantern Hill, Connecticut. There will be intrigue and suspense around every corner.

The Bounty Hunters!!

Beautiful Bounty by MJ Nightingale

(Book 1 in The Bounty Hunters – The Marino Bros.)

Ronnie Sears has a college degree, a promising future, a boyfriend, and a plan. But, her perfect life comes crashing down around her in the blink of an eye. Arrested, framed for drug smuggling, and facing years behind bars, Ronnie sees no choice but to run. Only she can prove her innocence.

Nikko Marino is a sexy, devastatingly charming bounty hunter. His job, as told to him by his older brothers, is to keep an eye on the curvaceous blonde. Make sure she doesn't run. But what his brothers don't know is that he and Ronnie have a past. He and the Ice Princess are more than mere passing acquaintances. She makes his blood burn, and he knows how to warm up this woman.

Nikko wants to prove himself, but this beauty might just take him down. With his reputation on the line, will Nikko, the hot-blooded youngest Marino, fall for this temptress? Will he be able to protect this beautiful bounty from herself, from the man who framed her, but most importantly can he protect his heart?

Beautiful Bounty is the first book in *The Bounty Hunters – The Marino Bros.*

Suspenseful, erotic, and romantic, these books are packed with passion, sex and characters you will love. What more could you want?

Beautiful Chase by MJ Nightingale

(Book 2 in The Bounty Hunters – The Marino Bros.)

Bella Chase led a simple life. She was a good girl who worked hard at a job she loved, had good friends, and enjoyed her life. She just fell for the wrong guy. A bad boy with a bad reputation. When he maliciously involves her in a crime that goes awry, and someone is killed, it is her life on the line. She has no choice, but to flee. She not only faces life in prison, she faces a death sentence if she talks.

Blaze Marino is done with women. They can't be trusted. Period. Not even the good girls. When his next case lures him to the hills of Tennessee, hunting down another "good girl", Blaze is torn between taking down this natural beauty, and losing himself inside of her. He, who has vowed to never love, or need again, is drawn to Bella and he just can't help himself.

Terrified, Bella doesn't know which way to turn. She doesn't know who to trust.

Jaded, Blaze can't fight the pull of attraction. He doesn't know if he can trust her.

He has to chase her for his job. Or so he keeps trying to tell himself that.

Beautiful Chase is the second book in *The Bounty Hunters – The Marino Bros.*

Suspenseful, erotic, and romantic, these books are packed with passion, sex and characters you will love. What more could you want?

Beautiful Regret by MJ Nightingale

(Book 3 in The Bounty Hunters – The Marino Bros.)

Lisa Rasmussen, formerly Lisa Raphael, has had enough of her manipulative abusive husband. He has forced her to his will, tortured her both physically and psychologically, and she wants out. Her sham of a marriage to Albert, son of the blue blooded Rasmussen's of Manhattan, has to end. But, Albert has vowed to never give Lisa her freedom. He owns her. Body and soul. Her plans to blackmail him to get out, will not go unpunished. Albert will strike first.

Gio Marino knows Lisa. He knows of Albert. After all, Lisa left Gio to marry the son of the luxury classic car dynasty. So when Lisa calls him begging for help, he is floored. Not only because she called him, but because of what she has been accused of. Attempted murder! She had meant everything to him, but after what she did nearly a decade ago, he knows not to trust her, but the temptation to see her in an orange jumpsuit is just too hard to resist.

Lisa is full of regret. She has a lot to feel guilty about. But, she doesn't have any one else to turn to. She needs Gio. He is the only one she can trust even though he might never be able to trust her again.

The minute he walks into Riker's and sees her, he knows he has made a big mistake. The emerald eyes, the flawless skin, the fiery hair, bring it all back. Especially the regret. Can he help her? Does he want to? And why, after all these years, does he find her beauty so hard to resist?

Beautiful Regret is the third book in *The Bounty Hunters – The Marino Bros.*

Suspenseful, erotic, and romantic, these books are packed with passion, sex and characters you will love. What more could you want?

Beautiful No More by MJ Nightingale

(Book 4 in The Bounty Hunters – The Marino Bros.)

Catarina Stone is a woman of mystery, and she likes to keep it that way. But she is thrust into the limelight when two of her "girls" are slain by a serial killer. The Tampa Madame, as she has been dubbed by the press, is being hounded by the media who want to find a connection between the killer and her. She reaches out to Andreas Marino of The Marino Bros.

Cat has done her research, and knows she needs a professional, a person experienced in catching psychopaths. She needs Andreas. The police are baffled, and the killer must be caught before another one of her girls is mutilated, then murdered.

Andreas Marino, the striking eldest Marino, does know serial killers. It used to be his job. But not anymore. Not since one of those sick bastards claimed his parents' lives, and destroyed his own. He doesn't want this case, not at all. Not until he sees her.

The strikingly elegant Madame intrigues him. She is an enigma. And, Andreas can't get her out of his head . . . and the need to have her in his bed. When she shows him copies of the note left by the killer, signed "Beautiful No More," the thought of her exquisiteness destroyed reignite a flame in him he thought long dead. He must catch a killer. He must save the girl. If he doesn't, Andreas will be lost this time . . .

forever.

Beautiful No More is the final book in *The Bounty Hunters – The Marino Bros.*

Suspenseful, erotic, and romantic, these books are packed with passion, sex and characters you will love. What more could you want?

What is Next for MJ Nightingale?

Mystic Nights!

Chances (Book 1 of Mystic Nights Series)

Mystic Nights Casino is the newest gambling hot spot to hit Lantern Hill, and Tawny Sassacus runs it. For her people, the Eastern Pequot Tribal Nation, she is determined to make it a success despite trouble with politicians, and a rival tribal nation. With the help of her children, she is determined to fight for what is right.

As Vice-Chair of Mystic Nights, Jonathan Sassacus doesn't have time to chase women. He only likes a sure bet. When he crosses paths with the new dancer, things change. Tall, with legs that won't quit, she's a distraction he doesn't need, but can't resist.

One night of passion is all it takes. Aliya Chance can't get the sexy as sin Jonathan out of her head. His powerful and domineering ways are not what she needs in her life. She has her own dreams that don't include giving private dances to the boss.

Jonathan has much to do. He has to hunt down skimmers and embezzlers in his casino before the big audit. The trail he follows leads him down a road filled with murder and betrayal that brings danger to his very door. When his faith is rocked by the woman stealing his heart, will it be too late to save them? Or, will he risk throwing the dice by taking the biggest chance of all?

Triple Diamonds (Book 2 of the Mystic Nights Series)

Mystic Nights Casino is the newest gambling hot spot to hit Lantern Hill, and Tawny Sassacus runs it. For her people, the Eastern Pequot Tribal Nation, she is determined to make it a success despite trouble with politicians, and a rival tribal nation. With the help of her children, she is determined to fight for what is right.

Joseph Sassacus, corporate attorney for his reservation's casino, would rather be fighting for justice for his people, but the casino sucks him in time and time again. A dark haired beauty with almond eyes, might be able to alleviate some of the stress he is feeling. He can't help but imagine doing things to her he shouldn't, but her allure keeps him coming back for more.

A life altering tragedy prevents Jewel Diamente from pursuing her dreams of her own restaurant. She finds herself doing things she never thought she would have to do. She has no time to pursue her own ambitions, let alone Joseph Sassacus. But the man with the sexy smile, and electric touch, has her pulse pounding and her senses reeling.

A rash of robberies at the casino, an increasing drug problem on the reserve, and Jewel Diamente will test Joseph's loyalties when the three collide. With all the signs pointing to her, will he risk his family, people, and ambition? Is his 'diamond' the real deal? If he goes with his gut, gambles and wins, he just hit the jackpot, but he could also lose it all.

Lucky Strike (Book 3 of the Mystic Night Series)

Mystic Nights Casino is the newest gambling hot spot to hit Lantern Hill, and Tawny Sassacus runs it. For her people, the Eastern Pequot Tribal Nation, she is determined to make it a success despite trouble with politicians, and a rival tribal nation. With the help of her children, she is determined to fight for what is right.

Eve Sassasacus loves the night life. Sometimes more than she should. Music, dancing, drinking, and partying are more than just sport for her. It's her livelihood as well. As entertainment director for the casino, it's her job to bring in the hottest talent to Mystic Nights. She'll do anything to bring the sexiest rocker she's ever seen and heard to Lantern Hill. Anything.

Levi Stryker is the hottest and most in demand up-and-coming rocker in the northeast. Knowing his music and his band is about to explode, when Eve Sassacus tells him she'll do anything to have him come play for her. He is tempted to find out just how far she is willing to go. From the moment he sees this beauty, he knows how far he wants to go.

Eve fears she has made a deal with the devil when she becomes involved with her new headliner. And the more he pursues her, the more things begin to go wrong. Determined to find out the truth, Eve is led on a twisted and dangerous journey in the behind the scenes music industry. Can she survive it? Can her heart survive it? Is she another notch on a very cluttered bedpost, or will she be the one to hit pay dirt. Will she strike out, or get a lucky strike?

Black Jack (Book 4 of The Mystic Nights Series)

Mystic Nights Casino is the newest gambling hot spot to hit Lantern Hill, and Tawny Sassacus runs it. For her people, the Eastern Pequot Tribal Nation, she is determined to make it a success despite trouble with politicians, and a rival tribal nation. With the help of her children, she is determined to fight for what is right.

Dawn Sassacus wants to help her family even if it means looking for trouble at the casino as a dealer on the floor. No one steals from her people and gets away with it. No one. Especially not a smoldering hazel eyed con-man who counts cards. Even if he makes her body burn.

Jackson Black is a working man. Using several aliases, he conducts his business across the country undetected until one young, bookish black jack dealer threatens his game. And he knows he's the best game in town. But looking at her, he knows she is a game he would like to play. With his cover in jeopardy, he needs to do something drastic. With single minded focus, Jackson sets his sights on pleasantly distracting the woman with the cherry lips, and sexy smile.

Dawn knows she's in deep. Deep trouble and love. Her gut tells her to trust Jack even though she still can't figure him out. He's hiding something from her. She knows it. Should she risk her heart? Can she play his game, or will she find out that Jack's heart is as black as his name?

Playing for keeps (Book 5 of the Mystic Nights Series)

Mystic Nights Casino is the newest gambling hot spot to hit Lantern Hill, and Tawny Sassacus runs it. For her people, the Eastern Pequot Tribal Nation, she is determined to make it a success despite trouble with politicians, and a rival tribal nation. With the help of her children, she is determined to fight for what is right.

She is a task master. A woman who raised four determined, driven children on her own. With them all grown, making choices on their own, her focus becomes her business and her people once more.

But when one of her children becomes sick, all that she has struggled to build is in jeopardy. Why? Because she will be forced to reveal a 30 year old secret to her children. And no one will be happy about it. With her secret unravelling, Tawny starts to receive threats against herself, her children, and grandchildren. She'll either have to give it all up and give in, or someone will have to pay the price.

Disappearing to keep her secrets seems like the only way to protect them all. But instincts warn her even that may not be enough. So she gambles it all. And goes public. This time Tawny won't accept second place. This time she is playing for keeps.

About the Author

MJ Nightingale has been a teacher for over two decades. Writing is her new career, and something she has wanted to do for a very long time. But reading has been a part of her life since she was a child. She has been an avid lover of romance novels, and they have always held a special place in her heart. When not working, or writing, or spending time with her children, she devours books all summer long, and any type of fiction; thrillers, crime, suspense, contemporary, and drama.

She has published five novels, all contemporary romance, and her new series, The Bounty Hunters, will add an element of suspense to her already complicated character portrayals. Fans of MJ will not be disappointed.

She currently lives in Florida with her wonderful husband, and sons. And, she loves to hear from her readers.

Follow her on Amazon to get all the latest on her upcoming new series; Mystic Nights. Five new romantic suspense books that follow Tawny Sassacus and her children who help her to run Mystic Casino Nights.

You can contact her on Facebook, twitter, and Instagram, or visit her website.

Facebook:
www.facebook.com/pages/MJ-Nightingale/185806224943537

Website:
mjnightingale.weebly.com/contact.html

Made in the USA
Coppell, TX
09 July 2022

79758212R00134